CALLING MY CHILDREN HOME

The Bishop Smoky Mountain Thrillers
Book 5

LAUREN STREET

STERLING & STONE

Prologue

SHE RUNS past a briar bush and a big thorn scratches her leg. Ouch! It *hurts*. She looks down and sees that it's bleeding. She wants to cry. She wants her mommy, but she keeps running.

She can't let him catch her.

She feels the leaves crunching under her feet, bangs into a tree and cries out, but doesn't stop. He'll catch her if she stops. He's bigger and can run faster than she can. She'd squeezed through a window opened only halfway, could fit through because she's so little. She's never been glad to be little before. But they know by now that she's gone and they're looking for her. Maybe he's running right behind her in the woods. She turns to look over her shoulder, trips over a root and sprawls on her face in the dirt, skinning the palms of her hands and bloodying both knees. But she doesn't have time to sit in the dirt and cry, so she jumps to her feet and keeps running, cries while she runs. She's never run this fast for this long. Her side *hurts*. She can barely breathe. There's nobody in the woods. How will she find anybody to help in the woods?

And then she remembers the poster of the big black bear on the wall in the grocery store. There are bears in these woods, and she's out here all alone. Will a big black bear come and eat her? Will it jump out from behind a tree, growling? She's whimpering and crying and panting all at the same time, making little noises like a kitten. Her nose is running, and the scratch on her leg hurts, and the knees she skinned hurt, and her hands hurt, but mostly she's just so afraid.

Up ahead, she can see a break in the trees, and it looks like... yes, there are cars. It's a parking lot. She has to make it to the edge of the woods. She didn't think she could run any faster, but she does. She runs faster and faster, breaking out of the woods into the parking lot, looking around frantically. And she sees a man and a woman, older, like grandparents, standing next to a camper in front of one of those signs that has a map of the Smoky Mountains on it. And she races across the parking lot and throws herself at the woman, almost knocking her down.

"What in the world?" the grandmother woman cries. "Who are—? What's the matter, honey?"

The man asks her what's wrong too, but she can't talk. She's panting so hard, gasping for breath, can't speak.

"What are you doing out here all by yourself?" the grandfather man asks.

He's bending over her, but when he straightens up, he looks back into the woods where she came out. Then the woman looks that way, and the little girl turns around and sees him. He's standing in the edge of the woods on the other side of the parking lot, looking at her.

She has to talk now. She has to speak. She gasps in a breath and manages to whisper, *"That man's not my daddy!"*

She says *man-th* instead of *man's* because she's missing her front teeth.

That's all she can say, but she sees from the looks on the faces of the grown-ups that it was the right thing to say. She turns and watches the man walk across the parking lot toward them. He's looking at her, shaking his head.

The woman she grabbed around the waist is hugging her. When the man who walked out of the woods gets close, the grandfather man steps slightly in front of them and says, "She says you ain't her daddy."

The man from the woods stops, hangs his head, shaking it sadly.

"That's right. I'm *not* her daddy."

There's a pause, and hope bursts inside the little girl so fierce it's almost as painful as being afraid. But then the man from the woods keeps talking.

"I'm *trying* to be. I'm doing the very damn best I can to be. But bless her heart, she just misses Jack so much."

He smiles, sticks out his hand to the grandfather man and introduces himself, says he lives in the white house right around the bend.

"You must have seen it. Margaret's bicycle's laying in the driveway — pink, she likes pink. I just got finished painting the walls in her room pink." He gestures down at his paint-splattered britches. There are all colors of paint — red, blue, white, and yellow splotches, but he points to the pink ones. "Her mama calls it Pepto-Bismol pink."

He looks down at the little girl and his face is sad.

"Her daddy was my best friend, the finest man I ever knew. I'd have taken a bullet for Jack." His voice is thick and tear-clotted. "He was a lineman for the electric company, and a little over a year ago, he touched a hot wire and …"

He doesn't finish, just looks down at the little girl and shakes his head.

Then he keeps talking. "When I married his widow, I

thought everything would be fine, you know, because Margaret already knew me. I wasn't some stranger and I thought Margaret would accept me as her daddy." The man sighs, "But she didn't. I've tried everything I know, and just when I think I'm making progress, just when I think she's opening up, she does something like this. She runs off, tries to get somebody to take her away."

The man from the woods gets down on one knee so he's looking her in the eye.

"Margaret, we got to go home now, sweetheart. Mommy's worrying herself sick about you."

Then he notices the scratch on her leg and her skinned knees. He pulls a handkerchief out of his pocket and wipes away the snot from her upper lip and uses the edge it to dab at the blood from the scratch. "We need to get you home and get a Band-Aid on that arm and on those skinned knees."

The little girl can't speak. She's still panting, but that's not why. Her throat has locked up. She shakes her head no, frantically, tightening her grip around the old woman's waist.

The man looks up at the grandparent couple. They look back at him sympathetically. He looks back down at her and only she can see the glint in his eyes.

"You know that black puppy I showed you — the one with white paws like he's wearing socks?"

The little girl remembers the black puppy alright. He'd shown it to her and that's why she'd gone with him. He'd said he had a box full of puppies and asked if she wanted to see them.

"You can't have that one cause it's spoken for, but you can have your pick of any other puppy in the litter. There's a real cute white one with a pink nose and one black ear. It's a female, and you can name her anything you want."

4

She clings to the old woman, trembling.

The man from the woods stands, reaches down to take her arm, and pulls. "Come on, Margaret. It's time to go home, and we'll go get that puppy. Would you like that?"

The grandmother and grandfather don't see that he's squeezing her arm too tight. So tight it hurts. But she doesn't have the air to cry.

The grandmother woman pries the little girl's arms away from her waist and gently shoves her toward the man from the woods.

"Go on, now sweetheart," she says. "Your mama's worried about you."

The man takes her hand then, and he squeezes it too hard too, just like he squeezed her arm, hard enough to make a bruise. The grandfather man smiles and gently pats her on the shoulder.

"You wanna see that puppy, doncha? Why, I bet your daddy will let you sleep with that puppy!" He winks at the man from the woods.

The man from the woods smiles. "I bet he will, too!"

He holds her hand too tight, thanks the people for being so kind, then turns away.

"Mommy baked an apple pie. When we get home, it'll still be hot out of the oven. And we got some vanilla ice cream in the freezer. You can put ice cream on top of it."

The man from the woods talks about the pie and the ice cream and the puppy as he pulls her along beside him across the parking lot, holding her hand so tight it hurts. She turns back once to look at the old couple beside the camper in the parking lot. They smile and wave at her, but she doesn't wave back.

He waits until they are so far into the trees that you can't see the parking lot anymore before he stops, turns her toward him, and looks down at her.

"Don't you *ever* do nothing like that again, you got that, little girl?"

She can't do anything but nod dumbly.

"You will be very, *very* sorry if you do!"

Tears spill down her cheeks, but her chest is too tight to cry. And she's sure he won't like it if she cries.

"Your name is Margaret, you understand me?"

She nods her head.

"Then say it, say your name."

"My name is Margaret," she whispers.

"Say it!"

"My name is Margaret." She speaks the words in a tiny, shaking voice.

He takes her by the hand again and drags her off through the woods, but not toward the white house on the hill with a bike in the driveway. The other direction, down toward the valley where the trailer house is tucked back behind trees so far you can't see it from the road.

As he leads her away, she reaches into her pocket and squeezes the locket the kidnappers don't know she has. It's the kind of locket that opens. Inside there's a picture of her real Mommy and Daddy.

Chapter One

THE SLENDER young woman in the bright red shorts and fashionably retro Led Zeppelin tee shirt fired a serve over the net that would have made Serena Williams proud.

Rileigh Bishop captured the moment, froze it in digital eternity. She was pretty sure she'd captured the look of studied concentration on the blonde's face, maybe even the sheen of perspiration on her forehead, if she was already sweating. It wasn't really all that warm yet. Rileigh sat back, snapped the 180mm lens off the Nikon and replaced it with a 50mm portrait lens. She fired off three shots with that, capturing the woman playing tennis, of course, but also the sign out front that identified the court in Rutledge Park. The tennis courts in the park were new, opened a couple of weeks ago. That and the time/date stamp on the photo would prove the picture wasn't one taken years ago, before the traffic accident that had left Crystal Collins disabled.

Located far in the back, right by the woods, the tennis courts were impossible to see from the road, but Crystal knew how to negotiate the little winding road that led to them. She ought to. She had been there bright and early every morning this week. And Rileigh knew that because she had taken pictures of her there every morning. She didn't park right in front of the courts, but halfway up the hill, so she had a good view down with the sun at her back.

Crystal was annihilating the young man who was her opponent, driving shots low over the net or landing them in one corner or another, wherever he didn't happen to be. An amazing display of physical prowess from a woman whose injured back made it impossible for her to get around without a walker. After a lawsuit settled out of court, she had collected a tidy little nest egg from the insurance company for said disability.

Whack!

The sound of the racket hitting the ball square was carried in through the open windows of Rileigh's old Honda on a breeze perfumed by dogwood blossoms and the little bunches of white flowers that had begun to bloom in the bushes. Rileigh inhaled a big lungful of the fragrant air and let it out slowly. If there was anything in this life that Rileigh Bishop loved, it was springtime in the Smoky Mountains. It looked to her sometimes like an artist had seen the brown landscape slowly turning green and daubed little white and pink dogwood-tree blotches of color all up and down the slopes of the mountains for decoration.

There was a cherry tree at the entrance to Rutledge Park, but it hadn't started to bloom yet. Cherry blossoms apparently took a little longer, but the wait was always worth it.

Whack!

That must have been the killing blow, because the young man trotted up to the net laughing as Crystal strode confidently toward him, racket in one hand, a tennis ball in the other which she tossed up and down as she walked. Rileigh could tell that she was razzing the guy hard, but he appeared to be taking it well. Rileigh fired off two more shots as the pair stood talking at the net, then popped the 180mm back on the nose of the camera to catch shots of the woman going back to her car, opening the trunk, and putting her tennis racket inside. She closed the trunk and looked around. She might even have noticed Rileigh, because she stood still for a moment, looking her way. Rileigh kept the camera tucked low so you couldn't tell she had one.

Mama had asked Rileigh why she had to use some fancy kind of camera when you could take a picture with your telephone. Why, Mama had seen a television show just yesterday right after *Family Feud* where teenagers made movies, all kinds of movies, just using their iPhones. Rileigh had explained that when you held your phone out in front of you, it was obvious you were taking a picture. And the subjects of her pictures would likely not take kindly to being photographed.

Crystal continued to look up the hill in her direction. So she set the camera down in the passenger seat, cranked up the Honda, and crunched over the gravel through the gate of the park.

Rileigh glanced at her watch and realized that if she didn't hurry, she was going to be late. She had to go by the house and pick up Mama, then drive into town to Black Bear Forge Elementary School, where Mama was in charge of the Spring Carnival. Mama had volunteered Rileigh to help her operate the balloon-pop booth. Rileigh had tried to beg off, but Mama said she really needed the help "since Rhett ain't gonna be around to carry the heavy stuff."

Apparently, Mama had broken up with Rhett Butler.

Weren't many women in the world who could say that, including Scarlet O'Hara.

The carnival started at eleven in the morning and would end at one in the afternoon, in time for the kids to return to their classrooms before being dismissed for the day.

Rileigh still had to load all of Mama's paraphernalia into the trunk of her car to haul to the school. Once the carnival was over, she would deposit Mama back home, then drive into Gatlinburg and drop off the company camera at the office of Gatlinburg Investigations, the Good GIs, and let Wally Hansford know that she'd have the final report for him in his email first thing tomorrow morning. The report would detail the activities of the poor young woman who'd been rear-ended in an accident eighteen months ago, a woman who claimed her life was completely destroyed because of her back injuries. According to court depositions, she'd been active and athletic before the accident, played tennis and golf. She'd even been a rock climber. But afterward, she'd been confined to bed, only able to move around slowly using a walker. Otherwise, her life had been ruined.

The photographs accompanying Rileigh's report would prove otherwise.

Rileigh headed toward home, windows down, inhaling crisp morning air so fresh it might have been scrubbed with lye soap and hung out on the line to dry in the sunshine. The aroma of springtime was somehow more than the sum of its parts. It wasn't just particular flowers or blooming trees. You could add all those scents together and it still wouldn't smell as good as the air smelled every spring in the mountains. If a company could manage to capture that aroma in a dryer softener sheet, they'd make a fortune.

Turning off Bent Twig Road and up the driveway toward Mama's house, she performed the feat of driving dexterity required to make it all the way up the driveway and over the hump at the top without crashing through the fence. She wasn't the only person in Yarmouth County who had to perform some manner of driving magic to negotiate the landscape. These were mountains, after all. Driveways were steep. Streets were steep. She and everyone else in the county were grateful that the winter had been as mild as it was. Aside from the nasty ice storm in January that had locked the whole county down.

Rileigh had been on a paddle wheel boat in the middle of Big Puddle Lake during that storm, then had gone straight to the hospital with Mitch, who'd been seriously concussed as a result of his heroics. By the time she'd been aware of what was going on out in the wide world beyond Mitch's hospital room, the ice had melted and nothing remained but the stories of those who'd had to go out and negotiate icy mountain roads. And everyone had a story, told with an underlying sense of pride, the way folks in Maine shrugged off blizzards and Texans dismissed twisters.

As soon as Rileigh got out of her car and closed her door, the child-guard locks snapped and locked all the doors. For a frantic moment she was afraid she'd gotten locked out *again* — but she had the keys in her hand. There was a short somewhere in the car's electrical system that made every door closure an adventure. She had to get it fixed, as soon as she could afford it. In the meantime, she'd best pocket her car keys as soon as she turned off the ignition or she'd be making nice with the guy from Triple A again.

Mama came out onto the front porch.

"I got all the stuff we need piled up in the living room. Open up your trunk and let's get it loaded."

Over the years, Mama had been in charge of various booths — the ring toss, the water gun squirt, the fishing pond. Consequently, she had accumulated the paraphernalia associated with those booths, and she hauled it all with her to the school every spring, in case this year's new crop of volunteers needed anything. Loading it all took longer than Rileigh had hoped.

"You was up with the chickens this morning," Mama said. "Where'd you go so bright and early?"

She'd had to be in position up the street from Crystal's house when she came tripping out the front door and hopped into her car, poor disabled wretch that she was, on her way to go play tennis. Rileigh was looking forward to writing this report, not only because she could nail the woman dead to rights, but because this was the first big case the Good Guys had assigned to her since Wally Hansford had given her a full-time job a few weeks ago. In a few days she'd get her first paycheck from her first full-time employment in almost a year. If she could just manage not to get dragged into some kind of ... *adventure*, she could finally start putting her life back together.

Chapter Two

WHILE MAMA USED the bottle of compressed air to start filling up balloons, Rileigh made a beeline for the machine at the far end of the carnival site, following the sweet, hypnotic aroma of cotton candy. Rileigh had been addicted to cotton candy for as long as she could remember. It was like eating a cloud, a pink cloud, or a blue cloud, or a purple cloud. And it was pure sugar so what was not to like?

"I'll take two of those, please," Rileigh said, digging in her pocket for change.

"I don't take money. You got to go buy you some tickets."

Right. All the little kids at the carnival would be using tickets as money, which they'd been accruing ever since they got back from the Christmas break.

You could earn a ticket by helping the teacher wash off the whiteboard, by standing politely in line and refraining from jumping up and down, wiggling, pulling somebody's hair or poking somebody in the side. You could earn a ticket by turning in your homework or getting an A on a spelling test. And you could earn tickets by doing absolutely nothing at all. Every child had been issued a ticket for each day's attendance. The teachers kept up with the tickets for the children, knowing that there wasn't a five-year-old on the planet who could keep track of a small piece of paper for three months. When the children were dismissed from class to come out to the carnival, they'd be given all their tickets to spend however they liked.

"Be right back," Rileigh said, making her way to a woman dressed in a costume that was a cross between a fairy godmother and a New Orleans madam: Evelyn Foster. She and her husband Clive were natives, born and raised in Yarmouth County. Clive sat nearby in the chair part of a walker. He had a satchel at his side that held an oxygen tank, and slender clear tubing ran from the tank to an apparatus that fit in his nose. Clive Foster had black lung. Rileigh never was sure why some coal miners got it and others didn't, because they all breathed the same coal dust. But Clive was one of the unlucky ones. He had been disabled for fifteen years and she'd watched him slowly deteriorate, getting skinnier and scrawnier, coughing more, until he was dependent on the oxygen rig to leave the house at all.

"Yo, Evie," Rileigh said to Evelyn, "I need some tickets."

Evelyn cocked her head to the side. "Have you been a good girl?"

Rileigh shook her head. "Absolutely not."

"You know these tickets are only for good little girls and boys."

"If these tickets were only for good little girls and boys, there wouldn't be a kid here with any of them."

That got a laugh out of Clive, but then he started coughing.

Rileigh traded a five-dollar bill for a handful of tickets and stuffed them down into her pocket, hollered thanks over her shoulder, and made her way through the growing crowd to the cotton candy booth where she bought a pink stick of cotton candy *and* a blue one and carried them back to where her mother was filling up balloons.

Mama reached out for the blue cotton candy. "Oh, that was so sweet of you to get me—"

"Get your own," Rileigh barked playfully. She reached into her pocket, pulled out tickets, and gave them to her mother. "Both of these are *mine.*"

"You never were a selfish child." Mama shook her head and tsk-tsking. "All that training in generosity gone to waste." She nodded to the rubber hose that went to the bottle of compressed air. "Here, fill up balloons while I'm gone."

"I can't fill up balloons. I got a handful of cotton candy."

Her mother raised one eyebrow. "You'll figure something out."

The balloon-pop booth consisted of a big piece of cardboard with the balloons affixed to it with tape. Contestants had to stand behind a line chalked onto the grass and toss darts at the balloons. If they popped a balloon, they got the prize listed on a piece of paper taped to the cardboard behind the balloon.

Mama had brought along several folding chairs, so she and Rileigh could sit beside the table that displayed darts, and a small box to deposit the tickets the children paid to play.

The whole front lawn of the elementary school was quickly becoming a controlled zoo with parents and other volunteers scurrying around setting up booths. By the time Mama returned with her stick of cotton candy, Rileigh had already polished off her two and her fingers were sticky, making it hard to handle the balloons she was trying to blow up.

"Let me do that. You go wash your hands."

Rileigh obediently went across the front lawn into the parking lot, where a pickup pulling a big white trailer was blocking the way into the building. The lettering on the side of the trailer said, "The Foote Notes." Rileigh waved at Hank Foote as he hauled a set of drums out of the back of the trailer and a huge stand-up bass case so he could get to the other instruments.

Rileigh hadn't known there'd be a band. They'd likely play some country, too, but Rileigh's favorite was Blue-grass. If the whole band showed up, there'd be a guitar, a fiddle, a mandolin, a steel guitar, a five-string banjo, and a Dobro — different combinations of them for different songs.

When Rileigh stepped into the building, you could feel excitement thrumming like a harp string. By the time she got back outside, the Black Bear Forge Elementary School Spring Carnival had sprung up on the front lawn of the school like mushrooms after a rain. Besides the simple game booths, there were half a dozen hinky-tinky carnival rides: a Tilt-A-Whirl with its spinning booths, a small Ferris wheel, and a Hop Toad where giant frogs with little-kid passengers randomly leapt three feet in the air and then settled back to the ground. There was a traditional merry-go-round with plastic steeds — that always creeped Rileigh out. The horses' faces seemed contorted in pain, as if somebody really had poked a pole through their bellies. The pony ride with live horses was more her speed, though she feared the lambs and baby goats in the petting zoo would be sticky from cotton-candied fingers before the day was done.

She looked at her watch, then hurried back to her booth to be there when the tsunami of small children crashed over the carnival in three … two … one … *RING.*

The bell inside the building went off, and Mama grinned and rubbed her hands together. "Showtime!"

Half an hour later, the pandemonium had reached epic proportions. The entire community had been invited — parents brought younger siblings, while relatives, neighbors and friends came to support the school. Though the children had either earned or had been issued tickets to enjoy the games, the adults had to purchase theirs, the money going to fund the necessary expenses of future carnivals, renting the cotton candy machine and the popcorn machine, and purchasing various supplies. Squealing kids were running everywhere. Parents and grandparents urged their little ones on in the rousing competition of throwing a hoop over the neck of a bottle or a basketball into a wicker basket. And the din of laughter and conversation was the kind you could warm your fingers on when you came in out of the cold.

All of it was painted on a background of fiddle and banjo music as Hank Foote belted out, "I Am a Man of Constant Sorrows."

A little blonde girl appeared out of the crowd and cried, "Wi-leigh!" and came barreling at her, arms spread wide. Mayella Stump crashed into Rileigh, a little wrecking ball, almost knocked her out of the chair and upsetting the table of darts.

Rileigh hugged her while she scanned the crowd for Georgia, her best friend since childhood, and spotted Georgia looking around frantically for the little girl. Rileigh waved. Georgia turned and headed her way, dragging four-year-old Mason along beside her.

"Mayella, I told you to stay with me or you have to

hold my hand," she told the little girl, who smiled at her angelically.

"I promise I won't run off," Mason said, trying to pry his hand out of his mother's.

"In a pig's eye," Georgia scoffed. "I've chased you down twice and I'm done."

Georgia spied the remains of Mama's cotton candy on the table. "That looks good, where's the booth?"

Mama pointed to the other end of the carnival.

"You have to have tickets," Rileigh said, pulling a handful out of her pocket and giving them to Georgia. Georgia let go of Mason's hand to take the tickets and he stood obediently beside her.

"This thing is twice the size it was last year," Georgia said. The carnival had clearly outgrown the front lawn of the school.

Two little girls approached the booth, wanting to play. Mama got up to help them and Georgia nodded to Rileigh. "You're busy, catch you later."

She turned to take Mason's hand, but he was gone.

"Mason!" she cried, looking around. She grabbed Mayella's hand and headed off into the crowd. "I'm gonna skin that boy alive! *Maaason!*"

The little red-headed girl popped a balloon with her first dart.

"Good shot!" Mama cried, then gave her the necklace of plastic Mardi Gras beads she'd won and sat back down.

"Where's Georgia?"

"Chasing Mason."

Mama rolled her eyes.

Trevor Lane hurried past, bumping Mama's chair, and mumbling "Excuse me." He had a shiner and a split lip. Rileigh smiled. The last time she'd talked to him was right after he got into a fight with Jason Begley over a tourist named Veronica Langley — who was later murdered.

Smitty Arnold, the bartender at the Rusty Nail Tavern in Gatlinburg strolled by with his wife and newborn son. He smiled and waved. Zander Dowling was behind him. *Dr.* Alexander Dowling — the full-of-himself doctor Rileigh babysat as a child. He neither smiled nor waved.

Then Rileigh looked up and saw Yarmouth County Sheriff Mitchell Webster making his way through the tangle of children, booths, and volunteers. He arrived at their booth and held out a pair of handcuffs. "Either one of you ladies want to get locked up?"

"Not so's you'd notice," Mama said.

"The sheriff's department is running the jail." He pointed to an enclosure nearby made of two refrigerator boxes duct-taped together, not a whole lot bigger than a telephone booth, with a "window" opening cut in the side.

"I get to arrest people for doing all kinds of nothing, and I take them to jail. Then they have to pay to get out."

"Nice work when you can get it," Rileigh said.

Mitch leaned against the edge of the table full of darts and said, "I deputized three little boys to do all the work, so I could come over here to people watch." He looked from Mama to Rileigh, then back to Mama. "Your mission, should you choose to accept it, is to tell me the life stories of everybody who walks past in thirty seconds or less."

"Not hap'nin'," Rileigh said. "Not in thirty seconds or less."

Chapter Three

"You think we know every single one of these people?" Mama asked. "There's hundreds of them."

"But you do, don't you?"

Rileigh smiled. "There was a time when Mama probably would have."

"Not anymore," Mama said. "It used to be that you never bumped carts in the produce section of the grocery store with anybody you hadn't been bumping carts with your whole life. But it's different now."

"Why's that?"

"There are a lot more away-from-here's than there used to be," Rileigh said, glad that she no longer had to explain what that meant to Mitch. He had finally accepted his identity ... not with grace, but with resignation.

"And more of them every day," Mama said. "Tourists retiring to their vacation homes. People who work remote so they can live wherever they want. It used to be that we were so isolated and off the beaten path that nobody ever came here. But now ..."

"The Great Smoky Mountains National Park has more

visitors every year than any other national park in the country," Rileigh said. "More than fourteen million people last year."

"Not everybody's new," Mama said. She pointed with her chin toward a couple walking past the booth with several small children in tow. "That's there's Audrey and Hank Foote. Lived here all their lives. He's got himself a local band called the Foote Notes, plays at events all over the mountains. But he makes his living as a studio musician in Nashville —banjo, guitar, bass, any musical instrument's got strings on it, Hank can make it sing."

"And Audrey is a vocalist," Rileigh said. "You've heard her sing on country music albums for twenty years. She sang backup with Reba McEntire, Faith Hill, Dolly Parton, and the Judds."

"I asked Hank once if he ever wanted to be famous," Mama said. "Most of the musicians who go to Nashville are going there because they think they're going to be the next... who? Garth Brooks?"

"What'd he say?"

"He said he'd given up on that when he was twenty. He and Audrey started having kids and he wanted a normal life. Said he wanted to go in a Starbucks and get a cup of coffee without everybody mobbing him. He ain't rich and famous, but he makes a *good living*. Him and Audrey swapped out who stayed home when the kids were little. They got to make the music the good Lord gifted them to do, but they didn't have to live their lives on a tour bus and they was home most every weekend."

Rileigh caught Audrey's attention and called out, "Duelin' Banjos!"

Audrey smiled and gave her a thumbs up.

"They take requests?" Mitch asked. "I would dearly love to hear Country Roads."

"They'll start up again in a few minutes and you can go ask. Threaten to put them in jail if they say no."

Two women passed by in their early 50s. One had long straight gray hair. The other, her dark hair cut short and curly, was driving a motorized wheelchair. "There's Hannah and Betty Marie Forrester. Don't remember the last time I saw them, or Betty Marie, anyway."

Rileigh looked at Mama, who nodded. "It's been a year, at least."

"They're almost local," Rileigh told Mitch. "Hannah's parents had a vacation cabin and she spent every summer here when she was growing up. About five years ago, Hannah retired and moved here with Betty Marie, who's got ALS. She seems to be doing remarkably well."

"They keep to themselves, mostly," Mama said with a knowing look.

"Oh, Mama, nobody cares about that."

Mama shrugged. "Betty Marie raises the most beautiful roses you ever seen. Terry Collins, he's their mailman, told me that first thing every morning for four years there's been fresh roses in a vase on the porch. Never missed once, even in the snow. So they must be raising some indoors somehow, too."

A tiny old woman, baby-bird thin, approached. She held the hand of a little girl who was taller and heavier than she was.

"That's Granny Maggie," Rileigh said. "You can't get any more local than she is. She still lives in the house where she grew up."

The old woman saw Rileigh and Mama, smiled and dragged the child over to them.

"This here is my granddaughter, Shiloh," she said proudly. The little girl hung back, looking at the ground. She appeared to be about ten years old, tall and big-boned, with the kind of pale blonde hair you saw on toddlers before it got darker. Hers was parted in the middle and hung straight all the way down her back to her waist. Her skin was porcelain-white, and she stood as awkwardly as only a painfully shy child can.

"Glad to meet you, Shiloh," Mama said.

The girl glanced up and Rileigh got a brief look at eyes that were robin's egg blue before she fixed them on the dirt again and mumbled some kind of greeting.

"Hello, Shiloh," Rileigh said. "Welcome to Yarmouth County."

The little girl just nodded her head but said nothing, inching back behind her grandmother, looking for all the world like she wished she could sink into the ground and disappear.

"I'm takin' her round introducing her so she can meet some other kids …" The woman's voice trailed off and she reached up to her right ear, then her left, fiddling with something. "Gotta get me some new hearing aids! These uns blink on and off like a sign outside a beer joint, and I'm deaf as a post 'thout 'em." Her face brightened then, so apparently they'd blinked back on. "Where was I? Oh yeah, I was telling you Shiloh won't be starting school until the fall."

There were still six weeks left of the semester before summer break. Rileigh wondered why her grandmother wouldn't enroll the girl in school now.

Then Rileigh and Mama heard the music sweep through the crowd. They stopped and sang along with everyone else.

"Rocky Top, you'll always be … home sweet home to me."

By the time the song finished, the whole crowd was singing along.

POV: Elizabetta Harbour

"GOOD OLE ROCKY TOP," Elizabetta Harbour sang with the others. *"Rocky Top, Tennessee."*

Her eyes were closed, remembering the Osborne Brothers concert when she was thirteen years old, smelling for the first time that sweet smoke drifting with the music through the crowd. At twelve, she'd known what she wanted to do with her life. She wanted to be a marine biologist!

But that smell ... that smoke had changed everything.

"Miss Harbour, Amanda took my tickets and won't give them back," cried a gap-toothed little boy in front of her. "Make her give them back!"

Elizabetta ground her teeth, then draped a patient smile between her ears like a sheet on a clothesline.

"Ask her nicely," she said. "Say please."

The kid kept complaining but she ignored him, pinching the bridge of her nose to ease the throbbing of her head.

Elizabetta Harbour was in the wrong line of work. She'd figured that out too late, and now she was stuck. What made it so hard to bear was that it was her own fault. She'd picked it. She saw it coming ... and yet here she was. She liked that phrase the mountain people used — "the truth still in the husk." And the truth still in the husk was that Elizabetta Harbour flat out did *not* like children. Not little kids, not older kids, not teenagers. Elizabetta Harbour would be delighted to spend the rest of her life in the company of nothing but adults, not a single human being under the age of 21.

And yet she'd managed to totally screw up her life by becoming a kindergarten teacher. Go figure.

There was a reason for that, of course. She'd had a glorious time in college, after developing a fascination for weed at thirteen, and it had colored most every day of her life from then on. She also liked booze and drugs and men, a lot of sex — *let's par-tay!* The problem was that she never had time to study and she damn near flunked out. And if she flunked out, there went her parents' support. They'd made it clear she would either make it in college or she would get a job at McDonalds.

Not wanting to spend her life asking, "do you want fries with that order," Elizabetta had taken the path of least resistance. She would have majored in underwater basket weaving if that would have gotten her a degree. It wouldn't. So, she figured — a big, *big* mistake on her part, as it turned out— that becoming a teacher would be easy. And if you had to be a teacher, how hard could teaching a bunch of five-year-olds be?

She had strung her partying lifestyle out as long as was humanly possible. Her father liked to tell people, "Yeah, Elizabetta crammed four years of college into six and a half." But eventually, the ride was over. The next thing she knew, Elizabetta was standing on the stage in her purple gown, awaiting a diploma for her degree in elementary education.

She didn't have a friend in the world who could understand it. They all said, "Shit, Lizzie. You don't *like* kids."

Yet here she was in her first year of full-time employment, corralling twenty-five gap-toothed five-year-olds. God, how she hated it.

Three little kids ran past her squealing — her students. She glanced around. The rest of them were … well, *somewhere.* She saw other teachers cruising the sea of people like that little clown fish looking for Nemo, keeping some kind of tally of their students, she supposed. She couldn't imagine how. In this pandemonium, there was no way to keep track, so why bother.

A woman about her age walked past on the arm of a hunk, flirting and laughing. Oh, to flirt. Not here! Not looking like the Sea Hag! When you were a kindergarten teacher, you were supposed to wear those stupid sweaters that had apples and bees and cutesy little monograms. Her mother had actually purchased one of them for her and presented it to her before her first day on the job. It had brought her a great deal of satisfaction to stuff the ugly sweater in the first dumpster she passed.

That had been eight miserable months ago. Eight months of smiling, gritting her own teeth as little kids who had none threw up on her shoes, fought with each other, wet their pants, threw tantrums, and flat-ass refused to learn a damned thing she tried to teach them.

She'd started looking for some other career path after two weeks on the job and she had finally found something. It would be a pay cut, but she would cheerfully take a couple of thousand dollars less a year to get out of *this*. But it was still spring, weeks before the end of the school year. She would have to tough it out to the end. The last thing she needed was to somehow manage to get fired so that every future employer would know she'd crashed and burned at her first job out of the gate.

So Elizabetta had perfected the art of smiling when she felt like screaming, of grinding her teeth without being heard. She balled her hands into fists so frequently that she had scars on her palms from where her fingernails had cut holes. She let out a sigh that wasn't relief, not yet. But at least there was a light at the end of the tunnel, and it wasn't a damn train.

"Oh, look," said her teacher's aide, Trisha, pointing at a little girl in their class who had managed to smear half a stick of cotton candy all over her face and *in her hair.* "Isn't that the cutest thing?"

Trisha whipped out her iPhone and began snapping photographs of the sticky-faced child that Elizabetta would have to clean later. Goody.

"This carnival is such a fun idea," she gushed.

Where did they find these people who found sticky children and the smell of Elmer's Glue appealing?

"Oh, yes, she's absolutely adorable," said Elizabetta, knowing that the sarcasm was lost on the young woman who had been assigned to help her corral the little kids in her class.

She longed for a joint, very much needed to mellow out, but she had better sense than to smoke weed on the job. She was sure getting caught with "drugs" at an elementary school was a walk-the-plank offense.

She had to admit, she was grateful for the spring carnival. It got her out of the classroom for most of the day and allowed her to temporarily ignore the little urchins who were her charges. Parents and volunteers operated games for all her hyperactive children, and all she had to do was stand around and smile — a beatific smile — as if she were enjoying it. The job had taught her one thing. The reason for that enigmatic smile on the face of the Mona Lisa: Elizabetta was sure she'd been a kindergarten teacher who couldn't stand children.

Chapter Four

"WHEN I WAS A LITTLE GIRL, I's the only one in the class didn't know the words to 'My Homeland, Tennessee.'" Granny Maggie said, "and the other kids made fun of me. Might be it ain't the official state song, but I know every word of 'Rocky Top.'"

The old woman caught sight of somebody else she wanted to talk to and grabbed the little girl's hand. "Y'all have a good day now," she said as she dragged the child off to another introduction.

"I guess you'd call Maggie McCulloch a fixture in the community." Mama said.

"She's..." Rileigh searched for the word.

"Her dipstick don't touch oil," Mama finished for her.

Talk about the pot calling the kettle black.

"Maggie's ... different," was all Rileigh could think to say.

"Oh, come on, Rileigh. She's a screwy old lady, everybody knows that." Rileigh's mother's absolute lack of self-awareness was breathtaking sometimes. "Least ways Maggie's got her dress on right side out today. Last time I seen her, the tag was flapping in the back and I couldn't figure out how she got the buttons fastened."

"Her daughter Becca and I went to school together," Rileigh said. "Becca was the kid whose mother never let her do *anything*. Maggie was absurdly overprotective, came all the way into the building to Becca's classroom to get her after school every day, and kept huge dogs to guard the house."

"Made Becca afraid of her own shadow. And you know what happens to kids who have been locked down like that."

"Let me guess," Mitch said. "She rebelled as a teenager."

"Oh, that's putting it mildly! Drugs, sex, rock and roll. She was a wild child."

"Eventually, she ran away, and she's been popping in and out of Maggie's life ever since. Drove that poor woman to distraction."

Rileigh's cameo memory of her happened after they were adults. Becca had noted that career-military Rileigh was childless.

"She told me, and her voice was dripping in sarcasm, that I *had* to have children. She said, 'Mama's been putting the full-court press on me to have kids my whole life.'"

"You know there *is* something to be said for grandchildren ... not that I'm speaking from personal experience," Mama said, eying Rileigh.

"Tell him the rest of the story," Rileigh blustered as the three of them watched Maggie pull the little girl along with her from one booth to the next, introducing her as she went.

"A few years ago, Becca told her mother that she'd had a baby, a little girl," Mama said. "Maggie was so excited. Becca promised to bring the child home to Yarmouth

County, but she never did. Sent one picture of a blonde toddler in a stroller and Maggie 'bout wore it out showing folks. Becca moved around all the time, doing drugs and selling drugs and God only knew what else. About a month ago, though, Becca called Maggie and said she had some awful disease." Mama looked at Rileigh. "What did she say it was?"

"I don't remember exactly." But Rileigh did remember. It was syphilis. "I know that she was literally dying and asked Maggie to come get Shiloh."

"So, Maggie went out to California and came back with the child, said she drove the whole way there and back in that old pickup, slept in the camper on the back of it. Didn't nobody know she was gone until she was already back. I ain't never seen anybody more happy in my life than Granny Maggie, smiling so wide her false teeth liked to dried out."

"She's a little old to be raising a small child, don't you think?" Mitch ventured. "And if she doesn't have all her marbles…"

"She's better'n a foster home," Mama said. "They ain't no other kin to take the girl."

"How you, Lily, Rileigh?" called a middle-aged woman with paint splatters on her clothes as she hurried by.

"Fine," Mama called back. "N'you?"

"Can't complain," said the woman over her shoulder as she disappeared into the crowd.

"That's Cynthia Waters," Rileigh said. "She's doing the face painting."

"You should go have your face painted," Mitch told Rileigh.

"What exactly is it you would like for me to look like when she's done?"

"How about a great big daisy right on your cheek?"

30

"Cynthia was married to a man named Claude," Mama said. "Meanest son of a bitch you ever met. But he finally died, thank the good Lord. Cynthia moved back home to the Forge and has a good life, flits around like a hummingbird to flowers."

"She belongs to every women's group in the county," said Rileigh. "Teaches Sunday school. Makes quilts and baby blankets to give to the Red Cross, crochets scarves and doilies that they sell at the church bazaar before Christmas."

The first notes of Duelin' Banjos drifted into the air.

"Don't talk to me," Rileigh cried, waving Mitch and Mama quiet. "That's my favorite song!"

Mama left in search of a bag of popcorn as Rileigh listened. The song ended with a flourish and there was a smattering of applause from the crowd. Rileigh clapped and whistled.

A couple passed the booth then, pushing a stroller. Rileigh hadn't seen the man in years, barely recognized him — David Hicks, the man her sister Jillian had left standing at the altar, more or less, when she disappeared twenty-eight years ago. Rileigh knew that David was a licensed personal trainer and martial arts instructor who ran several gym/training facilities called Boot Camp, and Mama had told her he'd moved back home to the Forge from Nashville. But this was the first time Rileigh had seen him since he'd arrived. He was stunning. In his late forties, he looked ten years younger and was built like Arnold Schwarzenegger. Huge shoulders, muscled arms, ripped belly. She couldn't help the thought — it broke free of the armed guards that patrolled that part of her mind and leapt center stage under the spotlight. That could be Jillian there, walking beside him. It could be their child in the stroller. Then a yapping bark came from the stroller and the blonde woman beside him — whose big chest was squeezed precariously into a tight blouse with a plunging neckline — reached into the stroller and retrieved an odd-looking little dog. It was mostly hairless, but with long white fur on its head, ears and feet, plus a fluffy tail.

"That's a Chinese Crested," Mitch said, pointing to the dog. "I've seen pictures, but I've always wanted to see one in the flesh."

With that, Mitch leapt to his feet and approached the couple, introducing himself and oohing and aahing over the dog in the woman's arms. David's eyes met Rileigh's and she felt rooted to the spot, finally forcing herself to smile and nod a greeting. The woman giggled and Rileigh looked at her, really looked at her for the first time. Early twenties, too much makeup and … and she was *flirting* with Mitch. Not that Rileigh blamed her, but seriously? After what seemed an interminably long conversation, Mitch came back to the table and the pair moved on.

"Wow," Rileigh said, "what an *eye-catching* …" She let the pause dangle a couple of beats too long, then finally said, "dog." But the remark blew right past Mitch, who allowed that it was, indeed, a fine-looking animal. Mama returned from the direction David and the woman had gone, looking over her shoulder.

"That was David Hicks!" she said, and Rileigh nodded.

"I saw."

Mitch watched the unspoken words dance back and forth between them.

"What?" he asked, utterly clueless.

"He and that woman were having a … disagreement," Mama said, "and I didn't want to interrupt, so I didn't say hidey. She got mad and stormed off. And there wasn't no baby in that stroller. It was a *dog*, a funny-looking thing. Musta had the mange 'cause most of its hair fell out."

"I saw that, too."

An old man walked by, holding the hand of a young man of indeterminate age who would always be a little boy — Russell Henderson and his grandson, Buddy. The boy clutched a handful of toy cars in his free hand, which he gave to his grandfather to hold for him while he played every one of the games. A few minutes after they passed by, Rileigh heard the boy cry, "I won! I won!" from the other end of the carnival.

Ben Pendergast approached their booth, which now had a small line of children waiting to play. Ben was wearing an orange University of Tennessee baseball cap, which he tipped to the ladies before he nodded a greeting to the sheriff. "You seen Sylvia?"

Rileigh shook her head.

"Maybe she got locked up in the jail," Mitch offered, nodding toward the cardboard box building on the other side of the lawn.

"I'll go check." Ben turned that way.

Mama leaned over to Mitch. "Him and Sylvia lost a son in Afghanistan."

"I remember Joe," Rileigh said. "He was a freckled-face cereal box kid." She shook her head. "He joined the military so he wouldn't have to take over his father's pig farm. At the time, I didn't blame him at all."

Mama watched Ben as he searched for Sylvia. "They ain't never been the same since they lost Joe."

A dark-haired couple accompanied a little boy who wanted to try his luck at the balloon pop. Mama took his ticket, showed the little boy how to hold the darts, then helped him throw them.

"That's Ahmad and Leyla Kalel," Rileigh said. "He runs a store on Main Street in Gatlinburg. Sells rocks. Not jewels, rocks. Beautiful rocks. Crystals and geodes and stones from all over the world. Right next to the front counter is a quartz crystal that must weigh five hundred pounds. I don't know where he gets them."

Three squealing children came running past the booth, two of them chasing the first, who was weaving in and out of the bodies in the crowd like a receiver dodging tackles on his way to the end zone. Coming up behind them was a woman calling ineffectually, "Now you kids stop running. You're not supposed to run here, you know that."

The woman stopped when the kids vanished into the crowd and put her hands on her hips, then glanced over at Rileigh and sighed.

"What are you going to do?" she asked.

Rileigh gave her a commiserating smile. The woman shook her head and headed out through the crowd in search of the children.

"That's LaTisha Johnson. She teaches piano and voice lessons. You should hear her sing!" Rileigh shook her head. "I went to an Easter program at the A.M.E. Zion Church down on Pudding Lane and I swear, she's got a voice like Aretha Franklin."

"She ever sing with the Foote Notes?" Mitch asked, then looked past Rileigh as she answered.

"I don't think so. I heard she won't sing anything but gospel music."

"Who's that guy?" Mitch asked. He gestured to a man with a distinctive face — boney, all hard angles. His chin looked sharp enough to break a shovel on, but you couldn't tell for sure because he was wearing a medical mask covering the lower half of his face. What she was sure of was that she didn't know him.

She turned to her mother. "Do you know who that is?" Mama looked at the tall man. He was dressed in jeans and a plain black tee shirt.

"I ain't got no idea," Mama said.

The man was standing beside the Guess Who? booth where numbered pictures of babies and toddlers were affixed to a big board. The pictures were photographs of the teachers and other school personnel as children. The object of the game was to identify as many as you could and list them on the sheets of paper provided.

Rileigh saw that Mitch was studying the man.

"Something wrong?"

"Nothing's wrong." He shook his head. "Just he looks strong and healthy ... and there's a reason bandits in the Old West wore masks."

WHEN THE BELL went off inside the building that signaled the end of the carnival and the beginning of the end of the school day, the groan that went up from the crowd of children was matched in intensity only by the groan Elizabetta let out at the thought of having to go back into the building. It was bad enough when they went outside at recess, running around, playing in the dirt. This was even worse. Every one of them would come into the building stinking. Oh, how she hated the smell of little kids' sweat. But she smiled, nodded her head, and told all the children to "find your buddy" and "march into the building like good little boys and girls."

A little girl named Tally Masterson came running to her. "I can't find Chloe," she said. "She's my buddy and I looked everywhere."

"Oh, she's here somewhere, sweetheart." Elizabetta cooed, her words so slathered with molasses, they dripped sugar. "Look around, you can find her."

All of the other little kids were lined up two by two to go into the building, and here came Tally again.

"I've looked and looked. She's my BFF and she's gone!" she cried dramatically.

"All right, dear," Elizabetta gritted her teeth and took the little girl's hand. Damn, it was *sticky.* Apparently, she had wadded up a piece of cotton candy in her fist. Elizabetta let go and shooed the little girl toward her teacher's aide. "You go on into the building now with Miss Trisha, and I'll find Chloe."

The odd number of children, two by two except for one little girl, marched into the building and Elizabetta wandered around searching the remains of the carnival for Chloe Malone. She was like a china-doll, with long blonde curls, blue eyes, and no teeth in front. So small for her age, she looked more like a four-year-old than an almost six-year-old. If she were choosing to hide somewhere, playing some idiot game because she didn't want to go back into the building yet, she would be hard to locate.

Elizabetta saw the principal approaching and rearranged her facial features into concern.

"Mrs. Robertson," she said, "we can't find Chloe Malone. Her buddy looked all around before the other children went into the building and couldn't locate her. I can't find her either."

Mrs. Cora Robertson was a mummy from the elephant's graveyard of retired teachers. She had the whole thing going — the requisite ugly sweater with an apple on the pocket, a worm coming out of it to wind through the buttons. She wore a look of perpetual patience, and Elizabetta often studied her face so she could arrange her own features to look the same.

Creasing her forehead, Elizabetta looked around, and made her voice sound anxious. "I've looked in every booth, and I've asked most of the people running booths, and no one has seen her. I think she's hiding somewhere, playing some silly little game. But if she is, I don't know where else to look. Do you?"

Mrs. Robertson took the handoff and ran with the ball toward the goalposts.

"I'll handle it, Miss Harbour," she said. "You get Mrs. Hawkins and Mrs. Campbell to help." Those were the ladies who worked in the school office.

When Elizabetta returned with the others, Mrs. Robertson organized a search with the skill of Admiral Nimitz coordinating a massive assault from the sea. They searched the carnival area in front of the school from top to bottom, from bottom to top, and back again from top to bottom. There was no Chloe.

By the time they had searched the whole area for the third time, Elizabetta was genuinely concerned. That kid had been in her care, and if the little shit had run off somewhere and got lost, her disappearance was a chicken that would come home to roost in Elizabetta's hen house. That was the last thing she needed at the end of a miserable school year. Now she no longer had to fake the look of apprehension on her face. Fear fluttered in her belly. Where the hell was Chloe Malone?

From the carnival area in front of the school, Mrs. Robertson took the search into the building, assuming that Chloe had gone in to go to the bathroom or some such and was in there somewhere. And at the end of another half hour with no Chloe inside and nobody who'd even seen the little girl since the class was dismissed to attend the carnival, Elizabetta was scared pure D shitless. She had lost a kid! Damn, what did they do to a teacher who loses a kid? It wasn't her fault, but you think anybody would believe that? Hell no.

Mrs. Robertson, whose concern now manifested itself in a shaking voice and trembling hands, hailed her in the hallway as she was scurrying toward the library to give it yet one more look. Her words stopped Elizabetta's heart.

"I'm going to call the sheriff," Mrs. Robertson said. "I think something's happened …" She couldn't even get the rest of the sentence out, had to take a breath, then another one. "I think something's happened to Chloe."

The tears that sprang to Elizabetta's eyes and rolled hot down her cheeks were absolutely genuine.

Chapter Five

THE LITTLE GIRL is so scared. She's never been this afraid in her whole life. It feels like she's going to throw up, but she swallows because she knows she can't throw up. Throwing up would make a mess and she doesn't dare make a mess. And she needs to pee. Oh, how she needs to pee! But she can't work up the courage to ask if she can pee. She's afraid to ask for anything. She just wants to ... shrink, get smaller and smaller until she's invisible.

It has to be a nightmare. Things like this don't happen to real little girls, do they? But she'd been warned. Every child she knows has been warned. Mommy and Daddy told her over and over to be careful. But they also told her that she has to be polite. They said it is rude to yell or make a scene in public. They said she has to be a good girl. Her teacher said she has to be a good girl, too. So did her Sunday School teacher. She has obeyed, she'd done what the grownups told her to do because that's what good little girls did.

This can't be real. She squeezes her eyes shut as tight as she can and feels tears running down her cheeks. She's shaking all over, so she tries to stop shaking. If she can stop shaking and stop crying and go back to sleep, she'll wake up and it will be over. She'll be in her own bed in her own room with sheets that smell like sunshine because

Mommy hangs them out on the line to dry. Mommy says she wants her little girl to wake up smelling sunshine. The little girl drags in a ragged breath. Mommy! She loves Mommy so much. She wants to close her eyes and then wake up in her sunshine bed — and she'll leap out of it and run into her parents' room. She'll wake them up, but they won't mind when she tells them she's scared, that she had a terrible nightmare and now she's afraid to sleep alone. They'll hold out their arms to her and she'll crawl under their warm sheets between them.

The little girl squeaks out a sound of some kind. More like a mouse would make or a kitten, not a little girl. But she is afraid anyway that they heard and she doesn't want to draw any attention to herself, doesn't want them to come check on her. Making sounds will get her in trouble. She is sure of it. If she didn't know that making noise would get her in trouble, she'd start screaming and stomping, yelling and crying for help. But they'd hurt her if she did that. They'd hurt her if she made noise and somebody came and it was her fault.

The little girl starts to cry again and she can't do that. She grits her teeth together, sniffs and tries to stop shaking. She can't go back to sleep if she is shaking and crying. And unless she goes back to sleep, she'll stay here in this horrible nightmare.

Sticking her hand down into her pocket, she grabs the locket and squeezes it tight in her little fist. Mommy and Daddy gave her that locket for Christmas. It is a special locket, not just heart-shaped, but it opens. It has a tiny hinge and catch, and when you open it, there is a picture of Mommy and Daddy inside. The man broke the chain when he took her, but she grabbed the locket before it fell and stuffed it down in her pocket and nobody saw. Nobody knows she has it. And holding onto it makes her feel better, closer to Mommy and Daddy and home.

Sitting on the floor, crouched into a corner trying to make herself small, her ear is to the wall, she can hear what is going on in the next room. The grownups in the next room are talking and she can hear their voices. She doesn't want to hear what they're saying, but she can't help it. The woman is crying. And the man is trying to comfort her, telling her everything will be alright. The little girl doesn't know what the woman is crying about, but she thinks it has something to do with her.

Then she hears words that freeze her heart.

"Why would they look here?" he says. "It's the last place they'd expect to find her. She's all yours now."

The words echoed in the little girl's head, bouncing around in there like it's hollow.

"She's all yours now."

"No, no, no, no, no, no!" the little girl cries, screams silently. She isn't their little girl. She is Mommy and Daddy's little girl. They can't keep her.

She stops then.

They took her and nobody stopped them.

They have her and nobody has come to get her.

A thought occurs to the little girl that makes her feel empty inside, hollow, like everything below her neck is an empty room with the window open and the cold wind is blowing through it. What if Mommy and Daddy don't want her anymore? What if they don't care that she'd been taken away? What if ... what if maybe they are glad she is gone? She made messes, after all. She left her toys scattered out everywhere even after Mommy told her to put them up. She got grape jelly on her fingers and made the refrigerator door handle sticky and Daddy shouted at her. She left the lights on when Daddy told her to turn them off when she left the room. And sometimes she spilled things. She knocked her orange juice glass over at breakfast the other day and it went all over the table. And Mommy was sputtering and grabbing paper towels, and Daddy was cursing.

Mommy and Daddy might be glad that she's gone.

The little girl stops crying, stops shaking because she is frozen still by the thought. What if she does belong now to the people in the other room talking about her, the ones who'd taken her? What if Mommy and Daddy never came to get her? She can't even cry, can't make a sound, and when she feels the warmth spreading out around *her on the floor and realizes she's wet her pants, she can't pretend anymore that she is asleep and this is just a bad dream. She can't make believe she'll wake up in her own room hugging Mittens and smelling bacon frying in a skillet in the kitchen.*

She isn't asleep.

This isn't a bad dream. The little girl has been … kidnapped … and unless Mommy and Daddy come and get her, she will have to stay here.

She cries then, quietly, tears streaming down her face, knowing they'll be mad when they see she wet her pants, afraid of what they'll do when they find her. Will they hurt her? Little kids on television sometimes got taken away from their Mommies and Daddies, and the bad people who took them hurt them. Would they hurt her? The most painful thing she has ever felt is when Daddy pulled out her bottom tooth and it wasn't loose enough, and she screamed and blood went everywhere. Will the people in the next room hurt her like that? Will they make her bleed?

She scrunches down tighter into the corner, puts her hands over her ears so she can't hear, squeezes her eyes shut so she can't see, and tries not to be there at all.

Chapter Six

MITCH FLEW DOWN the twisting narrow roads toward Black Bear Forge Elementary School, code 27, lights and siren, with a terrible cold feeling in the pit of his stomach. He hadn't been gone from the school but a couple of hours, had been there at the carnival, sitting with Rileigh and her mother, watching the glorious chaos. There were probably thirty booths, maybe more than that, hundreds of people coming and going, little kids and parents and grandparents and teachers. Seen in a new light, however, the chaos was no longer glorious but ominous, a police officer's nightmare rather than a little kid's dream. So many unidentified people, so many vehicles, so many ways in and ways out. And to his knowledge, no surveillance equipment of any kind.

On the way back, he called his chief deputy, Jeb Rawlings, using cell phones so their conversation wouldn't go out over the radio. Rawlings said he'd locked the school down, all he could do since most of the carnival booths had already been taken down and the people were gone. Standard procedure, which they had to follow, even though

Mitch knew that was closing the barn door after the horse was long gone. Standard procedure kept you on the rails, even if you didn't know where the track was going, kept you from running off in all directions when you needed to proceed logically and thoroughly from one point to the next.

The missing little girl was Chloe Malone, five years old. Rawlings said he had already texted a picture of the little girl to all the neighboring sheriff's departments. A terrible clock was ticking. If the little girl had been kidnapped — and that was a call Mitch was far away from making — but if she had been, the first seventy-two hours were critical. Although stranger kidnappings were way more rare than most frightened parents would suppose, statistics did indeed paint a bleak picture. Sixty percent of kidnapped children who didn't survive were killed less than three hours after they were taken, eighty percent within the first two days. Hopefully, Mitch would get to the scene and gather more and better information, but right now he'd been told that no one had seen the little girl after the school bell rang to dismiss the students to the carnival … and that had been *hours* ago.

Deputy Rawlings was waiting for Mitch when he pulled up.

"I got Jim coming, called him a few minutes ago. We're lucky, he and his dogs were at his daughter's house, and it's not far from here."

Jim Baumgarden was an old farmer who had the best bloodhounds in the county, maybe in the whole state. He lived in Coon Track Hollow on the other side of Chalk Mountain. Mitch had used him and his dogs last fall when elderly patients went missing from the Carrington House. Baumgarden and his dogs had found nothing, because none of the patients ever left the hospital grounds — they all were murdered on the premises.

Jim and his dogs were as close as the Yarmouth County Sheriff's Department got to a K-9 unit. Besides locking down the school, Deputy Rawlings had set up a perimeter about 100 yards from the school, where officers allowed no one in or out. As soon as Jim arrived, the dogs would be taken immediately to the parking lot to inspect every vehicle. The animal wouldn't be trying to track scent in such a scent-polluted environment, but a trained dog could hear a human heartbeat in the next room with the door closed. They'd take the dog past every car trunk. If the kid had somehow gotten into the trunk of a car, unlikely as that was, she was in grave danger. It was a cool day, springtime in the mountains, but the temperature was already 75 and climbing.

After the parking lot was cleared, Jim would give his dogs a pair of the little girl's gym shoes from her locker and walk the animals around the school inside the perimeter that had been set up, but outside the playground, where scents would be too confusing. If a lone child had walked away from the school building in any direction, the dog would cross the child's path inside that perimeter and could follow the scent from there.

Mitch hadn't even made it into the building to begin setting up his own search of the premises when a car careened into the parking lot and came to a screeching halt in front of the school. Two people leapt out, left the doors open, looked around frantically, then came running at Mitch.

"Where's Chloe?" the man demanded.

"My little girl, they said she was *missing,*" the woman said.

Mitch wondered if he would ever stop being surprised

by how fast news spread in this town. How in the world the parents of that little girl had found out that she was missing already was astonishing.

The father turned and started toward the building, and Mitch reached out and took his arm.

"I'm sorry, sir, you can't go in there."

The man bristled. "I'm Jeff Malone, and you're telling me I can't go into my own daughter's school?"

His fear was making him hostile. Mitch understood, but it didn't matter. The man was not going in that building.

"Yes, sir, that's exactly what I'm telling you. We have the school completely locked down, nobody in, nobody out."

"But that's my little girl, and if she's lost—"

"Where's my baby, my Chloe?" the woman said, teetering on the brink of hysteria.

Mitch put one hand on the man's arm and the other on the woman's shoulder and leaned into them, spoke softly so they'd have to concentrate to hear what he said.

"I need for you to listen to me. I know you're frightened, and I get that — of course you are. But you have to understand that the very best thing you can do for your little girl right now is to let me do my job. Getting in my way, causing a disturbance, distracting my officers, will only keep us from concentrating on what's most important here, and that's finding your little girl. Do you understand that?"

Both of the parents looked stricken and terrified, but they nodded mutely. Mitch turned to Deputy Crawford and told him,

"Take these people somewhere quiet and get as much information from them as you can," he said.

Crawford took the couple by the arm like a pro and

walked them toward the stone benches in front of the school to sit them down. Then he began questioning them. Mitch was proud of him.

"Ma'am, I need to know what your little girl was wearing when she left for school this morning," Crawford said.

He didn't need to know any such thing. They knew what the little girl was wearing. They had a detailed description of her from the school. Crawford was simply trying to calm the parents down, keep them occupied, and make them feel like they were helping. He already knew the answers to every question he was about to ask them.

Mitch went into the building to organize his own search there. He formed up four teams of three people each. One teacher, one officer, and one administrator or janitor or office worker. Then he divided the school into four quadrants. Each of the teams was to search one quadrant. Then they would shift and search a different quadrant. When they were done, the whole building would have been searched four times by a total of twelve different people.

Mitch dispatched those teams, then turned to Mrs. Robertson, the principal. "I'd like to speak to you in your office in a little while, please."

Mrs. Robertson glanced toward a tall, slender woman standing nearby who looked absolutely terrified, and Mitch didn't blame her. He was sure teachers of young children fell in love with every kid in their class. For one of them to be missing must be something like their worst nightmare.

"This is Chloe's teacher, Elizabetta Harbour."

"We'll have questions for her as well. Give us a few minutes."

While Mitch waited for the results of the team searches of the building, he gave the property a quick walkthrough.

It wasn't like he expected that he would suddenly trip over the missing child, but he wanted to re-familiarize himself with the building. Mitch had toured every school building in Yarmouth County, knew the layout inside and out, and so did all of his officers. Walking slowly down the hallways, Mitch could hear the murmur of voices behind the closed doors of the classrooms he passed. The school had been locked down. The children would not be dismissed to get on buses and go home until Mitch was absolutely certain that Chloe Malone was nowhere in this building and that she was the only child missing.

Mitch looked out into the playground and smiled. It was not like the playground he remembered from his elementary school years by any stretch. In the school playground of his remembrance, there had been see-saws, monkey bars, wooden slat swings, a merry-go-round that squeaked and wheezed its way around in a circle, and all manner of other playground equipment that had fallen victim to safety regulations. He reflected on the fact that somehow his generation had managed to survive the mayhem of childhood that the kids closed up in this building had been protected from.

Mitch glanced at the big clock on the wall by the school office and shook his head. No one had seen Chloe Malone since the whole school had been dismissed to that carnival before lunchtime. Where could that child have been in the hours since?

As Mitch headed down the hallway to the principal's office, he looked at the photograph of the little girl that Deputy Rawlings had texted to all of Mitch's officers and to all of the sheriff's departments in nearby counties. She was an angel, had a sweet cherubic face and rosy chipmunk cheeks. Her wide smile, affixed to her face with deep dimples, revealed blank spaces that would be refilled by adult teeth sometime in the next year or so, but that were adorably empty right now. She had long blonde hair that hung in curls around her shoulders and blue eyes. She was wearing a blue blouse with lace around the collar, speckled with red and black-spotted ladybugs. He noticed that the blouse was the same color as the little girl's eyes, and he wondered if her mother had dressed her in the blouse to match her eyes for her school picture.

He would question the principal and the little girl's teacher because it was protocol. But Mitch knew in his heart that something had happened to that little girl, and the two people he was about to talk to had no idea what it was.

Chapter Seven

MAMA CAME into the living room where Rileigh was re-stacking the supplies they had brought home from the school carnival, sorting them out so that they'd be easy to access next year. When Rileigh looked up, Mama had tears running down her cheeks.

"Mama, are you all right?"

"I ain't never gonna be all right till my girls is home."

Rileigh mentally rolled her eyes, but managed not to manifest the behavior in a way Mama could see.

Just when you thought it was safe to go back in the water.

"Mama, I'm right here and I'm not going anywhere."

She knew she had teed the shot up perfectly for Mama to take the ball and run with it, pardon the mixed sports metaphors, but it was probably best to get it out of the way. Apparently, Mama needed to haul out her favorite delusion — that Rileigh's missing sister was coming home someday — and blow the dust off it again.

"I know *you're* here, sweetheart. Of course you are. It's Jillian who ain't, and I do miss her so, so much." Mama reached up and wiped tears off of her cheeks, then draped a smile on her lips. "But she's coming home soon. I'm just sure of it."

At this point, the conversation could go one of two ways. Route A was that Rileigh tried to reason with her mother, to point out for the umpteenth billionth time that Jillian wasn't coming home because Jillian was dead. She could dredge up all the evidence that supported that conclusion and make her case.

Route B was simply to smile, nod like a good little bobblehead doll, and keep her mouth shut. She picked route B.

"Mm-hmm," she said, and tried to change the subject. "Don't you think Betty Marie Forrester looks good? Maybe she's got MS instead of ALS. ALS progresses really fast, and she actually looks better than she did the last time I saw her."

Mama didn't take the bait.

"Truth be told, I wasn't crying about missing my girl. I was crying because you got so little faith and hope. And that's a sad thing for a mama to realize."

"Now, Mama, I —"

"You ain't got no hope that your sister's coming home. And she is, baby, I swear she is, I know she is." Mama patted a spot on her chest and continued. "A mama can feel it, right here, in the heart. I know you don't understand, you ain't never going to understand till you have kids of your own. But there's just this thing, like an invisible string. It's delicate as a little strand on a spider web and tough as cat gut. It attaches you to them as has grown in your belly. And there ain't nothing but death can de-tach them. Cutting the umbilical cord ain't the same thing. That string is always there. That's why I know Jillian ain't dead. Because I'd know if she was. I'd feel it if that string was cut. And it ain't never let go. That's why I know she's still out there."

Mama was on a roll, so Rileigh let her roll.

"She was there on that paddle boat in January. She was there in the room. I could feel her presence."

Mama had said she'd seen Jillian dressed as Cinderella. Had followed her downstairs into the bowels of the boat, then lost sight of her. Either right before or right after, she happened to notice the man digging a hole into the back of the safe where two million dollars that belonged to the casino was stashed.

"I know you think you saw her, Mama." Rileigh floated that out into the air between them.

"If she wasn't there, who put that postcard in your pocket? That postcard didn't have no postmark on it because it had never been mailed. She put it in your pocket. Do you realize that means your sister, your big sister Jillian, was right next to you? She was standing right next to you. You could have reached out and touched her."

Until that point, Rileigh had been able to blow it off. It was the same old, same old. But that stabbed home. She wanted to shout at her mother. If that were true, if Jillian really had been standing right next to her, Rileigh would have known it, too. Maybe there was no invisible thread like Mama talked about between a mother and a child. But Jillian was her sister, and there was no way in hell she was within arm's reach of Rileigh but Rileigh didn't even notice.

"Mama, there was no postmark on that postcard because *somebody* slipped it into my pocket. That doesn't mean it was Jillian. Somebody has been sending us post-cards ever since Jillian vanished. And when I finally find out who has been jacking us around for decades, when I finally catch the son of a bitch who's been making my mother think my sister is—"

"Ain't nobody trying to trick us. Why would they?"

"I have no idea why. But then I don't have a sick and demented mind, and there are a lot of those out there."

"Why have them postcards been getting closer and closer in the last few months? We got the one that was from Atlanta right before that party on that boat. She sent that to us so we'd be looking for her. She drove up from Atlanta to be on that boat."

"What for, Mama? To be on that boat so she could like sidle up beside me and shove a postcard in my pocket? That doesn't make any sense. Jillian would never have teased us for three decades. Whoever has been sending those postcards is a sadistic bastard and—"

Her mother actually put her hands over her ears and shook her head like she was a five-year-old who didn't want to hear it was bedtime.

"I'm not going to listen to that. You'll see. And you'll be sorry. One of these days, when she comes walking through the front door and wants to know if we believed in her, if we kept the faith, if we knew she was going to come home someday, what are you going to say to her then, huh?"

"If she's going to come home, she'll come home. It won't matter whether we believed she would or not."

"I got this feeling. I've been having it all week. It ain't like it was when we was on that boat and she was right there and I could feel her. It ain't that strong, but Rileigh baby, I swear by everything I hold dear in this world — and that's *you* — that your sister is somewhere nearby."

Rileigh didn't have a comeback for that. She never did. If getting the final word made you the winner of an argument, then Mama had won every one about Jillian for almost three decades.

Thankfully, Mama's phone rang in the kitchen and she went to answer it. If Rileigh was lucky, by the time she was finished talking, she'd have forgotten all about Jillian. At least for now.

Mama didn't talk for long, though, and when she came back into the room, she had a strange look on her face.

"What is it?"

"Dolores just told me there's a little girl missing."

"What?"

"She said that a little girl went missing from the elementary school during the carnival."

In all the time that Rileigh had been home in Black Bear Forge, Mama's grapevine of information had seldom been wrong.

"What else did she say?"

"All she knew was what Stella Herman told her she'd heard from—"

"I don't need to know the whole line of transmission, Mama. Just what did she say?"

"She said that when the teachers took the kids back into the building so they could get them all ready to put them on buses and send them home, they were one kid shy — that little Malone girl. I think her first name's Claire or maybe Chloe. A kindergartener."

Rileigh didn't want to believe it. A little girl missing? They'd been right there at that carnival themselves only a couple of hours ago. How could they not have noticed if something had happened to one of the kids?

But denial was not a river to sail on if you really wanted to go anywhere. Rileigh sat down the box she had been stuffing unblown-up balloons into and grabbed her purse.

"I'm going to go see if I can help," she said, and out the door she went.

If Rileigh had had any doubt about Mama's information, it was gone as soon as she got close to the elementary school. She had to park blocks away. Cars were parked along every street, blocking driveways, up on the sidewalks. Then she had to elbow her way through a crowd of people who were being held back from a police line by Mitch's deputies and several firemen she was sure had been pressed into service at need.

She spotted Pete Brady. "It's true then, isn't it? There really is a kid missing."

"Sure is. This is what she looks like." Pete held out his phone and showed her the school picture of a little girl with blonde curls and blue eyes and no front teeth. "Rawlings texted all the deputies, all the departments around here, all the volunteer firemen her picture. Then we got a call he needed help with crowd control."

If there was a little girl missing, Mitch needed help with much more than crowd control.

Pete nodded toward the building. "Mitch is somewhere in there." He moved aside so that Rileigh could pass through. She hadn't made it to the front door of the building before Mitch came out and motioned for one of the rescue squad members to pull a pickup truck into the bus lane in front of the school. He nodded to Rileigh, didn't smile, but she was sure she saw a look of relief on his face. Yep, the man needed all the help he could get.

Mitch climbed up into the back of the pickup truck, and Deputy Mullins handed him a megaphone, but before he had a chance to say anything, parents began shouting questions.

"There's kids missing, right? Whose kids?"

"Why won't you let us in the building?"

"Have they been kidnapped?"

"What are you doing about it?"

Mitch held his hand out for silence.

"If you'll give me a chance, I will tell you what I know. A kindergarten student, Chloe Malone, did not return to her classroom with the other students after the school carnival on the front lawn this morning. The premises of the school have been searched thoroughly, and there is no sign of the child." He paused, drew a breath. "I know you're all concerned about your own children, and I can assure you that every other child in this school is accounted for. There is only *one* child missing. Your children are safe, and you need to go home now. As soon as I'm finished speaking here, the principal is going to signal the buses. They'll be coming by the front of the school to pick up your children and take them home."

Several parents called out they would take their own children home.

"We're here. Why put them on a bus?"

"I will not release the children in this building helter-skelter. We'll dismiss school today by the book. Every teacher has a list of the children to put on each bus. Every school bus driver has a list of the children who are supposed to be on his bus. The teachers will check off the names of every child they release to a bus. The bus drivers will check off every child who gets on their bus and will check them off again when they let them out at their bus stop. We will be *sure* every child gets home safely."

There were rumblings of dissent in the crowd, but he held out his hand.

"This is a police matter, and it's not up for debate. I suggest all of you get back in your cars and go home, because your children will be arriving by bus on schedule. And there will be no school tomorrow." That announcement caused another rumble through the crowd, grumbling about having to arrange last-minute baby-sitting.

"How about day after tomorrow. Is school cancelled then, too?"

Mitch answered that one. "I don't know. The school will let you know."

He turned off the megaphone, and though other questions were called after him, he ignored them, gesturing for Rileigh to follow him into the building.

"I figured you could use some help," she said.

"I just issued an AMBER Alert."

Those two words, AMBER Alert, froze Rileigh's heart, putting a stamp of reality on the situation the way nothing else could.

"Too little, too late," he said.

Rileigh looked at him in alarm.

"The last time anybody saw that little girl was when she went out with the rest of her class to the carnival." He drew a breath. "That was hours ago."

A chill ran down Rileigh's spine. Hours. In a kidnapping. That could be the difference between life and death.

"And the FBI?" Rileigh was dreading his response, fearing he'd called in the Feds. She knew in a way she'd never be able to explain to him that a bunch of FBI agents in suits and ties would cause more problems than they would solve.

"They gave me access to all their resources. Missing children profiles, databases, facial recognition software—" He burped out a bleat of sardonic laughter. "You know, to identify all the people in the surveillance videos we don't have."

"And agents?"

"I just have to ask."

"And you didn't." It wasn't a question, but he answered it anyway.

"Not yet. Not ruling it out, but not yet."

She gave him an approving look she was sure he didn't notice. The away-from-here sheriff was becoming more like the home team every day.

Chapter Eight

"You said the last time anybody saw her was when she left the school to go to the carnival. Do you mean nobody saw her *at the carnival?*" Rileigh asked Mitch as they entered the building.

"Oh, I'm sure somebody did. We just haven't found them yet. We haven't talked to every teacher, certainly not to every volunteer who was on the premises at the time. I'm sure people saw her after that point."

Rileigh knew how important it was to establish that one fact. When was the last time the child was seen and where was she at the time? And who was nearby?

"I've lined up a group of people who need to be questioned and I'm hoping you—"

Rileigh didn't let him finish. "Tell me what you need."

"I think it would be best if you talked to the children." He glanced down at himself, a big man in a uniform. "I want them to be as at ease as they can be. and I'm scary."

Rileigh almost made a joke. "Yeah, you're scary alright." But she didn't. Now was not the time for jokes.

"I asked the teachers to gather up little girls in her class who might have been with her at the carnival. The principal has informed their parents that they'll be staying late."

Rileigh remembered the buddy system in school. It was easier to find two kids than one. And if you made the children responsible for each other, keeping track of them was easier.

"Chloe had a buddy, right?"

Mitch nodded. "The children were allowed to pick their buddies, and Chloe picked her best friend. Her name is Tally something. She was the one who first sounded the alarm. When she couldn't find Chloe, she went to her teacher and said so. That's when the search began. Besides Chloe, there are three other little girls that the teacher's aide said hung out together often. They were the ones who were likely near her during the carnival. Could have seen who she talked to, where she went."

The front lawn of the school where the carnival had been set up was almost as big as a football field, bordered on one side by the pickup lane where cars and buses brought and picked up children for school. The back side of the front lawn stretched out down the hill toward a creek. The street that accessed the school lay on the other side of that creek.

Mitch stopped and turned toward Rileigh. "You got any initial thoughts? You were here same as I was. You saw. There were hundreds of adults, children going and coming, cars pulling in and pulling out. That little girl could have been in any one of those cars."

"You're sure she didn't walk off?"

"I've done a perimeter search. Jim Baumgarden's dogs would have picked up her scent if she left on her own. I'm sure she didn't leave the building by herself and walk anywhere. That leaves only one explanation — she left the carnival in a vehicle." He paused. "Whether *voluntarily* or not, we don't know."

"So, are we talking stranger abduction?"

"That's not off the table, but the definition of stranger gets real muddy here. Stranger in the sense of *someone nobody knew* is a bit of a stretch. But stranger as in *someone who had no right to take the child*, well…" He spread his hands. "Hundreds of people. Your mother said it — used to be that everybody knew everybody else, but it's not that way anymore. Maybe we're not talking about 'stranger' by the classic definition, but some adult took that little girl and left the school premises with her. By anybody's definition, that's kidnapping."

RILEIGH LISTENED to her heels echo on the floor as she walked down the empty hallway to Room K-26, the kindergarten room that was missing one little girl. She stopped in front of the door and looked at the wall beside it, surprised — not by what she saw, but by she didn't see.

All the other kindergarten rooms had little-kid art on every bare wall near them — finger paintings, stick figure drawings, globs of either papier mache or wet toilet paper stuck to construction paper, probably in some familiar shape but she couldn't make out what. There were tables beside most of the doors, too, displaying other kinds of art projects, like buildings constructed using sugar cubes. Some were tall spires of sugar cubes, others squat little Quonset hut-looking buildings. One she thought was perhaps supposed to be an igloo and another might possibly have been supposed to be the Alamo. But maybe they weren't trying to recreate any existing building. Perhaps all of that was way too complicated for a bunch of kindergarten kids. Maybe they were just handed a box of sugar cubes and some Elmer's glue and told to go for it.

Another classroom she passed had unidentifiable artwork on the table by the door. Boats of some kind, she thought. The primary building material was wooden tongue depressors, and possibly they were building Noah's Ark or maybe the Titanic or maybe their grandpa's Jon boat that they went fishing in on the weekends.

But Elizabetta Harbour's classroom stood out. There was no table outside the door with art projects. There were no little kid drawings affixed to the wall around the door. The wall was blank and clean, and the only decoration at all on the door hit Rileigh in the solar plexus. Every time she saw a smiley face, she felt like someone had kicked her in the belly.

Rileigh knocked, then stuck her head around the door and asked the woman seated at the desk, "Are you Elizabetta Harbour?"

The woman leapt to her feet. She was a young woman, probably her first teaching job out of college. She was nervous and jittery, a reasonable response to having had a child kidnapped out of her class.

Rileigh put out her hand as she entered the room.

"My name is Rileigh Bishop. I'm helping Sheriff Mitch Webster gather information about Chloe Malone."

The young teacher gave her a deer-in-the-headlights look. When Rileigh looked deep into the young woman's eyes, she pegged her for a regular weed user, recreational, nights and weekends. Whether it was legal or not, Rileigh didn't care, but she'd learned to recognize the characteristics of regular users. Languid responses, a kind of disconnect, and of course, the slightly bloodshot eyes were a giveaway.

"I don't know how I was supposed to do it. I don't know how anybody could do it."

"Do what?"

"Keep track of all of them."

"I'm not sure what you mean."

The woman began to pace back and forth in front of the chalkboard beside her desk. Rileigh sat down on the edge of the desk and waited for the woman to let off whatever steam she needed to let off. She quickly realized that the young teacher believed she was going to be blamed for the disappearance of the little girl.

"Excuse me," Rileigh said, trying to interrupt the woman's stream of consciousness about all the children running in different directions and how it was impossible to keep track of where any one of them was at any given time, other than maybe putting electronic tags on them like you'd use to keep track of your car keys.

"Hit an icon on your phone and the tag buzzes," she said, "so you can actually dig the keys out from behind the cushion on the couch."

She paused to breathe there, and Rileigh saw an opening.

"Excuse me—"

The woman stopped pacing but continued her machine-gun fire monologue.

"You need to ask me some questions. Go ahead, ask, ask me anything you want to know and I'll tell you, but I can't tell you anything about Chloe Malone, because I don't have any idea what happened to her. I tried to keep track of—"

"Excuse me!" Rileigh put out her hand to indicate she wanted silence. The woman stopped talking.

"This isn't your fault," Rileigh said. "Nobody's holding

you responsible for the fact that this little girl is missing. Is that what you're afraid of?"

The woman's face froze for an instant, then crumpled. She plopped down into the chair behind the desk and looked up at Rileigh.

"Are you sure nobody's gonna blame me?"

That her greatest concern at the moment was whether or not she was going to take a fall for this struck a sour note with Rileigh. It seemed a singularly self-centered question given that the issue was a missing child.

"This is your first teaching job, isn't it?"

The woman nodded. "Yeah, and what do I do on my very first teaching job? I lose a kid."

"That's what I'm here to talk to you about."

"About Chloe."

"And Chloe's friends."

"Oh, Mrs. Robertson already asked about that. My teaching assistant, Trisha, gave her the names of the little girls who hang out together."

Hmm. The teaching assistant knew the children better than the teacher did.

"When was the last time you saw Chloe Malone today?"

"She and her buddy, Tally Masterson, were holding hands as they walked out of the building toward the carnival…," and then the woman's voice trailed off.

"During the carnival, when did you see her?"

"I didn't."

"So, during the whole carnival, you never caught sight of her somewhere playing a game or running around with other little girls?"

"Not that I recall."

"But you were there, right? You accompanied the children to the carnival?"

64

"Oh yeah, you had to be there."

"So, you were there for the whole time and never caught sight of Chloe a single time?"

"There were hundreds of children out there. I don't remember catching sight of any particular one of them."

Rileigh had her measure now. This young woman had seen the carnival as an opportunity to zone out —she'd been physically present,, but Rileigh was sure her mind had been a thousand miles away.

Rileigh didn't see the woman as negligent, but it was clear she was uncaring. She'd done the bare minimum her job required and nothing beyond that. Most teachers had a lot more emotional investment in their charges than this woman did.

"Tell me about Chloe."

"What's to tell? She was just, you know, a regular little girl."

"Did she have any problems with any of the other children?"

"Not that I ever saw."

"Did she ever talk about her home life?"

"Nope."

"So, you never heard her talk about maybe some grown-up in her life that she had a special relationship with?"

"Nope, never did."

"Was she the kind of little girl who would decide to run away?"

"I don't think so."

"Did she get along with the other children?"

"Seemed to."

"Did she ever come to school upset about something?"

"Not that I know of."

Rileigh ran out of steam. She'd get more in-depth

answers from a Magic Eight Ball. This teacher didn't know the students in her class, had invested no emotional energy into them. Mitch would get much more out of the teacher's aide, who appeared to have connected with the children.

"Thank you for your time. That's all the questions I have."

Rileigh stood up and the woman stopped her.

"So, you're *sure?* I'm not going to get the blame for this."

Rileigh looked at her coldly.

"You can relax. Nobody's going to say this was your fault."

The woman heaved a giant sigh of relief.

"Well, thank God," she said, and smiled.

"If you think of anything you forgot to mention, anytime you saw Chloe, or anything else that struck you as the slightest bit odd, you will let us know, right?"

"Yeah, sure. But I didn't see a thing."

True that. This woman didn't see a thing.

Chapter Nine

RILEIGH LEFT the kindergarten classroom and went to the principal's office, where three little girls had been gathered up for her to talk to. As soon as she walked into the inner sanctum of the principal's office and saw them lined up like blackbirds on a clothesline, their feet dangling from the padded bench because they were too short to touch the floor, Rileigh knew that this was not the best place to talk to children. Rileigh had never been comfortable in the principal's office, and she doubted that these kids were either.

"Is there somewhere else I could talk to the girls?" Rileigh asked. "An empty office, the counselor's office maybe, or the nurse's office."

The principal fell all over herself to be helpful, offered any empty room in the building that suited Rileigh's purpose. She picked the counselor's office a few doors down and then turned to the four little girls and asked, "Which one of you is Tally Masterson?"

"I'm Tally."

Tally Masterson's long brown hair was parted in the

middle and hung around her shoulders, almost to her waist. She had big brown eyes, a few brown freckles scattered on her nose, and a heart-shaped mouth. She was a beautiful little girl —and Rileigh suspected that she knew it. She was also a self-possessed little girl, and she didn't appear to be overly upset by all the commotion around her.

"My name is Rileigh Bishop," Rileigh said. "I'd like to ask you a few questions, if that's okay with you."

"It's about Chloe, isn't it? Chloe's gone."

"Would you mind coming with me to the counselor's office?"

"Sure."

Tally hopped down off the bench and reached her hand up for Rileigh to take it, then proceeded out the door, not exactly dragging Rileigh, but certainly not being led by her either. Rileigh didn't sit behind the desk in the counselor's office – instead, she pulled out a chair and asked Tally to sit across from her at a small table that had a bouquet of silk daisies on it that Rileigh moved to the side.

"They tell me you're Chloe's best friend. Is that right?"

"Uh-huh. We're besties."

"So that means what? You play together all the time?"

"Uh-huh. Being best friends means that none of the other girls are her best friend. I am. She sits next to me in the lunchroom and we stand in line together. And when we go out to recess together, we play, only us."

"Which one of you decides what you play?"

"I do," she said without hesitation. "Chloe sometimes needs, well, you know, somebody to help her make decisions."

The child said the words with such a sage wisdom Rileigh had to fight the smile itching to form on her face.

"Make decisions?"

"Yeah, you know. What game should we play? What should we should do? Which dolls — things like that."

"So you were her buddy, and you went out to the carnival together. Is that right?"

"Uh-huh." The little girl picked up a lock of her hair and was twirling it around as she talked. "And we went to the ring toss booth, the one where you put the ring around a flamingo's neck, and we played the basket toss. I won a little bear because I got the tennis balls in the basket, and then Chloe had her face painted."

"You didn't get your face painted?"

"I didn't want to spend a ticket just to get paint on my face."

"So Chloe got her face painted." The little girl nodded. "What did she have painted on it?"

"Some stupid butterfly thing. It was blue and purple. It looked silly."

"Did you tell her it looked silly?"

"Yes, but she wanted it anyway."

"When it was time to go into the building, you couldn't find Chloe, and you told the teacher. When was the last time you saw her, and where did she go after that?"

"Well," Tally said and sighed, "Chloe wanted to go to the football toss booth, but I wanted to go to the water balloon toss. I told Chloe to come back to the flamingo toss, where all the pink flamingos were, when she was was done so we could go get a ride on the pony."

"So, Chloe went by herself to the football toss booth. Is that right?"

"Uh-huh."

"Where did she go after that?"

"I don't know. She was supposed to meet me back by the flamingos, but she never came."

"Did you go looking for her?"

"No, I waited by the flamingos. She was supposed to come back."

"Did Chloe ever talk to you about her mommy and daddy? Was she happy?"

"Her mommy and daddy give her stuff, whatever she wants."

"And your parents don't give you what you want?"

Tally rolled her eyes. "My parents spend all their time watching my brothers play baseball and soccer. They like sports, but I don't."

"You don't?"

The little girl flipped her long hair over her shoulder in a gesture that was affected. Obviously, she'd seen some-body on television make that same move.

"You get all dirty and sweaty, and sometimes you fall down and skin your knee. I don't like to get dirty." The little girl reached out and smoothed her skirt.

"Did Chloe like to get dirty?"

Again, the little girl rolled her eyes. "Yes, she was all the time wanting to dig in the dirt or climb a tree. But I didn't like doing that, so we didn't do it."

"You didn't ever do it just because Chloe wanted to?"

"No. Chloe did things because *I* wanted to."

"Did Chloe and her parents get along?"

"Yeah, I told you. They bought her stuff. And Chloe's mommy makes her clothes sometimes. She had the best Halloween costume last year. She was Tinkerbell. Her mommy made these wings that were... you could see through them."

"Did Chloe ever talk about running away?"

The little girl started to wiggle around, pulled her foot up onto the chair, and rested her elbow on her knee. "No. Why would she run away?"

"I don't know. Do you know?"

"I don't think she ran away."

"What do you think happened to her, Tally?"

"She got lost."

"But if she got lost at the carnival, somebody would have found her and brought her back to school."

"Oh no. I mean she *just got lost.*"

"What does *just got lost* mean?"

"You know, she couldn't... Chloe needed me to help her, like in crowds of people and things, or she'd get lost."

"I don't think I understand."

The little girl sighed. "You know, Chloe would like... follow somebody... like a clown in a parade. She did that once. Just walked off behind him. And I had to go get her."

"Did you see her with any grown-ups?"

"No. ... yes. That lady who has roses in her yard."

Betty Marie Forrester, maybe.

"Do you know what they talked about?"

"I couldn't hear what they said."

"How about other children? Did you see her with any other girls?"

"Chloe was *my* best friend." Tally had made that abundantly clear. "She wouldn't play with anyone else. I waited for her. And I got mad, because the carnival was going to be over, and I wanted to play the roulette wheel and spin the bottle. But she never came."

"Is there anything that you can think of that would explain what happened to Chloe?"

"I told you — she got lost. She didn't have me to help her, so she got lost."

Chapter Ten

WHILE RILEIGH TALKED to Chloe's friends, Mitch talked to the teachers who'd been at the carnival that morning. He had just gotten to the last of them and none had added anything useful to what he already knew. Frustrating, but he wasn't surprised. He knew the key to finding that child did not lie within the school building. She'd been out there at the carnival with all those people and all those vehicles, and someone had taken her.

Deputy Crawford came up to Mitch almost apologetically.

"Sheriff, I know you're busy, but there's an old woman here who's demanding to talk to you, and she won't talk to anybody else."

"About the kidnapping?"

"She won't say. She just says she wants to talk to the sheriff privately, and I can't get another word out of her."

"What's her name?"

"Dolores Hanover."

"Do you know her?"

"I've seen her around is all."

"So, she's local?"

"Yeah, she's local. I tried to get her to talk to me. She won't talk to anybody but you — privately."

"Fine," Mitch said. He looked around — "take her to that classroom," he said, indicating an empty second grade classroom across the hall from the principal's office. "I'll be there in five minutes."

When Mitch went into the classroom, the old lady was looking around like she expected the boogeyman to jump out of a closet and gobble her up.

"Mrs. Hanover, I'm Sheriff Webster. What is it you want to talk to me about?"

"You ain't gonna tell nobody I said nothing, are you? You gotta promise me."

"Ma'am, I don't have time for games. What do you have to tell me? If it's not valuable, I have better things to do."

"Oh, it's valuable. All right. I know where that little girl is."

That got Mitch's undivided attention.

"You know where she is?"

She nodded her head, then peered around her, nervous and fearful.

"Where is she?" he demanded.

"You're gonna have to promise me you ain't gonna tell nobody I told."

"I promise you that if you *don't* tell me — right now— I'll arrest you for—"

"Ronnie's got her."

"And who is Ronnie?"

"She's Jeff's ex-wife."

"Jeff Malone, Chloe's father?"

"I'm Chloe's grandma, and I know Ronnie's got her."

"You *believe* she has her? Or you have information that proves she does?"

"I know Ronnie's got her. That's all you need to know."

"Tell me about this Ronnie person. Who is she?"

"Her name's Rhonda Jo. I don't know what her last name is now. She's changed it a couple of times since she's married to my boy. But she's Chloe's mama, and I know she come and got her."

"Chloe's *mother?*"

Mitch thought he had met Chloe's mother, but apparently he had met her father's wife.

"Chloe's mother's pond scum, pure pond scum," the woman said. "Ain't no woman could walk off and leave her kids like she done and not be pond scum."

"She abandoned her kids."

"Hell yeah, she abandoned them. Shit, that last baby was only 18 months old. She left him in a playpen and walked out the door."

"Let me get this straight. You're saying that Chloe has brothers?" Mitch had been told that the little girl was an only child.

"Not really brothers — half-brothers or whatever they call it. They all got the same mama, but different daddies."

"Your son was married to her?"

"My son was an idiot for ever gettin' involved with that woman. I told him, I said, 'Jeff, ain't you got no eyes on you? Can't you see what kind of person she is?' But you know how it is. She had a pretty face and a big chest, and my son was always a fool for women with big tits. He fell for her, and it didn't matter to him that she'd already left one little boy with her first husband and another with her second. Well, he wasn't her husband, he was her second hookup. Jeff was just crazy about her. And of course, she done him just like she done everybody else. She played with him. She got him to buy her nice things, and she flitted around, twitched that round little ass of hers, made my son think the Rapture had done come and he'd been caught up into Heaven. But when Ronnie got pregnant with Chloe, it got ugly."

The woman hissed the next part, disgusted.

"She was going to go get an *abortion!* She didn't even tell Jeff she was pregnant. He only found out 'cause the woman at Planned Parenthood in Gatlinburg was married to a man who worked at the same sawmill Jeff did. When Jeff found out, he went right home and asked if she was pregnant.

"And she rolled her eyes and said, yeah, she was pregnant, but it wasn't gonna be no problem 'cause she was going to 'get rid of it.' And Jeff, he's like, '*The hell you are!*' And they got into it, and it got real ugly. She was bound and determined that she was going to get rid of that baby, and she would have, too. Little Chloe wouldn't never have drawn a breath on this earth if it'd been up to her mama."

"How did your son keep her from getting an abortion?"

"He paid her off. He had one of them 401K's or whatever you call it at work, and he said he'd give her the whole thing — it was more'n ten thousand dollars! — if she'd agree not to get an abortion."

"So she carried the baby to full term?"

"Jeff was gonna divorce her, but he made her live right there in the house with him until the baby was born. She was known to drink and take drugs and the like. She took them weird drugs, not coke or crack, but something that was supposed to 'expand her mind.'" The woman made a humph sound in her throat. "If ever there was a woman coulda used more mind than the good lord give her it was Rhonda Jo! Jeff just about kept her under lock and key to keep her from doing something that'd hurt the baby."

"So, if she was determined to get an abortion and only had the baby because your son paid her off, why would she wait five years to kidnap Chloe from school?"

"'Cause she's crazier than a shit house rat, that's why," the old woman said, irritated. Clearly Mitch was not getting the drift of what she was saying nearly fast enough. "It's been a long time coming. Maybe it was all them drugs she took, or maybe she just got knocked around so much by all them boyfriends. But she plumb lost her mind. She went to some monastery up in Kentucky near Bardstown, Gethsemane Monastery, and stayed for two months in one of them rooms that didn't have nothing but a bed and a chair and a table, getting dried out and her head straight. Then she come back to town all pompous and said she was gonna collect her children, as was her right to do, raise 'em up proper 'in the fear of the Lord.'"

"So, she's tried in the past to come and take Chloe?"

"No, she never got as far as Chloe. She went after the little boy she had by her first husband, and he run her off with a shotgun. Then she showed up wanting to see the little boy she walked out on from that other fella. And the way I hear it, he beat the holy hell out of her."

"So, she never came to your son demanding to see Chloe or talk to Chloe or…"

"Like I said, she never got to Chloe. Between that last one she went after and Chloe, she got hooked up with that Gunderson fella. And he's mean as a pack of rabid dogs. He took her up the other side of Gray Squirrel Ridge, had him a cabin up there, and he wouldn't let her go nowhere or do nothing."

"How do you know all this?"

"My daughter is best friends with Ronnie's sister,

Aggie, and Aggie is the only one in her whole family that didn't abandon Ronnie when she started behaving like she done."

"Gunderson — what's his first name?"

"Hell if I know. They call him Gunny, I think. He was in the military, some kinda special something, knows how to kill people with his bare hands ten different ways. His people's from Wayne County."

Which, though it was right next door to Yarmouth County, still landed the man in that not-to-be-trusted strata of humanity labeled *away from here*.

"Gunderson warned everybody, even her family, that they best not have any truck at all with Ronnie, she was *his* and his alone. And anybody who tried to mess with him … well, they's lots of places to bury a body in these mountains. That's why I don't want you to tell who told. That son-of-a-bitch will come after me if he knows it was me done it."

"I still don't have this straight. She demanded to have her other children back, but she never demanded to have Chloe."

"Never even tried to see her. I don't think she's ever laid eyes on that child. Well, until she took her."

"Then why do you think she *kidnapped—*"

"You didn't let me finish. Ronnie got pregnant by this Gunderson fella, had a little girl, stillborn. If she had any marbles left, she lost 'em then. One of the neighbors lives up on Gray Squirrel Ridge said he'd see her out at night in a white nightgown running through the woods, crying out that baby's name."

"It wasn't three days ago that her sister told my daughter that Ronnie had got it in her head that her baby wasn't dead after all, that somebody come and snatched her, and she was by god gonna get her little girl back!"

"And you think—"

"Chloe's *her* little girl, Ronnie's own flesh and blood, just like the child she lost. And Chloe's *missing*. You add up them numbers and see if they don't come up to the same total. "

Mitch couldn't imagine how a woman who was apparently in the shape that this Rhonda Jo Gunderson or whatever her last name was, could have been at that carnival without somebody noticing her.

Apparently, the old woman had the same thought.

"I ain't sayin' Ronnie done it her own self. But if she talked that Gunderson fella into helping her, he coulda found somebody, bribed somebody or scared them into it."

"So you're telling me—"

"I'm telling you that if Ronnie wanted Chloe, she'd move heaven and earth to have her. Now you need to go get in your car and go get Chloe back!"

The woman had been running on pure adrenaline, talking so fast she was hard to understand, her eyes wild, her voice loud. But she stopped then and sort of caved in on herself.

"Why didn't you tell your son what you're telling me?"

She stood quiet and looked at him, and her eyes filled with tears.

"You ain't been listenin' to a thing I said, have you? My boy loves that little girl better'n life, and if he knew what I know, he'd a'gone after her. Jeff's a good boy. But he ain't big and mean like Gunderson. That fella could wipe up the floor with my boy 'thout breaking a sweat. If Jeff messes with Ronnie, sure as sunrise on Easter Sunday mornin', Gunderson will kill him. And if he finds out it was me sicced the law on him, he'll kill me, too."

Chapter Eleven

RILEIGH RETURNED Tally to the principal's office and asked the next little girl on the bench, "Are you Corey Jackson?"

The girl nodded "Uh-huh, that's me."

A black child with dozens of ball-ties in her complicated hairstyle and an adorable pixie face — her eyes seemed to sparkle with mischief — hopped down off the bench and headed to the door of the principal's office without bothering to take Rileigh's hand. "Mrs. Robertson said you wanted to talk to me in the counselor's office. It's this way."

Rileigh allowed herself to be directed down the hall to the counselor's office, then she sat back down where she'd been sitting and invited the little girl to sit in the chair where Tally had been.

"Do I have to sit down?"

"Not if you don't want to. I just need to ask you a couple of questions."

"Oh, I know." She plopped down on the chair. "You want to know about Chloe. You want to know if I know where she is, but I don't."

"Did you spend time with her at the carnival?"

"No. She's Tally's best friend." Corey said that as if it explained everything.

"So if she and Tally are best friends, she can't spend time with you? Is that what you're saying?"

"Well, it's kind of like that. Tally and Chloe and Aurora and I, we play together a lot. Chloe's mommy and my mommy are friends, and sometimes Chloe comes over to my house with her mommy and Tally's not there, and then we can play together. We play dolls."

She began to describe the kind of dolls she had — not baby dolls and not Barbies either. Rileigh didn't catch the name, but apparently their hair was various shades of purple and the tiny outfits that came with them were made of leather.

"Do you and Chloe play together at recess?"

"She and Tally play with us sometimes, but sometimes not."

"Did Chloe ever talk about her life at home with her mommy and her daddy?"

"I don't know about her daddy, but her mommy's nice."

"Did you see Chloe at the carnival?"

"Uh-huh."

"When did you see her?"

"I saw her getting her face painted — a big red butterfly. I wanted one just like it, but the lady made mine blue because she was out of red paint. Then she and Tally were at the ring toss booth. Chloe was in line in front of me at the cotton candy booth."

"Did you ever see Chloe when she was by herself?"

The little girl shook her head. "No."

"Did you see Chloe talking to any grown-ups?"

"No."

"How about other children? Did you see her talking to other children?"

"Wait, I do remember some grownups. She ran into them and spilled her popcorn, and I think they bought her another bag."

"Do you know their names?"

Corey shook her head.

"What did they look like?"

"Old. And he had one of those tanks, like scuba divers wear."

Evelyn and Clive Foster.

"She talked to another little girl, but I don't know her name."

"Does she go to school here?"

"I don't think so. She had long blonde hair."

Shiloh King.

"But no other children?"

"Nope."

"Did you see her leave the carnival?"

"Uh-uh."

"So the last time you saw Chloe was when?"

"She and Tally were at the ring-toss booth. I think Tally won something. Then we had to go back into the building. That's when Tally couldn't find her, and the teacher started looking for her, and everybody started looking for her."

"So you didn't see her leave?"

"No."

"You didn't see her, like, get into a car with anybody?"

"No."

"Do you have any idea where she might be?"

"No. If you want to know things about Chloe, you need to ask Tally."

Rileigh escorted Corey back to the principal's office,

where the last little girl waited with Mrs. Robertson, who had given her some crayons and paper so she could draw.

When Rileigh came into the room, the principal looked up and asked quietly, "Did either one of them know anything?"

Rileigh shook her head. "I don't imagine any of the children knows anything that they know they know. If they did, they would tell the teachers. I'm just hoping that maybe I can find out something they don't know they know. Something they noticed, maybe. That's the best I can hope for."

Rileigh smiled at the last little girl, a chubby blonde with rosy chipmunk cheeks and no front teeth at all, on the top or the bottom. Mrs. Robertson started to say something, but didn't, just told Aurora Pettigrew to go with Rileigh to the counselor's office.

Aurora started talking as soon as they left the principal's office.

"Our dog just had puppies. Eight of them."

"I bet they're cute."

The little girl nodded her head, then looked stricken.

"But we can't keep any of them. Mommy said we have enough dogs."

"How many dogs do you have?"

"Four." She paused. "Well, five if you count Trader. But he's my big brother's dog. He just stays at our house sometimes when Robbie's working out of town and can't take care of him."

"I always wanted an older brother."

"I've got four."

"That's a big family."

"I've got four big sisters, too. Hannah said when I was born it meant the girls won, because there are more of us than the boys."

"So, you're the youngest."

Aurora nodded, then sighed. "Unless mommy decides to have another baby."

Nine children already. Rileigh couldn't imagine that the woman was contemplating yet another.

Rileigh sat down with Aurora and started asking questions.

"So, you and Corey sometimes play with Tally and Chloe. Is that right?"

"Uh-huh."

"Are you and Corey best friends?"

"Yes. Well, no. Not like Tally and Chloe are. Tally and Chloe are BFFs."

"Did you see Chloe talking to any other children at the carnival? Besides Tally, I mean."

"Just Tally."

"How about adults?"

"Yeah, she talked to some grown-ups."

"Who were they?"

"I don't know."

"Can you describe them to me?"

"One of them was a man and he had on a baseball cap."

"What color was it?"

"Red." The little girl thought, "No, it was orange. It was a University of Tennessee cap."

She was quite proud of herself for remembering that.

"So Chloe talked to a man in a University of Tennessee baseball cap." That would be Ben Pendergast.

"Is he the only grown-up you saw Tally talking to?"

Aurora shook her head. "No."

"Who else?"

"The piano teacher lady."

Rileigh tried to recall who at the carnival was ... then

she remembered. LaTisha Johnson. She taught piano and voice.

"Anybody else?"

"Uh-huh. I don't know what his name is. He was tall and he had black hair that had, you know, spots in it. Gray spots."

Rileigh thought about the man that had looked familiar to Mitch, but who he couldn't place.

"What was he wearing?"

Aurora crinkled up her brow. "He had on, like, like a tee-shirt that had some words on it. And jeans."

"What color was the T-shirt?"

"Black."

That fit the description of the man Mitch couldn't place.

Rileigh sat back. "You've been very helpful, Aurora. Thank you."

"That's not all," Aurora said. "Do you want to know about the man who had on the black sweatshirt?"

"Tell me about the man in the black sweatshirt."

"He talked to Chloe. He was just a man and he had on a black sweatshirt, the kind that has a hood on it, and he had the hood up and I couldn't see his face."

Rileigh froze. A man in a hoodie. Nobody else had mentioned that.

"Where did you see him talking to Chloe?"

"They were standing by the street and the man had a black van and he took Chloe's hand and led her around to the back of it and I think she got in. I don't know. I didn't see that part."

Rileigh's heart was hammering in her chest.

"Aurora, honey, tell me all that again. Very slowly and tell me everything you remember."

The little girl described the man again. She couldn't

see his face. He was wearing a black hoodie, and he was standing next to a black van, and he took Chloe's hand and perhaps led her into the back of the van.

"Why didn't you tell anybody about this sooner?" Rileigh asked.

Aurora looked uncomfortable. "I don't know," she said.

"Let's go over this one more time," Rileigh said, wanting to be sure she'd gotten all the details that the girl could remember. "Tell me again what you saw."

"There was this man and he had on a black sweatshirt that had a hood on it and he had the hood up and he picked Chloe up and set her in this black van that was parked beside the street and then he closed the door and—"

"Whoa, whoa, whoa, whoa," Rileigh said. "That's not what you said before."

"Oh, I forgot that part. But he picked her up and set her in the seat of the van, and then he closed the door, and then he went around and got into the driver's side and drove away."

Rileigh's heart was beginning to sink. "So now you're saying that the man in the black hooded sweatshirt put Chloe into the van and drove away with her?"

The little girl smiled broadly. "Yes, that's what happened. He put her in the van and drove away with her."

"And you didn't say a word about this when everyone was looking for Chloe?"

"Well, I forgot," she said. "I forgot about that part, and then I remembered it when you asked me, so I told you."

"So, when everyone was trying to find Chloe, you forgot that a man drove away with Chloe until just now, when you remembered."

She nodded her head up and down. "Uh-huh, I remembered."

"Do you remember anything else about the man?"

"No."

"Think about it. Anything else at all?"

"Well, um, he... had red hair," Aurora said.

"I thought you said the hood on the sweatshirt was up, and you couldn't see his face. If the hood was up, you couldn't see his hair either."

"Well, the hood was up, and then he pulled it back, and it wasn't up anymore."

"Did he pull it back before or after he put Chloe in the van?"

"After."

"So after he put Chloe in the van, you saw his face. Is that right?"

"No, I didn't see his face, but I saw his hair, and he had red hair."

"So the man who put Chloe into a van and drove away with her had red hair, but you didn't see his face."

She smiled broadly. "Yes, red hair."

"Are you sure it wasn't blond?" Rileigh said.

"No, it was red."

"Are you *sure?*"

"Well, I guess it could have been blond."

"So he could have had red hair or blond hair."

The girl nodded and smiled. Every time she smiled, her gums glistened in the blank space between her teeth.

"Can you tell me anything else about the van?"

"It was black."

"Are you sure it wasn't white?"

"No, it was black."

"So you're *sure* ...?"

"Maybe it was white," Aurora said, "but I think it was black."

"So, it could have been a white van or a black van."

"White or black."

Rileigh let out a sigh of disappointment and held out her hand to the little girl.

"Thank you so much for all of your information, Aurora," she said, stood, and led the child out of the room and back to the principal's office. Aurora's parents were waiting out front for her, and the principal got one of the office workers to take the child to their car.

Mrs. Robertson was looking at Rileigh carefully, studying her.

"You were going to tell me something before I took Aurora to the counselor's office to ask her questions," Rileigh said. "What was it?"

"I was going to give you a heads-up about Aurora."

"A heads-up that she's got a wild imagination."

The principal sighed and nodded her head. "Aurora has a *very* vivid imagination."

"She told me a wild tale about a man in a black hooded sweatshirt whose face she couldn't see, but then she could. Had red hair, or maybe blond, and he walked behind a black van with Chloe, or he took her by the hand and put Chloe in the front seat of the van. Or—"

"Or it could have been a red van or a green van." The principal sighed. "And it might possibly have sprouted wings and flown away."

Rileigh sank down on the bench where the children had been seated. "Yeah, something like that."

"Aurora is the youngest of nine children."

"So she told me."

"By the time a mother gets to the ninth child, she doesn't have a whole lot of energy or time or attention left."

"So Aurora makes up tall tales to get attention?"

"Right. You have to take everything that child says with a whole shaker full of salt."

"So, all that about the man in the hooded sweatshirt in a van was bogus, but does that mean the other things she told me weren't true?"

"What other things?"

"She saw Chloe talking to some other grown-ups."

"I don't know," Mrs. Robertson said. "Maybe she really did remember." She sighed. "It's equally possible she made the whole thing up."

When Rileigh left the principal's office, an office worker gave her Mitch's message. Gray Squirrel Ridge … he wouldn't be back for hours. It was time for Rileigh to go home.

There had been a few minutes there when she'd actually believed she had a lead. Now she didn't know if a single word Aurora Pettigrew had said to her was the truth.

Chapter Twelve

"Define climbable," said Deputy Beau Mullins as he and the other deputies gathered around the county map spread out on the teacher's desk in an empty first-grade classroom to discuss the best approach to Gunny Gunderson's cabin on the other side of Gray Squirrel Ridge.

"Can *you* climb it?" Mitch asked.

Mullins looked at Deputy Tony Hadley and then to Deputy Jeb Rawlings. Both of them shrugged.

"I imagine one of the other of us could make it to the top, but it certainly ain't a done deal."

Rawlings looked at his watch. "It's getting late, ain't but a couple hours of light left, and it sure as shit ain't climbable in the dark!"

Mitch knew what time it was. His internal clock was keeping track of every second. It was after 6 p.m. and Chloe Malone had left the school with her buddy to go to the carnival more than seven hours ago. The sun would set about 8:30— on the flat. It'd be dark in the mountains a long time before that.

Deputy Billy Crawford tapped another spot on the

map. "How about a plan B, Sheriff?" he said. "Instead of climbing up Gray Squirrel Ridge and coming up behind that cabin, we could come at it from the north and the south. The mountains on both sides of the ridge are steep, but they're definitely climbable. I could go up the north side, Beau could go up the south side, and you, Jeb, and Tony could hit it from the front."

Mitch looked at the map where Deputy Crawford had his index finger on a piece of real estate that didn't even appear to have a road leading to it.

"How do you get up to this place?" Mitch asked.

"I think that's the point, that you can't get up to it," Crawford said. "That's why he built the cabin there."

"Well, if he wanted to pick a 'you can't get to there from here' spot, he gets the blue ribbon," Deputy Jeb Rawlings said.

"I think the north side would be easier to climb." Crawford looked at Mullins, who nodded assent. "We could both climb up there, get to the top of the ridge, split up. Beau could go south. Then we could come down the back side of Gray Squirrel. We'd have the house surrounded."

"How long will it take you to climb to the top?" Mitch asked.

"Maybe half an hour," said Crawford.

"Make that forty-five minutes," Mullins said, patting his beginning paunch. "My hiking skills are a little rusty. But that side of the mountain is closer to the Forge, easier to get to than Gray Squirrel Ridge, so if we leave together, we'll all get there about the same time."

Mitch tapped the map at the top of Gray Squirrel Ridge. "You guys will end up right here, right?"

Both men nodded.

"You'll go south across the ridge," he said to Mullins.

"And when you're in position, you call in and you can both start down at the same time."

Mitch had a thought. "Can we get radio reception up there?"

Rawlings nodded. "The problem with reception in the mountains, radio and telephone, is down in the hollows, not up on the top. You'll get a clear signal."

Mitch took a deep breath. "I don't have to warn you that this guy's dangerous and—"

"You sure don't have to warn *me!* He beat the shit out of my brother in a bar fight, put him in the hospital for a week."

"So, watch yourselves. He could be out in the woods, squirrel hunting."

Mullins shook his head as all the deputies shared a smile. "Contrary to what its name might imply, Gray Squirrel Ridge is a terrible place to hunt squirrels. The best place is Tallow Creek Hollow."

"Or anywhere east of Sydney Point," said Tony Hadley.

"You let me know when you're in position. It'll take—"

Mullins answered the question before it was completely formed. "Twenty, maybe thirty minutes to come down the other side."

"I'll give you half an hour to get in position around the cabin before the rest of us approach."

Mitch made eye contact with each of the deputies in turn. "We good?"

They all nodded, turned, and left the classroom. Rileigh was still talking to Chloe's friends, so Mitch asked one of the office women working at the desk in the principal's office to let her know where he had gone and why.

Mitch and Deputy Tony Hadley drove together, flashing lights but no siren, to Gray Squirrel Ridge, with

Jeb Rawlings in a second cruiser behind them. They made their winding way with no lights at all up the gravel road that led to Gunderson's cabin.

The gravel gave way to a rocky dirt path for the last couple hundred yards. Mitch parked about half a mile down from the cabin and waited for a signal from Crawford and Mullins before he and the other two approached the house cautiously, making their way toward the big stand of scrub bushes where they could see only the roof of the cabin beyond.

It was gloomy now, twilight. Mitch used hand motions to direct Deputy Hadley to the left, as he and Rawlings went to the right around the bushes.

The log cabin didn't look like the old log cabins or the ruins of cabins that you saw scattered all around the mountains. This one was new, and Mitch had been told that Gunderson had felled the trees on the land and built the cabin himself.

If he had, he was quite a carpenter. The cabin had the kind of touches only somebody who knew what they were doing could have provided. The cedar shake roof came out over a broad front porch that stretched across the whole front of the cabin. The railings were hand-hewn, but the steps leading up to the cabin were poured concrete and there was a flagstone walkway. A black Ford 150 extended-cab pickup truck was parked out front.

There were two windows on the front of the cabin with light streaming out in a golden glow. Mitch was sure there was a back door, but there was no way to get around the cabin to check it out from where he and the others were standing without being seen. Deputies Crawford and Mullins, who'd come up behind the cabin, would stop Gunderson if he made a run for it.

This was a small cabin. If the crazy woman inside had

managed to get somebody to snatch her little girl out of the school carnival this morning, then this was already a hostage situation before Mitch ever said a word. He had been assured that Gunderson would be heavily armed.

When Mitch was sure all the other deputies were in place, he called out, "Mr. Gunderson, I'm Yarmouth County Sheriff Mitchell Webster, and I'd like to talk to you, please."

There was nothing but silence from the house.

Mitch called out again. "Mr. Gunderson, I'm the county sheriff, and I need to talk to you on an official matter. Would you please open your door?"

"Get off my land," came a growling voice from inside the cabin. "You ain't got no right here."

"Mr. Gunderson, we will not leave until we talk to you. This is an official matter."

"What do you want to talk to me about?"

Mitch considered how he ought to answer that question, but he supposed there was no sense in pretending that he hadn't come here about the little girl. If they'd taken her, they knew that much. If they hadn't, maybe they could all get out of this without it getting ugly.

"We're here to talk to you about Chloe Malone," Mitch called out.

"What about her?"

"She's missing."

"Missing? What does that have to do with me?"

Mitch heard a woman's voice then, speaking to the man inside, but he couldn't make out what they were saying. Then she cried out to Mitch, "What's happened to Chloe?"

"Ma'am, we're not going to have this conversation shouting. I need for you to open the door and come out on the porch."

"We ain't gonna—"

The door flew open, and out came a woman in a long white nightgown. Her hair was a bird's-nest mess. Her face looked haggard, and the nightgown was wrinkled and soiled. She stopped at the top of the porch steps beneath the bright porch light and cried out to Mitch, "What do you mean, Chloe's missing?"

Mitch had his gun drawn, pointed at the ground. At that point, he returned it slowly to its holster.

"Ma'am, there was a carnival at the elementary school this morning, and when the children went back into the building, Chloe wasn't with them. We have searched the grounds and the school, and there's no sign of her."

The woman sucked in a cry. "My little girl's missing?"

"Yes, ma'am."

"What are you doing to find her? What do you want here?"

Gunderson came out the door to stand behind her. He was a mountain of a man, broad and thick, with shoulders like a lumberjack and a head of long curly black hair atop a face mostly covered in a huge black beard. Backlit from the light from inside, he loomed like a dark apparition behind the woman.

"What'd you come out here for?" he asked. The way he was standing behind the woman, it was impossible to tell if he was armed.

Mitch looked at Deputies Hadley and Rawlings and motioned for them to step back. They complied, kept their weapons drawn but pointed at the ground.

"We were given information suggesting that—" Mitch paused because he didn't know what to call her. Perhaps the two were married, perhaps not. He decided to err on the side of married. "—Mrs. Gunderson might have been involved in some way in the child's disappearance."

"Me?" the woman cried. "You think *I* took her?"

"I didn't say that, ma'am. I just said that—"

Gunderson stepped out from behind Rhonda Jo then. He had a shotgun that looked like a toy cradled in his huge arms. But he made no effort to lift it or point it.

"Is that it? You come all the way out here because you think we took that little girl?"

"We're contacting every one of Chloe's relatives. Grandparents, aunts, uncles, anyone related to the child." Mitch turned to Rhonda Jo. "And your name is on that list. As I understand it, you are Chloe's biological mother. Is that correct?"

The woman started to cry, put her hands over her face, and her shoulders shook. In a remarkably tender gesture, the big man put his arm around her shoulders.

"Yeah, she's Chloe's mama. But that is the beginning and the end of what we know about that kid. Ronnie ain't seen her in..." He leaned toward the woman. "When was the last time you seen her?"

The woman didn't respond, just shook her head and continued to cry.

"If you come out here to find out if we're the ones who took her, you done wasted your time and ours. She ain't here. And we don't know nothing about her being missing."

Mitch took a slow step forward. "If she's not here, then I imagine you wouldn't mind me looking around to confirm that."

The man took a step toward the porch steps but kept the shotgun cradled in his arms. "The law ain't got no right here and you ain't coming in my house."

It could get ugly right now, Mitch thought, and needlessly so. After seeing the woman and the house, he was convinced that Chloe was nowhere around.

The woman surprised him then. She shoved the man out of the way and stepped back to the door of the cabin, pushing it open. "Go look for yourself. She ain't in here. Ain't no kids in here."

Mitch walked slowly up the flagstones to the bottom of the porch. He tipped his hat. "Mr. Gunderson," he said.

Gunderson swore under his breath but stepped back so that Mitch could go past him and the woman and into the cabin. The reek of marijuana smoke that slammed into him when he stepped inside was so powerful that he feared he'd have to let Deputy Hadley drive back into town. He went methodically through the small cabin. It took no time at all. The cabin was one big room divided into a bedroom, kitchen, bathroom, and a small room off the kitchen with a fireplace. He looked into the two closets, pulled back the curtain on the shower stall, got down on his knees and looked under the bed. There was no little girl here.

He stood and went back out onto the porch past the woman who was still sobbing into her hands.

"Thank you for your cooperation, Mr. Gunderson. You have a good evening now," he said, then walked down the steps and toward the flagstones.

"Who was it told you we had that little girl?" Gunderson asked.

Mitch turned back to him. "We have been collecting information about the missing child from—"

"I know who it was. It was that busybody Hanover woman, Chloe's grandmother. That woman's crazy as a shithouse rat," he said. "Ronnie's tried over and over again to go see that little girl, just see her. And that woman had a shit fit about it, wouldn't let Ronnie anywhere near. That ain't right." He put his arm back around the sobbing woman at his side. "That little girl's Ronnie's flesh and blood." Again, the man surprised him. He appeared almost to choke up. "We had us a little girl, me and Ronnie, but she died. Ever since then, Ronnie's been thinking about Chloe, about how she'd just like to see her. That's all. Just see her. Maybe not even talk to her. Just look at her. But they wouldn't have none of it."

"You can go to court and request visitation rights," Mitch said. "And if you are awarded them, no one can stop you from seeing the child."

The man snarled then and spit on the porch.

"Go to court. Right. Like some judge would rule in our favor." He snorted a laugh and waved his hand. "Now go on, get the hell off my property and don't come back."

The big man went back into the house and slammed the door. Mitch saw first one, then another flashlight come on in the gloom behind the house as Deputies Crawford and Mullins switched on flashlights to come down out of the woods to the cruisers.

Chapter Thirteen

MITCH CALLED Rileigh when he got back to town to find out if she'd learned anything. And to tell her he had come up snake eyes.

"I have some names," Rileigh told him. "One little girl named Aurora noticed more than the others." Mitch was momentarily hopeful. "She also made up more than the others, said she saw a guy in a black hoodie put Chloe into a white van and drive away with her."

"Sounds like half a dozen different television kidnapping scenes."

"The principal said Aurora was likely to make up all kinds of wild tales, but she did tell me about seeing Chloe with several adults at the carnival— people I saw there, too. It's all in my notepad— names of everyone she saw. Well, not every name. One of them has no name."

"Only one?"

"Only one that Aurora saw. It was that fellow you saw. The one you said looked familiar, but you couldn't place."

"He stuck out here like a sore thumb," Mitch said.

"Might as well have had a flashing sign on his chest—'Away From Here! Away From Here.'" Mitch shook his head. "A total stranger in a medical mask shows up and somehow manages to kidnap a child under the suspicious gaze of two hundred locals? It doesn't pass the sniff test. But I still need to find out who he was and what he was doing here."

"I ran out a little ahead of my headlights here," Rileigh said, almost apologetically. "But I knew you were going to want to talk to every volunteer who was there, right?"

"I do. I need to compile a master list of every person who was on the school property when Chloe went missing."

"I had that pegged. I'll meet you at the school about eight tomorrow. The volunteers are set to start showing up at eight thirty."

"Because …?"

"Because I did what I knew you'd do but you were busy. I put out a notice on the local radio station, WBBF, requesting that anyone who had been a carnival volunteer yesterday please return to the school at nine tomorrow morning."

Rileigh paused. "And I asked Mama to make a few calls."

Mitch would be willing to bet the pension he didn't have yet that most of the people who showed up would be there because they got a phone call on that mysterious phone tree, the notification system Rileigh's mother was hooked into that told her every time somebody painted their outhouse — while the paint was still wet. It kept the community of Yarmouth County as close-knit as steel wool.

Mitch and his deputies and Rileigh were ready for the

flood of people when they came the next morning. Deputy Mullins was a whiz at organization. He took the names of people as they arrived, then used a blackboard in one of the classrooms to put together a chart of the available officers to work through the crowd as quick and as efficiently as possible. He kept track of the master list of volunteers Rileigh's mother gave him and checked off the names as the people showed up at the school. If they had to, they'd go track down any volunteer who didn't come in voluntarily, but Mitch doubted there'd be any.

Mitch sat behind the principal's desk in her office, waiting for one of the office workers to bring in the first volunteer. As he looked around, he thought that things got to be a cliché for a reason. An office full of Precious Moments figurines was exactly what he would have expected to find at this little school.

An older woman came into the room, her short white hair so thin on top you could see pink scalp through it. If she'd had one more wrinkle, she would have had to hold it in her hand. Her face was deeply gouged with lines around her eyes, and the ones around her mouth were smile creases. Her name was Evelyn Harper and she'd been operating the basketball toss booth.

"Chloe come to the booth with her friend, Tally Masterson," the woman said. "Tally was the one who won the bear, then she told Chloe where to stand and how to hold the ball and how to toss it so she could win one too, but she missed." The old woman rolled her eyes.

"So, Tally Masterson was bossy?"

The old woman smiled at him. "Let's just put it this way — it was real clear who crowed and who laid eggs in that chicken yard."

Mitch's mind stumbled briefly trying to catch the train of that analogy before it left the station without him.

Rileigh had said that Tally Masterson was a force to be reckoned with, and apparently when she told her BFF Chloe Malone to jump, Chloe asked how high.

Mitch didn't like what that implied about Chloe Malone: that she was used to being told what to do, used to having someone else make decisions for her, accustomed to being compliant and obedient. In other words, a perfect victim.

Mitch asked the old woman if she'd seen Chloe again after that. She replied that many children had run around the booth all morning, including Chloe and Tally.

"Do you know when you noticed she wasn't there anymore?"

"I saw Tally just standing next to the flamingos, and I asked her what she was doing, and she said that Chloe was supposed to meet her there, but Chloe never showed up."

"What time was that?"

"It wasn't long before the bell rang and the kids all went back into the school. Maybe fifteen minutes?"

"Was there anyone else that you can remember being nearby when Chloe was playing at the basketball throw booth?"

The old woman rattled off a list of names, and Mitch obediently took them down. Some of them were familiar, people Rileigh and her mother had pointed out to him. A man named Hank Foote. A woman named LaTisha Johnson. Granny Maggie and her little blonde granddaughter. And a fellow named Ben Pendergast, who was either the man with an oxygen tank who had black lung or the man who had lost a son in Afghanistan. Mitch wasn't sure which; he would have to ask Rileigh.

"Then there was that fella I didn't know. He was standing there."

"What fella you didn't know?"

The old lady cocked her head at him. "Now how can I tell you what fella I didn't know if I just told you I didn't know?"

Mitch granted her a small smile. "Let me rephrase that. Will you please describe for me the man you saw there that you didn't know?"

"Well, he was the one wearing the mask."

Several people at the carnival were wearing masks. After all the dust had settled from the mask-no mask controversy of the COVID years, almost everybody he knew had stopped wearing them. Masks made sense for people who had some kind of health condition that would make it dangerous for them to contract any illness, of course. But the stranger at the carnival appeared to be young and healthy. So why the mask — to prevent germs or prevent scrutiny?

Mitch thanked Evelyn Harper for her help and nodded to the deputy to send in the next volunteer. People orbited in and out of his office long enough that he lost track of time. He asked them all the same questions. Some had seen Tally and Chloe. Some had only seen Chloe. Some had not seen either one of the children. Some had seen them more than once. He kept a running list of the people who were nearby their booths when those little girls were playing those games. And the list became the usual suspects. The same adults in different combinations, in a different order, were standing around at that carnival all morning. He would have to talk to every one of them.

As the afternoon wore on, Mitch saw the shadow of the mountain begin to stretch out farther and farther to the west, darkening the world, granting the mountains twilight when it wasn't yet sunset out there on the flat. Each time he waited for the next person to come in, he watched the big, long red second hand slowly ticking around the clock face. Tick, tick, tick.

And every tick on that clock was a second that kidnapped girl was in danger. If she was even still alive at all.

Chapter Fourteen

THERE WERE several security cameras inside Black Bear Forge Elementary School, trained on the doors, and one in each hallway. But there were none outside the building. So not only did they not have video of the kidnapping, they didn't even know what cars were parked there during the carnival or their license plate numbers. Every one of the volunteers and every one of the adults in attendance had driven to get there. The kidnapper had come to the carnival in one of those vehicles. But without surveillance footage, they were flying blind.

Well, not exactly blind. There was Buddy Henderson.

Rileigh asked Deputy Mullins to bring Buddy and his grandfather Russell to her as soon as they arrived.

Russell Henderson was a gnarly old coot who embodied the phrase "bark is worse than his bite". Truth be told, Russell probably didn't have a bite, certainly didn't have any teeth in it if he did. He was of indeterminate age, somewhere between fifty and five hundred years old. Rileigh remembered him from when she was a teenager, and she could swear he hadn't changed a bit since then. His gray-streaked black hair didn't appear to have grown a single additional gray hair. His beard was scraggly — he was one of those men who should never have tried to grow a beard at all. Though she'd never looked at him close enough to be sure, she thought that the scraggliness was due in large part to the pockmarks on his face from what must have been a hellacious case of acne when he was younger.

The old man lived in an ancient cabin on Crooked Creek, off a dirt road that started where the gravel road ended ... the gravel road that replaced a one-lane paved road when the asphalt ran out, and that one lane road wound through the mountains for miles before it fed into the state highway. Nobody passed by Russell Henderson's house on their way somewhere else. He lived in a cabin with his adult grandson, who was mentally disabled. Rileigh didn't know the boy's real name — everyone just called him Buddy, and he likely had a functioning IQ between 70 and 85.

Rileigh looked up to see Russell standing in the doorway, holding Buddy's hand. As soon as he let go, Buddy began to make a circuit around the room, looking at the floor, as if he were following some invisible trail around and around.

Russell sat down, looking silly in a child's school desk, scratching his scraggly beard, a plug of Shoal chewing tobacco swelling his jaw as it had every time she'd ever seen him. Today it appeared to be mint or wintergreen flavor, from the smell of it.

"I sure wish I could tell you something that would help you out," Russell said. "But I didn't see nothing. Me and Buddy spent most of the morning at the duck pond. He liked that, won half a dozen bears, and when he wasn't looking, I'd give the prizes back."

The duck pond booth was a plastic swimming pool full of water with a couple of dozen yellow rubber duckies bobbing around in the fake puddle. The game was for very small children, kindergarten, first grade. None of the older kids would be interested. Well, except for Buddy. Each child was handed a fishing pole with a magnet on the end of the line rather than a hook. The rubber ducks had magnets as well, so all the child had to do was swing the end of the line out over the flock of ducks, and one or more of them would leap at the magnet on the end of the line. The child won a prize based on the number on the bottom of the ducky. A board posted beside the booth described what prizes had been assigned to what members. The booth had been on the outside edge of the carnival, which is what Rileigh wanted to talk to Russell about.

"Here's what I'm wondering, Russell." Rileigh turned toward Buddy, still making a circuit around the room. "Could you get Buddy to tell me what he remembers about the cars in the parking lot?"

Buddy Henderson loved cars and trucks, never went anywhere without a handful of toy ones in his pocket. He was a savant on that subject, could tell you the make and model of any car he saw, had a perfect memory for the details of vehicles he'd only seen once, years ago.

Russell smiled, "Oh, he remembers all right. Trick is to get him to tell you."

The old man called the younger one to his side and told him to sit at one of the desks. Buddy had a red car, the Matchbox kind, in his hand and he began to drive it across the desktop, making motor sounds as he did so.

"Buddy, you 'member being at the carnival this morning, doncha?" The boy did not reply. "You won a bear at the duck pond, remember?"

The boy raised his head and looked in the direction of his grandfather, somewhere over the man's right shoulder, not making eye contact.

"I won! I won!"

"You remember the duck pond?"

"I won!" the boy said, driving his car back and forth.

"You remember the parking lot, where we left the truck?" The boy didn't answer. "You helped me find the truck when we were ready to leave, remember?"

"It was beside the 2021 blue Dodge Ram Laramie with the cracked side mirror."

Rileigh wrote down the vehicle name.

"What was the car on the other side?"

"A red Ford Fusion, 2021. It was over the white line, so I couldn't open the door all the way. I bumped it, but I didn't leave a scratch."

Rileigh wrote "2021, Ford Fusion, red."

Buddy never looked up as he spoke, just ran the car back and forth across the desktop.

"Do you remember the car parked on the other side of the Ford Fusion?"

"A Chevrolet Colorado, 2018. It was white, with an extended cab. The tires were muddy."

And so Buddy went, from one vehicle to the next to the next. Rileigh noted when she recognized the vehicle. The green Honda Civic belonged to Evelyn and Clive Foster. The black Accord, she'd seen Cynthia Walters getting out of. Granny McCulloch's old Ford pickup with a camper in the truck bed. A CRV with a wheelchair rack on the back bumper — that belonged to the Forresters. The black Dodge Charger belonging to the Footes, pulling the Foot Notes instrument carrier. Buddy described a white panel truck from Parker's Grocery store that delivered supplies to the popcorn machine and the cotton candy air blower, and two other panel trucks — Mathews' Plumbing Supplies and Wakashaw's Dry Cleaners.

Buddy reeled off bumper stickers, too. A Marsha Blackburn for Senate sticker on Clive Foster's Honda Civic. A sticker that read "Forest Fires Prevent Bears" on Granny McCulloch's pickup. An old Biden/Harris sticker on the Forresters' CRV and a sticker with the face of Donald Trump and the words, "Miss me yet?" on Ben Pendergast's Hyundai.

Rileigh was interested in all the cars in the parking lot, of course, but particularly those near the carnival. It wasn't likely that whoever took Chloe walked her all the way across the parking lot to some vehicle. Whoever took her had been parked near the carnival, near enough that she could travel from the carnival to the car without being noticed.

Rileigh had had to scramble to keep up with the boy as he described one vehicle after another, and she didn't want to interrupt him for fear the flow would be broken and he wouldn't be able to go on. When he got to the 2021 blue Dodge Laramie, he just stopped, like you'd turned off a faucet. It took her a moment to realize he'd gone all the way around the lot and back to the vehicle parked beside his grandfather's.

Sitting back in the chair, Rileigh looked down at the list of vehicles Buddy had provided. Maybe not as good as a surveillance camera, but certainly amazing.

"You want to know what I think happened to that little girl?" Russell asked, and Rileigh looked up from the notepad.

"What?"

"I b'lieve she walked out of there holding onto the

hand of somebody she knew, somebody she trusted. That's the only way it works. If she put up any protest at all, folks would have been right on top of her. That little girl went along willingly with her kidnapper." He leaned over and said softly. "And the kidnapper was one of *us.*"

Chapter Fifteen

MITCH, Rileigh, and a full complement of deputies spent the whole day talking to the people who'd been at the carnival. At some point somebody had brought Mitch a sandwich for lunch. When he finally noticed it late that afternoon, the chicken salad had made the bread mushy, and he chucked the whole thing into a trash basket.

The only bright spot was halfway through the morning when Rileigh appeared at the door of the principal's office and announced: "Here's a complete list of every vehicle that was in the parking lot for the whole morning." She ripped a piece of paper out of her notepad and handed it to Mitch. "It's all there."

He ran his eye down the list, looked at her in surprise, then went back to the list.

A Red Ford Fusion 2021, a Chevrolet Colorado 2018, white, an extended cab. He looked up over the paper as he read the next words. *"And the tires were muddy?"*

"Buddy notices everything," Rileigh said. And then she told him the story of the handicapped young man who was a savant about cars.

Mitch had heard about a kid somewhere who was the same way about trains, and who had in his head the schedules of every train on every track in the whole country. Knew the names of the different train companies and what was written on the sides of the train cars, everything. But he'd never heard of one who had that kind of eidetic memory about vehicles.

"So, you knew this, and you asked to talk to him?"

"I knew what Buddy could do and I saw him at the festival. You did too, remember? I pointed him out. He was the young man who squealed, 'I won, I won,' after he passed by our booth."

Mitch remembered him.

"He kept his eyes on the ground. That was him?"

Rileigh nodded.

"So when we put out the call over the radio—"

Mitch interrupted. "Over your mom's grapevine."

Rileigh took up where he had interrupted. "—that we needed all the volunteers to come back to the school, I asked the office ladies to bring Buddy and his grandfather to me as soon as he showed up." Rileigh pointed toward the list she had just given to Mitch. "If I knew whose car it was, I noted their name on the list."

"So, we know the makes and models of the cars. We just don't know the license plate numbers."

"But we wouldn't know those even if we'd had security footage. Usually it's not clear enough for you to read plate numbers," Rileigh said.

"True."

Rileigh cocked her head to the side. "You know what I could do? I could give that list to Mama and have her put it out over her phone tree, see if we can't figure out who those cars belong to."

Mitch shoved the list back across his desk toward Rileigh.

"Do it," he said.

She stood. "On it."

Then they'd both gone back to questioning the volunteers.

By the time the last volunteer had had their brain picked clean, Rileigh's mother had put the name of the owner to every vehicle on that list. He gave the list to one of the office workers to pass on to the FBI for vehicle checks and background checks on the owners. Then he and Rileigh sat down for a cup of coffee to regroup.

"Hear you went out to talk to Rhonda Jo and Gunny," Rileigh said.

They hadn't had a chance to talk about his "swing and a miss" yesterday afternoon.

Mitch nodded. "It was a colossal waste of time."

"Yeah," Rileigh said, then closed her mouth as if she'd intended to say more but changed her mind.

"Go on, spit it out."

"Well, I just wish you'd mentioned to me where you were going and why, because I might have been able to save you the trip."

"How so?"

"I know the backstory on Jeff Malone's mother, and I'm not sure I'd believe her if she told me that the sun was going to come up on Easter Sunday morning."

Mitch let out a huge sigh and rolled his eyes. "And you know that backstory how?"

"One word for you, Sheriff Webster," she said, "Mama."

"Is there anything about anybody that your mother doesn't know?"

"Not that I know of."

"Seriously, none of my deputies had any idea she wasn't reliable."

"Their wives probably did."

That stopped Mitch in his tracks. "What are you saying?"

"I'm saying that there are things the women in this county know that the men don't. As is true all over planet Earth, there are things that women know that men don't and won't ever know unless women tell them." She held up a hand as if to ward off a protest. "And I'm not taking about some kind of Nazi Feminist I-am-woman-hear-me-roar bullshit. I'm just commenting on the nature of the universe as I see it."

"And you know something I don't about Mrs. Hanover?"

"She and Mama worked together for a while at the park."

Mitch knew that Rileigh's mother had worked at Great Smoky Mountains National Park for decades, and had run the back country information office there before she retired.

"Mama hired Dolores about ten years ago to work the reception desk in the Oconaluftee Visitors' Center. She appeared to do pretty well for a while, then she went totally off the rails."

"As in?"

"As in she decided that one of the park rangers was making inappropriate advances to the tourists and she turned him in."

"Was he?"

"Nope. Mama investigated and there wasn't a thing to anything that Dolores said. So she called Dolores in and wanted to know why in the world she'd made such an allegation when it wasn't true. And Dolores pretty much exploded all over her. Said that Mama was blind. That she was covering up for the park ranger. Hinted that there were way more things going on with this touchy-feely park ranger that Mama was also ignoring. Claimed she was the only one who really knew what was going on."

"So your mama had this woman pegged as a totally unreliable hysteric. Why did you think the deputies knew nothing about it but their wives did?"

"Because women talk about such things among themselves." And she looked at Mitch and just shook her head. "Trust me on this one. Your deputies are great guys. They really are. You're lucky to have them. Jeb Rawlings and I went to school together. Tony Hadley was a couple of years older than I am, but he was one of the best basketball players I ever saw."

"Tony? He's barely 5'11."

"He went under all the long arms of the tall guys, right to the basket."

Mitch shook his head and tried to refocus, forced his mind not to dwell on the ball he'd dropped with Dolores Hanover and move on.

"I'm trying to put all of the resources of the FBI to good use. I've been sending them lists of names, the people who were volunteers, the teachers, the principal, the parents. Just let them run the whole batch of them through NCIC and see if anything pops."

"Good plan. Anything popped yet?"

"Nope." Mitch sighed. "I could use their facial recognition software, too — if I had any faces that needed recognizing. With no surveillance video..." he let the end of the sentence dangle. "You know, it surprises me. You'd think an elementary school would have surveillance video of everything."

"In Black Bear Forge, Tennessee, surveillance video in a school is at least slightly frowned upon."

Before he could say anything, Rileigh shrugged her shoulders. "These are private people, Mitch. They don't like the thought of Big Brother looking over their shoulders."

Mitch smiled a little. "And who needs big brother when you've got Buddy Russell?" Mitch had been thinking all day about the gold mine of information that the handicapped young man had provided — and about the fact they'd never have accessed it if it hadn't been for Rileigh. If Rileigh had been consulted about the reliability of the woman who'd sent him on a wild goose chase yesterday, he could have saved himself and the deputies hours of useless work.

That cinched it. He didn't know how she'd respond, but as her mother was fond of saying, "You have not because you ask not."

"I've got a proposition for you," he said.

Rileigh lifted an eyebrow. "Okay. And it is?"

"I'd like to offer you a part-time job as a sheriff's deputy."

Rileigh looked at him like he had just grown a third eye.

"What in the world?" she stammered. "Why?"

"Because I need your help on this case."

"I'm helping. You can't get any more of me than you've already got."

"I think it needs to be official. I want you to have a badge and all that goes with it."

"What for?" She was totally confused. "Why? Is it about using my firearm? You know that's not a problem."

He did. Rileigh had clocked in ten years on the job as a police officer, and that entitled her to privileges under

LEOSA, the Federal Law Enforcement Officer Safety Act. The law had been part of the old Patriot Act passed shortly after 9-11. The powers that be had determined that the retirement of police officers meant fewer guns in the hands of people trained to use them, and in the political climate in America at that time, that was not a good thing. Rileigh could use her firearm as a retired police officer legally, could have even if Tennessee hadn't been a state without a concealed carry law.

"No, it's not about your weapon."

"Then why? I mean, you have deputies, good ones. I told you Jed Rawlings was in my kindergarten class." She stopped and smiled. "He used to terrorize Georgia with bugs. She's arachnophobic. But it doesn't have to have eight legs to send her up the wall. Six, four, ten. She doesn't pause to count, just freaks out at anything creepy-crawly. He'd put rubber spiders on her shoulder. He and Tony Hadley have lived here their whole lives. What can I do that they can't?"

"You've done two things today that they couldn't … or at least didn't."

That stopped her.

"You knew I shouldn't have listened to Chloe's grand-mother. And you got a list of the cars in the parking lot during the carnival. I need you to be part of the team, Rileigh."

"Can you even do that? Hire a deputy? Doesn't the mayor or the county council have to–"

"Nope. Emergency authority. Think of it like a battle-field promotion. I can hire part-time help if I need it … temporarily. When the dust settles, yeah, those higher up the food chain will have a say." He shook his head. "I'm hoping by then we could talk about a permanent full-time position."

The department was understaffed and after all that'd been thrown at them since he took over the job, nobody would deny the need. He was sure the council would be squarely in Rileigh's corner.

He offered a small smile. "Remember, I'm only the 'interim' Sheriff."

Mitch knew that designation itself was temporary. He had replaced the elected Sheriff Mumford so that Mumford could have double-knee replacement surgery. The surgery had not gone well, and the man had put in his paperwork for early retirement with more than two and a half years left on his four-year term.

"I don't see the job as temporary, though. You've earned this and we need you. But all that's for another day. I'm asking for right now. What do you say?"

Rileigh stared at him and didn't say anything at all. And in those beats of silence, Mitch recognized the offer for what it really was. Oh, he'd made it for the reasons he'd told her. He just hadn't told her *all* the reasons. The truth still in the husk was he just worked better when she was working with him. He did everything better with Rileigh at his side. And the implications of that were ... nothing he could think about right now. But soon. Soon he would.

Chapter Sixteen

It was not possible that Yarmouth County Sheriff
Mitchell Webster had spent almost a year in Black Bear
Forge, Tennessee and didn't know what had happened to
Rileigh in Memphis that had sent her running home to the
mountains with her tail between her legs. He had to know.

Well, he had to know *something*. But she doubted that
anybody in the county really had the story straight. Maybe
they did when it was all fresh news, but not anymore.
When Rileigh was making headlines in Memphis, she was
a celebrity of sorts, she supposed, in Black Bear Forge. But
of course, that part didn't last. And what opinions people
had formed about her after, with only fragments of information at their disposal, she didn't know. But she could tell
by the way people greeted her, by the unguarded looks on
their faces, that at this moment in time, a full year later, the
population of Yarmouth County, Tennessee knew only one
thing about Rileigh Bishop that mattered to them: she was
local. She was the home team. And whatever had
happened to her out there in the wide world didn't change
that.

There were a lot of things in life you could lose. You could lose your car keys. You could lose your wallet. You could lose your citizenship. You could lose your mind. You could lose a fight or a game, your sense of smell, or your canary. Most everything in life was something you could lose, but what you couldn't lose was where you were from. You owned that. Everybody owned that. Black Bear Forge, Tennessee belonged to Rileigh in the same way she belonged to Black Bear Forge. And there was nothing that could take the designation of "local" away.

That was what had started the healing process for her. The unconditional acceptance of mountain people for their own.

All week long, Rileigh had tried not to know what day it was. Told herself she wasn't counting down the days. But she wasn't a very good liar, not to herself or to anybody else. Today was exactly one year to the day after Rileigh's whole world exploded into a thousand tiny pieces that drifted down around her head like confetti.

And Mitch had chosen this day to offer her a position as a deputy. A law enforcement officer. She refused to make more of it that it was … but she didn't believe in coincidences.

She had to tell him. He needed to know how she had gone from being a sergeant with a spotless record to a shattered woman who needed to slink home and put herself back together one piece at a time. If that process was indeed complete, if Rileigh had come back yet again, healed by the Smoky Mountains of the wounds the rest of the world had inflicted, then yeah, it was time. What was it they say in AA? You're only as sick as your secrets.

"I don't know how much you know about what happened to me in Memphis," Rileigh began. Mitch started to speak, but she held up her hand and continued,

"I don't care what you know, because whatever it is, it's probably not accurate. My past has been a closed book, but you need to read that book. I think you're entitled to know what really did happen before you walk out on the end of the plank and offer me a job as a law enforcement officer."

"I'm not offering a job to the person you used to be. I'm offering a job to the Rileigh Bishop who's sitting here, the woman who has been through more in the last twelve months than a lot of people do in lifetime, and still comes out swinging. That Rileigh Bishop is a good cop. She may not have had a badge for all this time, but she's never stopped being a good cop. And right now, I need the help of a good cop."

"With your eyes wide open, Mitch," she said. "Wide. Open."

She took a deep breath and stepped back in time to that spring morning in 2023. She remembered that she could smell jasmine in the air and magnolias. Maybe she had imagined that part, but she was certain that she remembered what she could hear -- the sound of a calliope on a riverboat in the Mississippi River a few blocks away. She'd always loved the sound of a calliope.

A scene flashed through her head like a comet across a black sky, bright and then gone. She was in her dress uniform, sitting by herself at a table. The officers questioning her are in suits and ties. She'd wondered at the time why they made everybody dress up for this.

"You used lethal force. Is that not correct, Sergeant Bishop?"

Well, duh. That's why we're all here, isn't it?

"Yes sir, I did."

"Will you please explain to the Internal Affairs board

why you believe the circumstance warranted such an extreme measure?"

You mean why did I decide to shoot the man who had a gun pointed at me, the guy who just murdered two civilians and shot my partner? Is that what you're asking?

Of course, that's not what she'd said. She told the story she was about to tell Mitch. When the internal affairs officer had asked her that question, she had still been operating under the erroneous assumption that the facts in the case mattered, that what had really happened mattered, that the outcome of the investigation was in some intrinsic way linked to reality. All of those assumptions had proved false.

"It was a beautiful spring day and I could smell flowers," she said. "And afterwards, I felt ... *offended* somehow that the whole world, the whole universe could come crashing down around my shoulders on such a beautiful spring day."

It had all been so ... *ugly*, like finding a cigarette butt in an offering plate.

"My partner was a new recruit. His name was Tyrell Crocker, and the two of us had been sent to do a well check on a woman in an apartment. Her name was Mrs. Pearl Van Dyke." She gave a little laugh. "Isn't it funny? I still remember her name, though I never met the woman. Tyrell and I never got that far."

She shook her head and went back to the story. "We'd been dispatched to do this well check because an old woman had fallen off the radar. No one could get in touch with her. Her children tried to reach her. Her neighbors knocked on her door and nobody answered." She shrugged at Mitch. "You know as well as I do how those things turn out. The best you can hope for is that the subject hasn't been dead so long the reek knocks you down when you open the door."

She paused.

"But like I say, we didn't get that far. We drove past a liquor store on the way. Atkinson's Liquor and Spirits. And I just glanced at the building, but when I did ..." she smiled at him again, "all sorts of unconscious alarms started going ding, ding, ding. There were cars in the parking lot, but there was not a soul visible through the windows in the building. And there was no clerk behind the counter."

"So you and your partner went to investigate," Mitch said.

"Yes, we went to investigate."

She had accompanied Crocker when the call came in because this would be his first time. It would likely be ugly, and she wanted to be there to help pick up the pieces, if he needed it.

"But the well check and all of that went out of my mind as soon as I saw that empty building. I told Crocker to pull down to the end so you couldn't see the car from inside the building. We parked beside a white SUV with tinted windows, so it totally blocked the cruiser from view.

"I stepped out of the vehicle, and that's when I heard screaming from inside the building. Shrieking. It was a woman's voice. Screaming. 'No. Please. No.' And then the sound of the word was cut off by the sound of a gunshot. Then I heard a man's voice. I was already moving by then. He was screaming, 'Help me, somebody, my wife—' And then there were two more gunshots and silence. And after that, it all slowed down."

Mitch nodded. "I know that slowed-down feeling."

"I pulled my weapon, and as I did, a man came running out the door of the liquor store. He had something in his hand which could have been a beer bottle or could have been a weapon. I turned, drew down on him, and called out, 'Stop, this is the police.' He didn't stop. He turned and fired. When I put it together in my head and replayed the whole thing, I remember glancing at the street behind him, and there was nothing but a hedge on the other side. No people. No cars. The guy fired blindly, a wild shot in my basic direction. And I heard Crocker grunt as he went down."

Rileigh saw the scene in front of her as if it were a movie playing on a screen, a movie she wished she'd gotten up and walked out on before the bad parts started.

"I fired three rounds. The suspect lurched backward at the first shot, the kill shot. Second bullet got him in the groin and the third missed. Hit the asphalt in the parking lot and ricocheted. I remember watching the gun fly out of his hand into the air, sliding away under a parked car. That's as long as it took. Seconds."

Rileigh didn't notice until that moment that she was pacing back and forth across Mitch's office or that the palms of her hands were sweating. She wiped them on her jeans, but didn't sit down.

"So, I grabbed my mic and called it in: 'Officer Down.'"

She lost her breath for a moment at the horror of those words — *officer down*.

"I didn't know the address, so I gave dispatch the name of the liquor store and the name of the street. Then I ran to Crocker, rolled him over on his back. He took a round in the belly. An inch higher and it'd have hit his Kevlar. He was bleeding badly. I grabbed a towel out of the back seat of the cruiser." She paused then and grinned. "The reason I had a towel in the back seat was because somebody had chalked graffiti on the trunk of the cruiser. I suppose it was supposed to say, 'die pigs,' but it was smeared and all you could see was 'D-I-P-I-G.' I was using that towel as a pressure bandage when I heard the screaming. I think I'd heard it from the beginning, but I didn't attend to it until then.

"The screams didn't come from inside the store. I looked up, and there was a commotion on the other side of the street, on the other side of *the hedge* that was behind the suspect. It was the most awful screaming. I've heard it before. It's the sound of outrage and agony and gut-ripping emotion. You don't hear it often. In Afghanistan, women screamed like that when they found their children blown apart."

Rileigh was quiet then, sinking into the memory, hearing the scream in her ears.

"You hit a civilian."

"Uh huh. A through and through. The kill shot that stopped the subject went right through his heart, and across the street and through the hedge."

She heard Mitch make some kind of groaning sound at that.

"It wasn't long before the second unit rolled up and the third and the bus. I couldn't leave Crocker. So, I watched from where I was kneeling on the ground. I watched the crowd gather around the sound on the other side of the hedge. And I knew it was something awful. And I knew it was my fault."

"Whoa there. Let's talk this 'my fault' thing through."

She held up her hand. "Been there, done that. Fault as in my responsibility, not fault as in wrong. But it was my responsibility. In the end, the facts of what really happened didn't matter. The fact that this man had just murdered two people in cold blood and shot a police officer. That part didn't matter. The only thing that mattered is that a police officer's bullet went through the side of a stroller and into the head of a nine-month-old baby girl."

Mitch was silent then. The gravity of it closing his lungs. Rileigh let out a long breath.

"That's the 'what happened' story. The 'what happened after' story is just as ugly for different reasons. Within an hour after it was all over, the facts of the situation were totally discarded, and a new narrative was built to take their place."

"And you took the fall for that narrative."

"I did indeed."

"I tried to fight it. Hired a lawyer." She barked out a laugh. "I'm still trying to pay that man's bill, by the way. They told me you get what you pay for, so I got the very best. But I didn't get what I paid for, because I paid for him to make the whole thing go away, and he didn't do that. What went away was Sergeant Rileigh Bishop. I ran."

She paused for a beat.

"Not from the scandal or from the suspension or from the ugliness. I didn't run away *from* anything. I ran away *to* the mountains, because the mountains have been my touchstone my whole life. I was like a sick old dog. I crawled into a familiar hole, curled my tail over my nose, and tried to pretend the world wasn't there anymore."

She let out another long breath and shook her head to shake the gauzy fabric of memories out of her mind.

"I was not fired from the Memphis Police Department. I would have been. The 'defund the police' mob smelled blood in the water and they were circling for a kill. But I resigned before they could fire me. So, take that for whatever it's worth. When you tell Mayor Southerland that you've hired a disgraced—"

"Disgraced, is that what you are?"

"Let it go, Mitch, just let it go. That's the word that's

going to be used, and the mayor's going to throw it in your face."

"You still haven't given me an answer."

"I said when I took off my badge and gun that I'd never put on another badge as long as I lived."

She looked for a long time out the window and then turned toward Mitch. Her gaze was long and searching, looking for doubt and finding none. When she spoke, she kept her voice light, not showing that the import of the words shook her to the core. "But hey, a girl can change her mind, right?"

Chapter Seventeen

RILEIGH WAS PROFOUNDLY grateful Mitch wasn't bent on some kind of official swearing-in ceremony. This had been too sudden for her to screw herself up to a public announcement. He just gathered up the handful of deputies who happened to be at the station, plus the dispatcher, the office workers, Circuit Judge Ansel Hawthorne to administer the oath ... and some guy named Higgins who happened to be in the office to fill out an accident report.

Mitch had a Bible in his desk. Rileigh didn't know that until he brought it out for her to place her hand on as she swore. "I, Rileigh Joseph Bishop, do solemnly swear that I will support The Constitution of the state of Tennessee and The Constitution of the United States and that I will perform with fidelity the duties of deputy sheriff of Yarmouth County, Tennessee; that I will preserve, protect and defend its citizens, so help me God."

It was that simple. And that profound. Mitch gave her a badge — in a flip case until she had a uniform to pin it on. That was it.

Of course, that wasn't it. Not by a longshot. The distance between "I'll never put on a badge again" and "I will preserve, protect and defend …" was wide and deep and full of piranhas and sharks and other man-eating denizens of the deep. She hadn't looked down into those deep, dark waters in more than a year, and the darkness of those depths filled her with an inexplicable dread. What if she hurt somebody *again*?

"I'm going to talk to the Malones, and I'd like you to come with me," Mitch said, dragging her out of her reverie to the reality that they had a missing child to find.

When Mitch pulled his cruiser onto the street where Jeff and Celine Malone lived, Rileigh didn't quite know how to feel about what she saw. The street was jammed with cars. Cars were parked in the neighbors' driveways and on the side of the road. It looked like somebody on the street was having a Super Bowl party. But Rileigh knew this was no party.

"I wasn't expecting this," Mitch said as he found a place for his cruiser on a side street and got out.

"I was," Rileigh said, "more or less. It's one of those things in mountain culture that have always given me ambivalent feelings. On one hand, it's glorious to know the kind of support you have when anything bad happens in your life. Your neighbors will suit up and show up."

She paused.

"Of course, the flip side of that is that there's no privacy. If what you really need is to be by yourself to come to grips with what's happening, or to process how you ought to feel, you're shit out of luck."

She gave him a sidelong look. "If you're local, that is. If you're from away from here, nobody cares what happens to you."

Mitch shot a glance, checking to see if she was serious and grinning when he saw she wasn't.

As they walked uphill toward the tidy brick home set back into the trees from the street, Rileigh told Mitch, "In a town like Black Bear Forge, Tennessee, you can count on your friends and neighbors to show up at the significant events in your life and to look for you at the significant events in theirs." She shook her head. "But this is a pretty big turnout. I guess everybody just feels like they want to show they care, so they bring a dish."

"Bring a dish?"

Rileigh nodded. "Of course. Every one of these cars contained a cake, a casserole, a salad, soup, chili, or pinto beans."

Mitch and Rileigh made their way through the jammed living room into the kitchen where Jeff and Celine were seated at the kitchen table. Jeff leapt to his feet as soon as he saw Mitch, read the look on Mitch's face, and sat back down in resignation.

"You don't know anything, do you?" Jeff asked him.

Mitch shook his head. "Not yet." Mitch looked around the room, and Rileigh saw him catch sight of Dolores Hanover.

"I paid a visit to your ex-daughter-in-law this afternoon, Mrs. Hanover," he said.

Jeff Malone's eyes opened wide. "You went to see Ronnie? What for?"

Mitch kept his eyes focused on the old lady. "You were mistaken, Mrs. Hanover. Rhonda Jo did not take Chloe."

"Mama," Jeff demanded, "did you tell the sheriff that Ronnie—"

"Hell yeah, I told him Ronnie had her. I thought she did. You don't know it, but she told her sister that she was going to come get her little girl and—"

"That's enough, Mama," Jeff said in disdain. He looked at the sheriff. "I'm sorry you wasted your time going out to talk to Ronnie. She's never wanted anything to do with Chloe—" he shot a glance at his mother on the other side of the room "—regardless of what my mother may have told you."

Mitch looked around at all the people gathered in the kitchen and asked if there was somewhere they could talk privately.

Jeff got to his feet and told a man who looked remarkably like him, "Danny, get everybody out of the den." Then he led Mitch and Rileigh down a short hallway, and it was like swimming upstream against school of salmon as people flowed out of the room in the small spaces. The den was an add-on to the first part of the house or perhaps a converted garage. There was a fireplace on one wall and the mantle was jammed with pictures — all of them, Chloe. Chloe as a baby, Chloe as a toddler. Chloe in Santa's lap when she was about three.

Jeff took his wife's hand and sat down on the couch, while Rileigh and Mitch sat in chairs facing the couch.

"I just wanted to spend a few minutes with you, hoping to find any little detail we might have missed."

Celine spoke then for the first time. "She was the most perfect little girl you've ever seen." Her voice was soft. Celine had strawberry blonde hair pulled back in a ponytail and bright green eyes and enough freckles for three or four people.

"Celine and I got married when Chloe was only four months old," Jeff said. "Celine's her mommy."

"Mr. Malone, did Chloe ever run away?" Rileigh asked.

Both Jeff and his wife looked shocked. "Run away? Hell no. Why would she run away?"

"Kids do that," Rileigh said. "Most of them don't get a whole lot farther than the end of the block. We were just wondering."

"No," Celine said. "Chloe never ran away."

"Does she have any kind of special relationship with any adult outside her family?"

"Don't you think we've thought about that?" Jeff said, and the pent-up emotion crept out before he was able to clamp it back down. "There's nobody. Chloe loved her Sunday school teacher, Mrs. Everett, but she's an old woman in a wheelchair and she lives by herself. Celine called her as soon as we found out Chloe was missing, and she was devastated."

"She loves my brothers," Jeff continued. "All three of her uncles put that little girl on a pedestal. They'd give her anything. They're all sitting out there tonight worried sick about her."

"I'm sure you've already racked your brain to consider this, but has anything odd happened in your life or Chloe's life in the last few days?" Mitch asked.

Celine and Jeff exchanged a look. Jeff shook his head slightly, but Celine ignored him.

"I know this isn't anything at all, but if it would help bring Chloe home..." she stifled a sob and Jeff took her hand.

"Don't do this, sweetheart," he said. "You know it has nothing—"

"I have to." She turned to Mitch. "My brother is about three years older than me and he's a druggie. He buys drugs, he sells drugs, he uses drugs. His whole life is about drugs. He sort of orbits in and out of my life, and my sister's, and my mother's. Shows up when he needs money or when he's destitute or needs a place to sleep. It's been awful to watch him go downhill in the past few years. He can't live much longer like he's living."

She drew in a ragged breath. "He was here two days ago, out of the blue. We never know when he's going to show up, but we came home from the grocery store —it was a Saturday afternoon — and he was sitting on the front porch, whittling."

Jeff said, "He looked like death on a cracker."

"He did look awful, like he hadn't had a bath or washed his hair in a week—"

"A month!" Jeff put in.

Celine shrugged then and looked at her husband. "We don't know why, but for some reason Chloe has always adored her Uncle Jimmy. She took one look at him when we got out of the car and went running across the yard and threw herself into his arms, so glad to see..." Celine had to stop then to collect herself to keep talking. "Jimmy's mostly unaware of Chloe. He's unaware of anything that's not about drugs."

"Then he did what we knew he'd come here to do, which was ask for money." Jeff shot his wife a look. "We made an agreement about a year ago and we've stuck to it, that when he shows up, we will give him coupons for McDonald's. We bought a whole book of them, over a hundred dollars' worth."

"I couldn't stand the thought of him being hungry, but I knew if I gave him money, he wouldn't spend it on food."

"We had probably $50 left of McDonald's certificates and we gave them to him." Jeff's face turned hard. "Drugs will change a person and they sure have changed Jimmy. He used to be the nicest guy..." and he let his voice trail off, then started over. "He got mad, demanded that we give him money. When I told him no, he lost it. Came running at me, knocked me down, had his fingers around my throat, like he would have killed me if he could have."

"I was crying and trying to drag him off," Celine said. "Chloe was standing on the porch and she had the most awful look on her face, watching her uncle act like an animal."

"He's so skinny, he couldn't win a fight with a nun from Little Sisters of the Poor," Jeff said. "I threw him off easy and told him to leave and not come back."

"And that's when—" Celine began, then she stopped. She looked at Jeff, and Jeff finished for her.

"That's when he started threatening. He said we'd be sorry that we had treated him bad, that he would make us pay, that one day we would rue the day we had been so selfish and hateful to him."

"That's when Chloe came down off the porch, ran to me and threw her arms around my waist. And Jimmy …"

"Jimmy started yelling at *her*, telling her we were monsters, all of us, the whole family. He said he'd make *her* sorry—"

"That's when Jeff put his foot down. He grabbed hold of Jimmy, and literally threw him out into the street. Then we went in the house and closed the door. We heard him yelling for a while, and after he stopped, I don't know where he went."

"Do you really believe that your brother would harm Chloe?"

"I don't think my brother knew he'd threatened her five minutes after it happened. I don't think he has anything to do with Chloe being missing." She looked deep into Mitch's eyes. "But you asked if we knew anything — *anything* at all and …" She finished in a whisper. "There's nothing I wouldn't do to bring Chloe home."

Mitch thanked the couple for being so open and

badge in her pocket, she would be chomping at the bit to talk to Wally Hansford about the case that she had been working on. Like all the other cases she'd been given, this was a contract laborer position with no benefits. As a part-timer, she only got crumbs from the table, the leftover jobs that nobody else wanted. But she had sucked it up and taken them and done a good job on them, and had finally earned enough trust that she believed Wally had been willing to take her on full time – as soon as she'd completed the job with Crystal.

Now she was about to march into Wally's office, give him a really good, thorough, exhaustive report on the case she was working ... and then tell him she couldn't take any more contract cases for a while because she had just been hired as a temporary part-time Yarmouth County deputy to work the kidnapping case. She really needed the full-time employment, the benefits and the salary, to get out of the financial hole she was in and move out of her mother's house. Full-time employment with Gatlinburg Investigations would provide the means to do all of those things. Although working as a private investigator had never been her goal in life, until yesterday, it was the only option.

Now, however ...

Rileigh steeled herself for Stephanie Papadopoulos' screechy voice, smiled a greeting, and said she had an appointment with Wally.

"How are you, Rileigh?"

That woman's voice was fingernails on a blackboard.

"I'm good, and you?"

"I heard about that kidnapping in Black Bear Forge. Shoot, you'd think a little place like that would be a safe place to raise kids, that they wouldn't be in danger of being snatched right out of the school yard."

"I'm not sure that there's any place that's perfectly safe anymore," Rileigh said stiffly.

She knew what Aunt Daisy would say: *Life's tough, get a helmet.*

"Wally will be out in a few minutes. He has a client in there who wasn't on this morning's appointment schedule. I'm sorry it's going to make him late meeting with you. Would you like a cup of coffee? I just made some fresh."

"No, thank you."

"You take it black, don't you?" Stephanie said. "I remember. No cream, no sugar, just black."

The reason Rileigh took her coffee black was not because she liked black coffee, but because she would do just about anything to avoid an interaction with Stephanie that required verbal communication.

"No coffee at all this morning. Thanks."

Rileigh turned and stared out the window of the office, which overlooked a busy street in Gatlinburg and shook her head. She wondered if she'd ever stop being surprised and dismayed by the ever-growing crowds of tourists who surged like tsunamis up and down the streets of this little mountain town. She would swear that the street out there right now was more crowded than most streets in New York City, or London, or any other major metropolitan area. You had to stand in line to breathe in Gatlinburg during "the season," which now started in early spring and lasted until late fall. Every year, the tourist time grew longer and the off-season grew shorter. Eventually there would be no such thing as a season here, she was sure. It would be year-round clogged roads and noisy tourists. Oh, how she longed for the quiet sleepy little town where she grew up.

The door to Wally's office opened and he stepped out with a tall slender woman in spike heels and a business suit.

She smiled at Rileigh condescendingly, the way only women who believe themselves to be at the very top of the female food chain can smile. Of course, she was dressed for business and Rileigh was dressed for a stakeout. It occurred to her that there was no term for what you wore on a stakeout — nothing like "business casual."

Surveillance formal. Scrutiny casual. Reconnaissance traditional.

Wally and the woman shook hands, the woman clack, clack, clacked out on her spike heels, and Wally smiled at her and waved her into the office.

"I'm anxious to hear about Crystal Collins," he said, "and so is the Haversford Insurance Company, particularly if you've got good news for them."

Wally walked around his desk and sat down. He was a man in his late 30s who was losing his hair, but doing it with grace. He was always tanned year-round, and as far as she knew, he didn't spend long vacations on beaches, which meant his was a tanning bed tan. It wasn't spray-on, she could spot those a mile away. Charlie Hayden had always worn a spray-on tan.

That thought snaked up out of her subconscious and bit her. The last person in the world she wanted to think about right now was Charlie Hayden.

She put him out of her mind and sat down at Wally's invitation, opened the folder in her lap, and gave him a brief overview of what she had learned in her two weeks of surveillance.

"Short and sweet, the woman is bullshitting the insurance company. There's not a damn thing wrong with her."

Wally made a fist pump in the air and grinned. "Tell me more."

"I can document with photographs and personal observation that she has no evident disability of any kind. She does not walk with a walker or a cane. She does not even limp. I have watched her play tennis, and she is as fast and agile as an athlete. A person with the spinal injury she has claimed could not have made it up the hill to the tennis court, let alone played the game."

"Pictures?"

"Absolutely. I have pictures of her playing tennis. I have pictures of her playing golf. I have pictures of her getting in and out of her car unassisted. I have pictures of her dancing in a nightclub. I have pictures of—"

Wally held up his hand. "You want me to applaud now or hold all applause till the end?"

"Oh, I have a grand finale. Definitely worthy of a round of applause."

"And that is?"

"Pictures of Crystal Collins rock climbing."

Wally's eyes grew wide. "You can't be serious."

"Serious as a heart attack, and the woman ain't a half-bad rock climber."

"The Haversford Insurance Agency is going to want to kiss your whole face, Rileigh-girl," Wally said, smiling. He reached out for the folder containing the report, and she handed it to him. Then both of them spoke at once. "Rileigh, I've decided that—"

"Wally, I was wondering if—"

They both laughed. "Let me go first," Rileigh said, because she feared that Wally was about to offer her a job, or at least engage her services in another assignment.

"I made no secret of the fact that I wanted to work for the Good GIs full-time—"

Wally smiled broadly and started to speak, but Rileigh held up her hand.

"And I really enjoyed this case—"

"Good, because I have a doozie for you!"

"But—"

Wally marched over her protests like Sherman through Atlanta.

"Brand new client ... and they picked *you!*"

Wally offered clients their choice from a roster of investigators.

"When they saw your profile — and with my whole-hearted recommendation — the Huntington Art Museum *in Knoxville* wants you to find out who has been swapping out real paintings with forgeries—"

"I can't."

"Can't what?"

"Can't take the job."

Wally looked totally confused.

"What do you mean you can't—"

"The Sheriff of Yarmouth Count asked me to become a part-time deputy while he is working on this kidnapping case."

She wasn't expecting Wally's reaction, which was that all expression fell out of his face. He sat there like a mannequin, just looking at her.

She hurried on. "You know about the case, everybody does. The little girl who vanished out of the carnival in front of the school. The sheriff has a very small department and needs boots on the ground who know the territory. That's me. He needs people with law enforcement experience, and that's me. I was looking forward to coming in this morning to find out my next assignment, but ... I'm sorry, I can't take another assignment right now."

Wally's voice was as cold as a stone in the snow.

"You think that's how it works? You get to decide for yourself what cases you'll take and which ones you won't? Work when it's convenient for you, but bail out on me when I need you? I went out on a limb, touting you as one of our top investigators, the best we have. And now I'm supposed to crawl back and tell my new clients that — what? You're *busy?* Maybe some other time? That you'll look at your schedule and get back to them? Maybe sometime next week or the week after?"

"Wally, I'm sorry. I—"

"So, working for me is just — what? A hobby?"

"No, it's not like that. I didn't mean—"

Wally got to his feet, cutting her off.

"I'm way too busy to engage in idle chatter. I have to get another 'top investigator' to put on this case and figure out how I'm going to explain the swap to my clients without looking like a fool."

"Wally, I—"

"I can't fire you because I never hired you. Key word in that sentence is 'never.' Never did and never will."

Chapter Nineteen

Rileigh wasn't aware of turning off the main road onto Carter's Mill Road. She didn't even realize she'd done it until she saw Georgia's double-wide trailer house up ahead. It was like her car was a horse going home to a familiar barn. She looked at her watch and scolded herself for wasting time coming here. She'd just stay a few minutes, then get on into Black Bear Forge to the Sheriff's Office. Where she was a *deputy*.

Deputy, deputy, deputy.

The word echoed around and around in her brain. She'd been so exhausted last night after Mitch swore her in, she hadn't had time for the emotional impact of it all to land on her. On the whole drive from the Forge to Gatlinburg in the wee morning hours today, she'd found herself patting the pocket where she had put the Yarmouth County Sheriff's deputy badge. She had no uniform. And she probably never would have one. But until she had a uniform to pin it to, *unless* she had a uniform to pin it to, she would keep the badge in a flip case in her pocket. It was what detectives did, how they carried their badges.

And she had so longed to be a detective all those years ago in Memphis...

Where you swore on everything you held dear that you'd never become a law enforcement officer again.

Rileigh didn't like that snide little voice. It poked its head up every now and then, and she wanted to whack it with a croquet mallet every time it did.

Yep. She had said she'd never be a cop again. And last night she'd changed her mind.

She pulled to a stop in front of Georgia's trailer. Liam, who was nine, and Eli, eight, were playing out in the front yard, chasing each other around with sticks. Maybe the sticks were supposed to be swords, or light sabers, or rifles. Or maybe, and this was also entirely possible, they were just sticks and the two were simply trying to whack each other on the head with them. Both boys stopped what they were doing and came running when Rileigh opened the gate and started up the sidewalk. They threw themselves at her and hugged her. Rileigh kissed Liam on the top of his head, but Eli wiggled away before she had a chance. When Rileigh first came home on leave from the military after Georgia had children, there'd been some discussion that perhaps they would call her Aunt Rileigh. Rileigh had vetoed that plan, but never told Georgia the reason. Though Georgia knew her well enough, she probably figured it out on her own. Rileigh didn't want to be Aunt Rileigh to anybody but her sister's children. And that would never happen.

"Your mama busy?"

"She's always busy," Liam said.

"She's always doing something," Eli said.

"Mason's in the corner in time-out because he bit Connor."

"Bit him?"

Rileigh had told Georgia that she had been sure she was about to be offered a full-time job at the agency.

"If Mitch hadn't offered me that job last night, I'd still have told Wally I couldn't take another assignment right now, while Mitch needs me to work on this kidnapping case. That would probably have pissed him off, and he'd still have fired me. So I figure I would have gotten fired either way, whether I'd gotten the deputy job or not. So I guess I should be grateful that Mitch offered me the job."

"I'm glad I was able to help you sort that out. Come back anytime. I charge by the hour, but I'll give you a discount if you redeem the best-friend coupon."

Georgia nodded toward the badge that Rileigh still held in her hand. "Seriously, Riles, how do you feel about that?"

"How I feel about it is…" Rileigh dug down deep into herself, searched her emotions, scooted them around, and looked under them to see if she'd missed anything. When she was done, she looked at Georgia and smiled. "How I feel about it is, I'm glad, I'm happy, and I'm proud."

Chapter Twenty

MITCH LOOKED AWFUL. Clearly he hadn't slept since Chloe went missing. His eyes were sunken in dark circles, like cigarette burns on his face. There was a bone deep weariness etched there, too. It was more than getting no sleep, more than worry and fear. It was all of them together, a combination painted on the canvas of his own sense of *responsibility* making all of it bigger than the sum of the parts.

Mitch sat behind his desk, while Rileigh sat in the chair across from him. Spread out on his desk was the Black Bear Gazette, Yarmouth County's weekly newspaper that was published every Wednesday morning. The headline was a single word: "Missing."

Rileigh remembered all the stories about what had happened to her in Memphis. How distorted they were. How they took one fact and left out all the information that would explain it. Because she had fired her pistol, and a bullet from it had killed a baby in a stroller. Just that much of the story without pointing out, "Oh, by the way, before the bullet hit the child in the stroller, it went through the heart of a killer who had just executed two civilians and shot a police officer."

"Read it to me, will you?" Mitch said wearily. "My eyes are so tired, the print is blurred."

Rileigh picked up the paper and settled back in the chair.

"Five-year-old Chloe Dawn Malone disappeared from the Black Bear Forge Elementary School carnival at approximately 11 a.m. on Monday." Though her school picture was beside the news story, the article still described the child. "Chloe has long blonde hair, blue eyes, stands forty inches tall and weighs thirty-five pounds. When she disappeared, she was wearing a white sundress with a yellow daisy on the front and bees on the skirt, a headband with a daisy on it and yellow clogs. She was last seen by her teacher and other students when she and the rest of the children in the school were dismissed to go to the carnival from their classrooms at about 11 a.m. Several adults and children saw her at the carnival, but no one saw her leave. When the children were called back into the school at one o'clock, Chloe was missing."

"I don't know what to say," said Elizabeth Harbour, her teacher. "She's the most adorable little girl you ever saw. Blonde hair and big blue eyes and no front teeth. None of the children in my class has any front teeth, but Chloe looks especially adorable without them."

Rileigh finally looked up from the newspaper she was reading and lifted an eyebrow.

"I talked to that teacher. When we spoke, the only thing on her mind was her own ass. Was she going to get in trouble because she 'lost a kid'? When I finally assured her that nobody was going to blame her, all her concern vanished. Clearly that woman needs to get into another line of work."

Rileigh went back to reading.

"The Yarmouth County Sheriff's Department has deployed every resource at its disposal to find the little girl. Her picture was sent to every law enforcement agency in the state within half an hour of her disappearance and an Amber Alert was issued, but by press time today, interim Yarmouth County Sheriff Mitchell Webster said that although they had checked out several promising leads, they've made little progress in the case.

"We know that she did not leave the school grounds on foot," Sheriff Webster said. "We've established that with coon dogs that tried to pick up her scent. She left the school in a vehicle."

"When asked why the FBI had not been called in to assist in the case, Sheriff Webster said that the case was not an inter-jurisdictional situation, and there was nothing to indicate that the child had been transported across state lines or was being held for ransom. I still called and the FBI gave me access to all the bureau's resources, databases and information," Webster added. "The sheriff did not rule out requesting further aid from the bureau at some point in the future."

"You said that? Told the newspaper you might call in the FBI at some point?"

"I did, and I might." He waved off her protest. "At this point, I genuinely believe a bunch of FBI agents poking around and asking questions would just muddy the waters. But I'm still open to it. I'm open to *anything* that will bring that little girl home."

"She's been missing for forty-eight hours," Rileigh mused, knowing that Mitch had not slept more than an hour here and there during that time. "We've chased down every lead that we have ... and still, snake eyes."

Rileigh skimmed the rest of the article. It noted that

the sheriff had asked for help from the community, listed the phone number to call with information, then added that the mayor, J.P. Rutherford had personally posted a $5,000 reward for any information leading to the recovery of the child. Thankfully, the paper had kept the mayor's words to a bare minimum. Rileigh was sure he had said way more than that when he was interviewed. The mayor had made only one effort to insert himself into the investigation and Mitch had stood up to him. Deputy Mullins had been there at the time and told Rileigh that Mitch had told the mayor to mind his own business.

"He said, 'Just stay out of my way and let me do my job,'" Mullins had told Rileigh. "And the mayor backed off." Mullins had grinned then. "I know people who'd have paid serious money to watch that show."

Five thousand dollars. Rileigh had to give him credit — she couldn't stand the man, but he'd been willing to put his money where his mouth is this time.

Rileigh laid the newspaper back down on Mitch's desk. "They stuck to the facts of the case by and large," Rileigh said. "That's —"

"Impressive," Mitch finished for her.

"The Gazette is owned and operated by the Hagerty family — they're local."

It had been founded by Elliot Hagerty, who grew up in the mountains, went to college, then came back home to start a newspaper for the people of the mountains. Not just *about* them, but a newspaper that described life in Yarmouth County and provide context for the events.

Rileigh added, "I knew the senior Mr. Hagerty, who died while I was in the military, and I've met his son, Samuel, who took over after that. Sam seems to be a fine journalist. If the Black Bear Gazette ever took a political stance, which to my knowledge it never has, it would be right of center, not far. From what I've seen since I've been back here, Sam steers clear of politics and biased reporting."

Mitch shook his head wearily. "Now if the New York Times would just do the same."

Truth was, it was a whole lot harder to get away with trying to doctor the truth in a small town than it was in a city.

"The people you're writing about in a small town are the folks you're going to bump carts with in the produce section of the grocery store every week. It's hard to malign people's character when you have to look them in the eye at church on Sunday."

"Did you hear the Malones on the radio yesterday afternoon?" Mitch asked.

"Yeah, I heard."

Rileigh's heart had broken for the couple who had gone on the radio station to beg whoever had taken their daughter to bring her home.

"Chloe can't go to sleep at night unless she has her Mittens," Celine had said, her voice breaking. "And you have to leave the light on because she's afraid of the dark."

Rileigh's conversations with Chloe's BFF, Tally Masterson, had convinced her that Chloe was indeed a sweet and compliant child who would have gone along, not the kind to make a fuss even when she needed to.

Jeff's voice had broken when it was his turn. He just asked, "Please, whoever you are, bring our little girl home. She needs her mommy and her daddy. And please, please—"

Her mother had broken in then. She was probably going to say something like, "Please don't hurt her," but her husband shushed her before she could.

Then, rather unexpectedly, he said, "Chloe, if you can

hear me, daddy and mommy love you." He'd paused. "I'll come get you, Sweetheart. You hear me. Daddy will come and get you!"

"You think pleas like that on the media do any good?" Rileigh asked.

Mitch shook his head sadly.

"The kind of people who are willing to kidnap a little girl are not likely to be swayed by the emotional appeal of her parents to bring her home."

Mitch rubbed his sore eyes.

"The entire population of Yarmouth County is on hyper alert. We've probably fielded three dozen calls from people who thought they saw her somewhere. They're looking for her. If she's still around anywhere nearby, they're looking for her."

Chapter Twenty-One

THE LITTLE GIRL can hear the voices of the grown-ups talking in the next room. For a while, she was in the basement, but now she's in a bedroom. There's a bed, and curtains on the windows and rugs on the floor. She's already checked, though. The windows have been nailed shut. She won't be able to do what she did before, get the basement window open just a little bit and somehow squeeze through it. The little girl suspects she won't ever be able to get away on her own again. Somebody will have to come and get her.

The grown-ups in the next room aren't fighting, but they are both upset and their voices are loud. She doesn't have any trouble hearing what they're saying.

"... see that story in the newspaper?"

That is the mommy kidnapper. That's how she has come to think of them now, as the mommy kidnapper and the daddy kidnapper. The mommy kidnapper's voice is easier to hear than the daddy kidnapper's. He has a low, deep voice that rumbles, and sometimes she can't make out the words.

She doesn't think she'll like what she hears, but she has to know.

As soon as the kidnappers started raising their voices, the little girl went to the door and sat down on the floor beside it. She can hear fine from there.

"What? You didn't think there'd be a newspaper story? Hell, I bet it's all over the news in the whole state, maybe the whole country."

"You don't mean that!" The mommy kidnapper sounds shocked and scared.

"Well, I mean, you know, it's a story. Stories go away. Something else will happen. It's always like that. Whoever is big news today is forgotten about tomorrow when something else happens."

"They ran her picture." The kidnapper woman says.

"Of course they ran her picture. Why wouldn't they?"

"I just didn't think that her face would be right there on the front page of the newspaper and..."

"She doesn't look like that anymore."

They had cut her hair off. She'd had long curls that hung down her back. Daddy loved those curls. When he sat her in his lap and read her a story, sometimes he would run his fingers through the curls in her hair. Mommy liked her long hair too. She liked to braid it and put ribbons on the ends of the braids. Sometimes she'd stacked the braids up on top of her head. They'd looked like a crown, and she'd looked like a princess.

But she doesn't have long hair anymore. They cut it all off. She hasn't seen her face in a mirror, and she doesn't want to. But she can't help seeing her reflection in the window when it is dark outside. And she is surprised that her hair doesn't look worse. She just looks like a little girl with a short haircut. Not like somebody had taken the scissors and whacked it all off. Oh, how she wished it looked like somebody had cut it off and didn't make it look cute. She doesn't want to be cute.

The mommy kidnapper had said everything would be alright. She wouldn't miss her long hair and curls. The mommy kidnapper had talked and talked while she cut it. But the little girl said nothing. She isn't sure if she can talk anymore. Her throat feels so tight. Maybe she can't make sound anymore. Maybe she can't make words anymore.

"You think we should color her hair?"

"Absolutely not!" The mommy kidnapper cries. "I've wanted a little blonde girl my whole life. A little girl with blonde hair and blue eyes. No, we're not going to make her hair some other color."

"You're right. She looks so different now with short hair, nobody would recognize her."

"Nobody's going to get a chance to recognize her." The mommy kidnapper says.

The little girl hears something like the rustling of papers.

"What are you doing?"

"I'm throwing it away," the mommy kidnapper says. "I don't want to look at her picture on the front page of the newspaper. A picture of a missing girl. She's not missing, she's right where she's supposed to be. She's right here with her mommy."

"Now sweetheart, don't get all upset. You know how it is when you get upset."

The sounds aren't the sounds of paper wadded up. She hears papers being torn apart. The little girl hears the sound of a chair scooting across the floor. Then the sound of someone sitting down in it hard. The mommy kidnapper starts to cry.

"You won't let them take her away from me, will you?" she pleads, "promise me you won't."

"Margaret is our little girl now, and she will stay our little girl forever."

"Do you promise?"

"I promise."

"If somebody comes and tries to take her away, if the police come—"

"The police aren't going to come. We've talked about this. They would never think to look here."

"But if they come, if somehow they find out and they come, I can't stand it. If they try to take Margaret away from me, I'll kill myself. Margaret, too—both of us. We'll go together."

The words stab a dagger of terror into the little girl's heart, and *she can't breathe for a few seconds. The kidnappers had not been mean to her when they found that she had wet her pants. She'd been so afraid they would be mad and maybe hurt her, hit her or slap her or do something terrible. But they didn't. The mommy kidnapper just gave her some clean clothes. The clothes were brand new; they still had tags on them.*

And after that, the little girl hadn't been quite so terrified. Now, the terror returns, bigger and meaner and scarier than it had ever been. They hadn't hurt her when she thought they would, but they would kill her if somebody came to take her away.

So when her daddy finally finds her, comes to get her and take her home, this lady won't let him. This lady will kill her before she'll let him take her.

The little girl feels hot tears sliding down her cheeks and dripping off her chin, but she isn't crying. She is too scared to cry. She doesn't have enough air to cry. You have to breathe deep when you cry, and she can't breathe at all.

She doesn't need to pee now, but she thinks about that and is suddenly afraid she will wet her pants again, not because she needs to go but because she is so scared. They hadn't been mean the last time. But now, knowing that the mommy kidnapper would kill her if some- body comes to take her away, maybe they are meaner than she thought. Maybe they are going to hurt her after all.

Reaching her hand down into her pocket, she touches the locket, feels it with her fingers but doesn't take it out. She's afraid they will find the locket. If they do, they'll take it away from her and she needs the locket — it's all she has to feel close to Mommy and Daddy and home. It's like a thread that keeps her somehow attached to them. If the kidnapper parents take it away, she will be ... like that boat on the lake last summer that came untied from the dock. Nobody was rowing it. It just floated away all by itself. The little girl will float away, too, without the locket to hold onto. She traces the letters of her name engraved on the back of the locket. That's who she is. Her name is not Margaret.

The picture of her real Mommy and Daddy is in the locket, and at night when the grownups are asleep, she takes the picture out and looks at it. She told the kidnapper Mommy that she was afraid of the dark, so now there's a night-light burning in her room. She crouches down around the light in the socket on the wall after they go to bed, looks at the faces of her Mommy and Daddy, and she pleads with them to come and get her. She doesn't want to stay here. She wants to go home.

Chapter Twenty-Two

THE DISPATCHER STOOD in the door to Mitch's office, keeping her voice calm and professional, but you could see the excitement in her eyes, the hope there.

"Sheriff, we just got an anonymous tip that there is a registered sex offender. Well, not registered, that's the point," she stopped and started over. "The caller said that there is a sex offender who lives in Yarmouth County. His name is Damian Eugene McCauley, and he was at the carnival Monday, but he's *not* registered."

Mitch glanced at Rileigh, who was seated in the chair across the desk from him, going through the files that had come back from the FBI, the background checks on all the people who had been at the carnival. Mitch had been surprised at the amount of information the FBI was able to gather up about so many people in such a short period of time. He had a bio on every man and woman, teacher, parent, aide, grandparent, uncle, every person whose name Rileigh had collected. Rileigh was now going through the background checks the FBI had returned to him.

Rileigh looked back at Mitch and said, "It's not listed in here. There's no Damien—"

"That's not the name he goes by here. In Yarmouth County, his name is Roderick Styles."

Rileigh began to shuffle through the files of the background checks and finally landed on the one she was looking for. She pulled it out of the stack.

"Roderick Styles," she said, and looked up at Mitch. "There's no mention here of a sex offender status." Rileigh flipped through the pages of information. "It says here that he's married to Amanda Styles and that they have two children, Jenny, who is five, and Alex, who is three." Rileigh was running her finger down the information on the page and her eyes shot back up to Mitch. "Jenny Styles is in Chloe Malone's class. And he must have been at the carnival, or his name wouldn't be on the list."

Mitch got to his feet as Rileigh. "What's the address?"

"Burnside Pike," Rileigh said, "that's on the south end of the county. I'm not as familiar with those roads as I am the ones in the north end, where Georgia lives."

Black Bear Forge was not in the center of Yarmouth County. It was in the northeast corner, and most of the county's rural farmland and mountains stretched out to the west and the south of the town.

Three of the other deputies showed up in the doorway to Mitch's office as if they'd been summoned by magical command.

"We heard we've got a lead," Jeb Rawlings said.

"Any of you guys know much about the geography of Burnside Pike?" Mitch asked.

"I do," Beau Mullins said. "My grandmother lives on that road."

"Tell me about the terrain."

Mullins shook his head. "Steep. It winds up through

Haneke Hollow and along the south side of Wilson Creek. What's the house number?"

When Mitch gave it to him, he said, "That's pretty close to where my grandmother lives."

"Let's go have a look at it," Mitch said, gesturing toward Rileigh to follow him.

On the ride to Burnside Pike, Rileigh was quiet. Then she turned to Mitch and said just the two words. "Sex. Offender."

"Not good news."

"But the bio said this guy's got a five-year-old daughter in Chloe's class. I can't make all that work in my head."

"You'll just get a headache trying. There's no way to understand the ins and outs of mental illness. It just is."

It didn't take Mitch and the other deputies long to size up the situation. Roderick Stiles/Damien McCauley and his family lived in a trailer house that sat back from the road beside a creek. There was a flower bed in the front yard, and on the little bit of flat land behind the trailer house, there appeared to be a garden. Mitch and Rileigh approached the house from the south side, Mullins and Rawlings from the north side.

Parked in the driveway was a white 2018 Chevrolet Colorado with an extended cab. And the tires were muddy.

The yard had children's toys scattered around it.

Rileigh waited at the foot of the sidewalk while Mitch knocked on the door. A small, dark-haired woman opened the door with a baby on her hip. Obviously, she had seen the cruiser out front and the officers in the yard, because she was already crying.

"Please ... don't," she said, looking back over her shoulder. "We haven't hurt anybody. We just want to be left—"

"It's alright Amanda," came a man's voice from inside the trailer. "Move away from the door, Honey."

The woman opened the door wide and stepped to the side. A man stood in the middle of the living room with his fingers clasped and hands behind his head.

"I'm coming out slow," he said. "No sudden movements. I'll keep my hands where you can see them."

A little boy was on the floor, stacking blocks.

"I not done, Daddy," he said. "Help me wiff the fence."

"Daddy has to go now, Alex," the man said. "Mommy will help you build the rest of the farm."

"You said you'd do it!" the little boy said, tuning up to cry.

The man looked at his wife.

"I'll help you make a big house," she told the boy, her voice breaking. "As soon as I tell your Daddy goodbye."

She stepped to where he stood, hugging him with the arm not holding the baby, struggling not to cry as she spoke to him softly.

The man didn't move his arms to hug his wife, but kept them behind his head as he'd said he would. He kissed her on the top of the head and moved around her to the door, which Mitch held open for him. Mitch took his arm and reached for the handcuffs on his belt.

Just then a little girl came running around the house from the back looking fearfully at the police officers, before she raced across the yard, up the porch steps, threw her arms around her father's waist and burst into tears.

The man didn't move his arms, just looked pleadingly at Mitch. Mitch took his hand off the cuffs, nodded his head, and the man knelt and pulled his little girl into his arms.

"It's okay, Jenny. Honey. I have to go with these officers

now, but I'll be back home as soon as I can." She said nothing, just clung to him sobbing. He finally had to peel her off to stand up. "You help Mommy with Alex and Erica while I'm gone, okay?"

She nodded her head, tears streaming down her cheeks, and looked at Mitch with unconcealed contempt and rage.

Mitch took the man's arm, nodded to Rileigh, then guided Rodney past her, toward the cruiser.

Rileigh stepped up on the porch, where the whole family now stood, watching Mitch lead the man to the cruiser.

"Mrs. McCauley," Rileigh said, grabbed the woman's gaze and held it. "Why don't you and the children wait out here while I–" Rileigh looked at her meaningfully. "–go in the house and look around … you know … to see those curtains you told me about."

The woman caught on and nodded. Rileigh knew she wasn't fooling the little girl, but the little boy didn't appear to be upset when Rileigh eased past them on the porch and went in the front door. She conducted a reasonably thorough search of the premises — because that was by the book — but she got out as fast as she could, finding exactly what she knew she'd find.

Chloe Malone was not there.

Chapter Twenty-Three

RILEIGH LEANED up against the wall beside the door of what passed for an interrogation room in the Yarmouth County Sheriff's Department. It was really the officer's break room, but it served as a place to interview prisoners when needed. Mitch sat on one side of the bare table, and Damien McCauley sat on the other.

Rileigh studied the man and couldn't peg him for a pedophile. She wasn't fool enough to believe that she could pick out that kind of thing just by looking at somebody. Still, he looked like somebody's daddy, an ordinary man who was tired and defeated.

"Mr. McCauley," Mitch said, "I've advised you of your rights and I need to ask you some questions about where you were Monday morning."

"How about I save all of us a lot of wear and tear on our nerves?" McCauley said. "I was at the carnival at Black Bear Forge Elementary School, and you know it as well as I do. Amanda and I took Alex and Erica to the school so that we could play those silly games with Jenny and the rest of her class. So yes, I was there at the school. Does that answer all your questions?"

"So, you know that there is a child missing from–"

"Of course I know there's a child missing!"

"Would you mind walking us through what you did yesterday?"

"Fine." He sighed and sat back. "I only got a couple of hours of sleep, went to bed late and got up early, both my fault. After supper, Amanda put the baby and Jenny to bed. Jenny had school the next day, but we let Alex stay up to see *Finding Nemo* as a reward for making up his bed, or at least trying, all week. I stayed up with him and we had popcorn. Of course, he fell asleep after the first fifteen minutes, but I stayed up to see the end. I put him to bed when it was over and barely got to sleep when he woke up — throwing up — because I let him eat too much popcorn. So I got up and cleaned the mess, gave him some Pepto, then just stayed up so I could give Erica her morning bottle and Amanda could sleep a little later before we went to work."

"Where do you work, Mr. McCauley?"

"You know where I work. You've checked all that out already. I work at Phillips Repair Shop out on Butcher Pike, and Amanda waits tables at Bubba's Diner." He paused, burped out a bleat of sardonic laughter. "She has a master's degree in biology, and she waits tables. And I have a bachelor's degree in chemistry, and I repair lawn mower and chain saw engines."

"If you have a chemistry degree, why do–"

"Can't we stop playing this stupid game? You know why I work in a repair shop and my wife is a server. Why we can't get any other kind of work."

McCauley let out a long breath.

"Here's how this goes," he said. "When we move into a

community, I have one of two options. I can report as required by law to the law enforcement agency in the jurisdiction in which I plan to reside. That's the first option. Option two is not to report. If I take option number one, the neighbors are notified that they have a convicted sex offender in the neighborhood, and nobody will talk to my wife and nobody will hire my wife, and I will get fired from whatever job I'd managed to land before the employer found out. Oh, and nobody will allow their children to play with my little girl.

"Or I can do what we have done for the past few years, which is move around a lot and take a fake identity. Then I don't register, and we have something approaching a normal life."

"Can't you just read this in my record?" McCauley looked at Mitch, then his gaze went to Rileigh. She tried very hard to keep hers noncommittal, not to let the compassion she felt for this man seep out. It didn't matter what she thought about him. What mattered was he had broken the law by refusing to report as it required him to do. And he was a suspect in a kidnapping case.

Rileigh shook her head. That was bullshit. No way in hell did this man have anything to do with Chloe Malone's disappearance. It really was all some stupid game they had to play because of his record.

"Why don't you just tell us your story," Mitch said, and the man sighed again.

"Amanda was a senior in high school and I was a first-year chemistry teacher in that high school. But she wasn't some giggling teenager, not like the rest of them. Her mother died when she was young and she'd stepped up. Cooked, cleaned and took care of her four little brothers. She gave up her childhood for her family."

"And so there she sat in my chemistry class day after

day." He let out a long sigh. "I fell in love with her. It was mutual." He cocked his head to the side. "But it wasn't allowed to be mutual. Not in her father's mind. When he found out that his daughter was in love with a black man, he went off like a bottle rocket."

McCauley barked out a sardonic laugh.

"Don't let anybody tell you that interracial marriages are commonplace now and nobody cares anymore. Because that is a pile of the warm, sticky substance you find on the south side of a bull going north. Her father had me charged with statutory rape. He owned the county where — drum roll, please — a *black* man had accosted his daughter. All my poor public defender could do was shuffle papers and tell me I ought to plead guilty."

He sat back in the chair.

"I refused. I didn't rape anybody. But never let the facts get in the way of lynching a black man. I was convicted. I served three years of an eight-year sentence."

He paused. "A sex offender in prison…"

After that hung in the silence, he continued.

"Amanda went to college while I was in prison, and when I got out, I made the second worst mistake of my life. The first was loving her. The second was marrying her — and sentencing her to life on the run with a … pervert."

"Let's go back to yesterday morning, Mr. McCauley. You have admitted that you were at the carnival."

"Of course I was at the carnival." He paused. "How about we cut to the chase? You want to know if I had anything to do with the disappearance of that girl in Jenny's class in school. And whenever something bad happens to a child, the law starts checking 'usual suspects' and my name's on that list."

"Actually 'Damien McCauley' isn't on any list."

"Of course I had to change my name. Come on, I

couldn't get a job. I couldn't pass a background check for a job. I couldn't find anywhere to live. The neighborhoods all have regulations about people with records as sex offenders." He let out a long sigh. "Try to arrange your life around draconian regulations about where you live. Find a house to rent that's not within six miles of a school, a park or a church, then figure out a way for your kid to go to a school that's miles from home."

McCauley stopped. looking up at Mitch. "You got an anonymous tip about me, didn't you?"

Mitch nodded.

"My wife's scumbag sister turned me in. She's a worthless druggie who came begging Amanda for drug money and Amanda wouldn't give her any. Turning me in was payback. Right now, she's out there getting high and selling drugs to kids and I'm locked up in here. Surely you can see the irony in that."

Mitch went back to the line of questioning he had begun. "So, you admit to being at the carnival and..."

"We've already gone over this part. Yes, I was there. Yes, I held my little girl's hand while she played the basketball dunk and went fishing in the pond. Did I at any time have contact with the girl who's missing? How the hell would I know? Maybe. Half a dozen little girls came to talk to Jenny. Maybe she was one of them. But it wouldn't have mattered if she was, because I'm not a pedophile. I don't molest children. Not her, not my daughter, not anybody's children."

The man sat back in the chair with a sigh. "I'm not doing this anymore," he said. "I want a lawyer. Go out there and find the poor schmuck who graduated at the bottom of his law school class and took the bar exam five times before he could pass it. I'm not gonna say anything more until he shows up to tell me I shouldn't have said anything in the first place."

He sat back and crossed his arms across his chest. Mitch continued to ask questions, but the man merely asked to be taken to jail so he could get some sleep. "The baby kept me up last night, too."

Mitch had called the Tennessee State Patrol; two officers were waiting outside to take McCauley to the jail in Gatlinburg. They escorted him down the hall past Rileigh, and when she made eye contact with the man, there was such anguish and hopelessness in those eyes, she wanted to cry.

She turned to Mitch then and shrugged.

"Well, that was a swing and a miss," Mitch said.

"Yeah. All we did by arresting him was make life miserable for yet another little girl."

Chapter Twenty-Four

IF GEORGIA COULD HAVE GOTTEN her fingers around Chigger's neck, she would have choked the life out of him. And he knew it. He didn't even want to talk to her, sent her a text. When she tried to call him, he didn't pick up. Oh, he would be so, so sorry. She fastened Mayella into her car seat next to Mason's, then she placed Connor between the two of them, because Mason and Mayella would fight if they could reach each other. Liam was in the front seat with Eli.

Chigger knew what a nightmare it was to go to the store with all five kids, and he'd promised he'd be home in time to stay with Mason and Mayella. Then he'd apparently decided that he'd really rather hang out at the I've Got a Spare bowling alley and drink beer with his buddies than come home and watch his children. So he'd pulled out the unassailable excuse —*"I've got to go make a deal."* A deal being a drug buy or a drug sale.

Georgia admitted she had to do a lot of mental gymnastics to think positively about her husband's line of work. He sold and bought drugs, *illegal* drugs, but only the soft, recreational kind — that was the deal they'd made when they got married, and as far as she knew, he'd lived up to his end of the bargain. He'd had a bad scare as a teenager, barely escaped going to prison as a persistent felony offender. He would have been locked away for twenty years, if it hadn't been for Rileigh. Of course, Georgia also owed her freedom to Rileigh, who had stolen the evidence against both Georgia and Chigger out of the evidence locker at the courthouse.

If you needed a bag of weed, Chigger Stump was the man to get it for you, and he could get you any kind you wanted, any quantity at just about any price. If you wanted some coke to snort at a party, Chigger Stump was the man to see. But if you wanted crack, or meth, or some pink lady, or any of the rest of the really bad-ass drugs, you needed to go elsewhere. Chigger had established a niche in the marketplace as the go-to man for the "harmless" drugs. There were plenty of other dealers who would sell you the shit that could kill you.

Unfortunately for Georgia, her husband's line of work offered him the perfect out for any task he didn't particularly want to perform. "Hey, I gotta go make a deal," he could say, and who was to say different? It's not like he got up in the morning at nine and came home at five.

All that being said, she'd really counted on him, and he had bailed big time. She had no choice. She *had* to go to the store. They were out of just about everything. Mayella had, for some unknown reason, decided to start wetting the bed again at age three. Georgia got tired of changing the sheets and put her back in pull-up diapers. They were completely out, and Georgia was sure she'd wet the bed again tonight. Basic groceries, bread, milk, and of course, the "you better not run out of it or you'll be sorry" bananas that kept her daughter from becoming a terror on wheels. They were out of that too.

So, Walmart it was — with All. Five. Kids.

Oh, she would so make Chigger pay.

The only way to successfully corral four-year-old Mason and three-year-old Mayella in a store was to put both of them in a cart. Unfortunately, she needed so many groceries today there wasn't room for Mason in the cart. And it really did require two hands to push a full grocery cart. You couldn't do it with one hand and hold on to the hand of a little boy with the other. What she needed was a leash. She thought it was an absolutely perfect idea. But Chigger had rolled his eyes and said the Department of Child Protective Services would be knocking on their doors if they ever saw Georgia out with their children on leashes.

She drove up in front of Walmart and parked, and before Eli and Liam and Connor could bail out of the car and go running into the store, she reached over and hit the child guard locks on the doors.

"Now hear this," she said, "I will NOT chase all five of you around this store today. Liam, you are in charge of Connor. If you lose him, do not come tell me that you've lost him. *Run away from home.* Go find somewhere to live in the woods like Tarzan. Call your grandmother and tell her I've kicked you out. Do *anything* — just don't you come and tell me you've lost Connor."

Eli had already started to protest because he could see what was coming. If Liam was being put in charge of Connor, that meant Eli was going to have to corral Mason, which really was the blind leading the blind. An eight-year-old trying to keep track of a four-year-old. Eli was a particularly conscientious eight-year-old, however, and he got along with his younger brother Mason, while putting Liam, the oldest, together with Mason, the youngest, was trying to mix oil and water.

"Eli, you're in charge of keeping up with Mason. If you lose him, if you can't find him—"

"I know, I know. Go out and live on the streets like a homeless person." He rolled his eyes and Georgia had to choke back a laugh. That boy was quick.

She focused all of her considerable force of will on Mason. "Mason, you have spent most of this week with your nose in a corner in time out."

"I'll be good, mommy. I promise, I promise, I promise." He began to babble. He'd already unfastened himself from the harness in his car seat, a feat no four-year-old should have the manual dexterity to perform, but that didn't stop Mason.

"Mason, you stay with Eli, are you listening?"

"I will, mommy. I'll stay right with Eli. I'll hold onto his hand the whole time. I promise, I promise, I promise."

And he started climbing out of the car seat.

"Stop!" Georgia yelled again and the car fell silent. "Mason, you need to understand me. You will spend the rest of the night in your room with no supper. And I'm making apple pie, but you can't have any unless you stay with Eli. Is that clear?"

"I will, Mommy. I will. I will. I will. I'll be a good boy."

Georgia sighed. She didn't believe that for a New York minute, but she really didn't have any choice.

She had to unhook Mayella from her car seat, because unlike her older brother, she was still too little to manipulate the clasps. But she had started to cry before Georgia ever even got her out and set her in the seat of the grocery cart. She watched the four boys walk ahead of her into the building. Eli had a death grip on Mason's hand. And although Liam was not physically holding on to Connor, he was within grabbing range, and that was about as good as it got.

She pushed the cart into the building and watched the boys disappear into the store. She gathered up her groceries, filling the cart to overflowing, keeping Mayella happy by stuffing her mouth full of bananas as she moved up and down the aisles, taking a detour from the food aisles every so often to go locate the boys in the toy aisles and the sporting goods section. She could always find the boys in one or the other.

She was finally ready to go through the checkout lane, which was a distinctly unpleasant experience with all the kids in tow, because the store saw fit to stock nothing but candy around the checkout lanes. All the kids wanted it and none of them could have it, or their dentist would kill Georgia.

Sighing, she set the laundry detergent on top of the pile in the cart and headed off to the toy department and the sports department to collect the boys. It wasn't hard to find Liam and Connor. Liam loved sports. If there was a ball anywhere, Liam was bouncing it. She found him in the sporting goods department, throwing a baseball back and forth with Connor. The aisle where the boys stood looked like a small twister had gone through it, balls and bats and gloves lying all around. Georgia would bet that the stockers at Walmart ran for the doors when they saw her and her children coming.

She told the boys to put the toys back where they got them, which Liam tried to do, but Connor continued to toss the baseball up in the air and try to catch it. Eventually, the aisle was at least safe to walk down, so she headed for the toy department to find Eli and Mason. She went down the big aisle that the toy aisles opened off of, looking down each. And she spotted Eli at one end of the superhero aisle. Mason was nowhere to be seen. Eli took one look at her and bolted around the corner. She was slow to follow because she was pushing a grocery cart and trying to make sure that Liam and Conner didn't make a break for it, too. After three attempts to corral Eli, she sent Liam after him. And a few minutes later, Liam brought his wailing brother to her, dragging him by the arm and threatening him the whole way. Georgia didn't have to ask what was wrong with him. Obviously, he had lost Mason.

"He was right there beside me, mommy. I was holding his hand and he asked me to show him how to move the arms and legs on a Spiderman action figure so it looked like he was climbing a building. So I did, but when I put the Spiderman doll back and turned around, he was gone."

Georgia took a deep breath and sighed. "Connor, you stay here with me," she told the six-year-old. "Eli, you and Liam go find Mason."

The nine and eight-year-olds went off in different directions through the toy department. Georgia picked a third direction and headed out that way, looking around corners and behind displays for a little boy with curly blond hair. Twenty minutes later, both Eli and Liam were standing before her. Eli was crying. Liam was keeping a stiff upper lip, only barely, as they reported to their mother that they couldn't find Mason anywhere.

Georgia looked at her watch. She had to get home to turn off the pot roast in the crockpot.

Chigger would be sorry. Oh, he would be so sorry.

Dragging the other children along beside her, Georgia went to the store manager and told him that she had misplaced a four-year-old named Mason Stump. Could he please announce over the loudspeaker for the boy to come to the front of the store? Before the man could make the broadcast, Georgia stopped him. "Say his Mommy's waiting for him." Mason would know how to translate that: *Mommy's ready to tan your little backside!*

"Will Mason Stump please come to the front of the store? Your mommy's waiting for you."

Five minutes went by. Ten minutes. At fifteen minutes, she told the store manager to announce again.

"Tell him to come to the front of the store because he won a free ice cream cone." The man looked at her quizzically. "If he's hiding, an ice cream will get him moving."

The man offered her a thin smile and picked up the microphone of the public address system.

"Will Mason Stump please come to the front of the store for a free ice cream cone," he said.

The other boys giggled. Mason would knock over little old ladies on walkers to get to an ice cream cone.

When Mason failed to appear ten minutes after the ice cream cone announcement, a little niggle of fear tickled in the pit of Georgia's stomach. Where the hell had that kid gone? Where was he hiding?

The store broadcast three more requests for Mason to come to the front of the store. By the second one, Georgia had become genuinely afraid. Where was Mason? She hadn't seen him since she'd sent him off with Eli. That was more than two hours ago.

What followed after that was an unfolding nightmare that grew worse and worse with every minute. The store manager had alerted all the employees to watch for the child after the second or third alert. Now the store manager called every employee, except the checkers, to the front of the store and dispatched them to go look for Mason.

They didn't find him.

Georgia stood frozen, clutching her cart, ignoring

Mayella's cries. The three other little boys stood quietly beside her, their eyes huge with fear. When the store manager approached after the last of the employees had reported that they couldn't locate the her son, she knew what he was going to say, and she gritted her teeth to keep from bursting into tears when he did.

"Mrs. Stump, I think we need to call the sheriff."

Chapter Twenty-Five

THE YARMOUTH COUNTY WALMART was probably six or seven miles from downtown Black Bear Forge, where the courthouse and the sheriff's department were located. Mitch made it in five minutes, lights and siren on, as Rileigh sat in the passenger seat of the cruiser trying to calm a hysterical Georgia Stump, who was babbling that somebody had taken her little boy.

He could hear Georgia's voice, the terror and hysteria in it, and Rileigh didn't even have the phone on speaker.

It was a stream of consciousness, a tale of a parent's worst nightmare, and it was becoming Mitch's worst nightmare too.

"... nothing else I could do. I couldn't put him in the cart. He wouldn't fit, there were too many groceries. And Mayella has to be in the seat. I couldn't carry her on my hip for two hours shopping and..." She dragged in a shuttering breath as the enormity of it hit her full force.

"He's gone, just *gone*. Eli was supposed to be watching him, and Eli turned around and he wasn't there. But I didn't know he was gone. Oh, Jesus, Rileigh, I didn't even know he was gone. The last time I saw him was when the kids were going into the store."

Another ragged breath.

"It's all Chigger's fault. It's his fault. Damn it, damn it, damn it. He was supposed to be home in time. He was supposed to be there to keep Mayella and Mason. He said he'd be there, and I put a pot roast in the crock pot, and I needed to get home to get it out, but I couldn't find... I couldn't find ... *Mason!*"

"Georgia, honey, calm down," Rileigh said. But she might as well have told a waterfall to flow upstream.

"There's not any other way to do it. I tried. I really tried. If you hold onto a little kid's hand, that only leaves you one hand to push a cart. Have you ever tried to push a full cart of groceries with only one hand? You can't. You run into things because you can't turn. It takes both hands to steer, which means I can't hold Mason's hand. And Eli was supposed to watch him. Eli was..."

She stopped for the first time then, calmed slightly.

"It's not his fault. He's eight years old. He should never have been made responsible for a four-year-old child. He's only eight. It's my fault because I didn't hold onto Mason's hand, and now he's gone. Where could he be? Who could have taken him?"

Mitch had listened to Georgia's hysteria the whole way from the courthouse to Walmart as he gave directions to deputies who knew what to do. They'd already done it once this week.

"Lock it down," Mitch said. "Nobody in. Nobody out."

But it was as hopeless here as it had been at the elementary school. Closing the barn door after the horse is already gone. Locking the place down and keeping everyone inside accomplished absolutely nothing when any fool could figure out that whoever had that little boy had taken him out of the building and put him into a car, probably before his mother ever even realized he was gone.

Mitch's hope, what he clung to like a drowning man in a raging sea, was surveillance cameras. Walmart had a camera about every three feet. There would be footage. There would be something that showed someone taking that little boy out of the building. The key was to get there fast and find it fast, and not waste time questioning a bunch of onlookers who'd have come forward by now if they'd seen anything.

Mitch came to a screeching halt in front of the store, which had already collected a crowd around it.

The employees and the manager had obviously been trained for various such emergencies because the manager had locked the place down even before Mitch and his deputies arrived. Mitch leapt out of his cruiser and ran full tilt into the building with Rileigh beside him, still listening to a hysterical Georgia via cell phone. When the manager opened the doors and allowed the two of them in, Mitch saw Georgia standing nearby, babbling on the telephone, unaware that Rileigh was twenty feet from her. When she spotted Rileigh, she gave a little cry and ran to her, flung herself in Rileigh's arms, and burst out sobbing.

Mitch looked at the three terrified little boys standing beside the grocery cart where a three-year-old girl was screaming her lungs out. Mitch was impressed when the oldest of the boys, who couldn't have been more than nine, reached up to his little sister, and she held out her chubby arms to him. He lifted her out of the basket. It was hard because she was a chubby little girl and he wasn't a very big little boy, but he managed it and held her in his arms, balancing her weight on his hip. And it was clear this wasn't the first time the boy had comforted his little sister. Mitch was grateful for his courage and fortitude.

He approached the semi-hysterical Georgia, sobbing in Rileigh's arms, then nodded to Rileigh over Georgia's head. Rileigh pulled back out of her grip and took Georgia by the shoulders.

"I know you're upset, but you have to calm down."

Mitch looked at Georgia's eyes, and they looked like the eyes of some terrified rabbit, darting back and forth, looking frantically for the predators who any second would descend upon her and rip her to pieces. He wondered if Rileigh might have to slap her to get her attention, and he knew that if Georgia didn't calm down quickly, Rileigh would do exactly that.

But that wasn't necessary after Rileigh shook her violently, got right in her face, and said, "Georgia, calm the hell down. You have to give us some information. You can go postal and be hysterical later, but right now we need to know what Mason was wearing. When you saw him last and where you saw him last, *get a grip*."

Mitch watched Georgia grab hold of herself and force herself to calm down.

In a trembling voice, she said, "Okay, all right, I can do this, okay." She took a breath and let it out. "Mason was wearing a pair of jeans. They were too big for him. They were hand-me-downs from Conner, and Conner was bigger than Mason was when he was four years old, so they didn't fit very well. I had to roll up the pants legs, and he had on a belt too because I had to buckle it tight enough to keep the pants from falling off."

Drawing in another shaky breath, she continued. "And a plain, white t-shirt. It was brand new and it fit just fine. My sister always gives the kids socks and underwear for Christmas, and it was too big, but when I pulled it out about a week ago, it fit just perfect."

"Shoes," Mitch asked.

"Sneakers and white gym socks. But they didn't match. I couldn't find any that matched, and I know all the teenagers wear unmatched socks, and it's a fashion statement, but I think it's a stupid fashion statement, and that's not why I..."

Rileigh patted her on the shoulder, squeezed, and Georgia let her voice trail off.

Mitch had been taking down the information as she spoke, as had Deputy Rawlings, who had come up to them as soon as he entered the building.

"Tell me when you saw him last and where you were."

"It doesn't matter where I was when I saw him last because that's not where he was when..."

"Georgia, tell me when you saw him last."

"Okay, I put Mayella in the seat of the basket, and I assigned the boys to look after each other. Liam was to look after Connor, and Eli was to keep track of Mason."

That didn't make sense to Mitch because the best he could remember, Liam was the name of the nine-year-old, the one who was comforting his little sister right now, and Mason was the youngest. Why didn't she put the oldest in charge of the youngest?

Georgia must have read the question in his eyes.

"Because Liam and Mason are oil and water, that's why. If you set the two of them beside each other at the table, Mason will immediately begin tormenting Liam until he can't stand it anymore, and he retaliates, he hits him. Then the other boys get into it, depending on—"

Mitch stopped her, held his hand up, and she hushed, literally clamped her teeth down to keep from speaking.

"So, the last person who saw Mason was his older brother, Eli, who is ... how old?"

"Eight," Rileigh said.

Georgia only nodded. The look of desolation in her

eyes was a terrible thing to see. It was like it had hit her anew, a wrecking ball, that her boy was gone.

Mitch left Rileigh to care for Georgia and went to the three little boys. Liam had managed to quiet his little sister by walking around in circles and bouncing her up and down. Conner and Eli stood next to the basket, their eyes huge with terror.

Mitch got down on one knee in front of the eight-year-old Eli. He put his hand on the boy's shoulder and could feel him trembling.

"Son, you need to understand that you're not in trouble. You didn't do anything wrong." His voice was so quiet Mitch could barely hear it.

"Yes, I did. I lost Mason."

"It wasn't your fault. You tried to keep track of him, but he ran away from you, didn't he?"

"We were looking at the superhero dolls, and I was showing him the doll - how the arms moved and the legs moved like at the knee - and he thought that was cool. I turned and I put the doll back on the shelf, and picked up the Superman doll, and I turned to show it to him." Eli lost his voice, looked at the sheriff with huge, frightened eyes that were filling with tears.

"... and he was *gone*. He wasn't there. He'd been there just a minute before."

Connor, who was six, standing nearby, put his hand on his older brother's shoulder. "He did it on purpose, Eli. It's not your fault."

The oldest chimed in as he bounced his sister up and down in his arms.

"He waited until you turned around and he ran. He was planning all along to make a break for it. You know how Mason is. It's not your fault."

Mitch could tell that neither he nor the boy's brother

had made any dent on Eli's guilt. If anything happened to Mason… Mitch let the thought go because he couldn't go there. He looked at Liam. "So, you think Mason planned this all along?"

Both Liam and Connor nodded their heads.

"That's just how he is," Liam said. "He thinks it's all a game. Anytime we go anywhere, if you let him out of your sight for a second, he's gone. He runs away. He hides behind things or under things. That's why we weren't afraid of anything when we couldn't find him, because we thought was playing hide-and-seek."

Then the hope drained out of the Liam's voice. "But that was before everybody looked for him. Even the grownups couldn't find him."

"Did somebody take Mason?" Eli asked in a tiny, trembling voice. " Did some grownup steal Mason?"

"We don't know exactly what has happened to Mason. That's why I'm here, to find your little brother."

"But you couldn't find that girl who went missing from school," Eli said, his voice still shaking. "She was in Mrs. Harbour's room, which is right down the hall from my room. So, I saw her sometimes. And you didn't find her."

"We haven't found her *yet*. But we will. We will find both of them." Mitch opened his mouth and found himself saying what he absolutely, one hundred percent should *not* have said. "Listen to me, boys. I'll find your little brother, just like I'll find Chloe Malone. I promise."

The words had leapt out of his mouth before he could stop them.

Mitch issued an Amber Alert for Mason Stump ten minutes after he arrived at Walmart. He would do the do. He would go through the motions, conduct a thorough, by-the-book search. He would dot every I and cross every T. But he was convinced that that child was nowhere in that building and that all their efforts to locate him would be futile.

The doors of the store suddenly opened, and a tall, gangly young man ran in, his eyes wild. He spotted Georgia, and she raced toward him, threw arms around him, and burst into tears again.

The man looked confused and frightened. "Georgia, what's going on? Where's Mason? They said Mason was missing."

"He's gone, Chigger. He's gone. I didn't... Eli was watching him, and he got away."

Mitch saw Chigger's eyes dart toward Eli and said a silent prayer that the father would not say something right now that would scar that little boy for life.

"Eli, come here, son," he said. The boy broke for him, raced to his father, and threw his arms around his legs, sobbing. Chigger got down onto one knee and held the little boy out from him. "It's going to be fine, buddy. Everything's going to be fine."

"But I lost Mason."

"No, you didn't lose Mason."

" Yes, I–"

"Listen to me, Eli. *You* didn't lose Mason. Mason pulled what he always pulls. That's not your fault. You didn't wander away and leave him. *He left you.*"

Mitch was sure that nobody had told Chigger the specifics of what had happened. He'd figured it out on his own.

"But Mommy told me if I lost him not to come and tell her about it. She told Liam that he should run away and live in the woods like Tarzan, and I should become a homeless–"

Chigger put his fingers over the boy's lips and silenced him.

"Mommy was teasing, Eli. You know she didn't mean what she said. She was just making a joke. Tell me you understand that, Eli."

Eli's lip was trembling.

"Son, tell me you understand that this is *not* your fault." Chigger's voice was firm, would brook no argument.

"Yes, daddy. I understand." Then he threw his arms around his father and started sobbing again. Chigger looked up with anguished eyes into Mitch's. And Mitch felt as helpless as he'd ever felt in his life. He pulled his cell phone out of his pocket and punched a number he had saved in favorites.

It was the number for the Nashville field office of the FBI.

Chapter Twenty-Six

RILEIGH STOOD HOLDING the sobbing Georgia in her arms, watching Chigger calm Eli, and at that moment, she abandoned every bad thought she'd ever had about that man. And there were plenty. She blamed him that Georgia and the kids lived in something approaching destitute poverty. Georgia never had any new clothes, had to scrape together enough money to buy shoes for all the kids. Rileigh faulted Chigger for that, found it outrageously absurd that every other drug dealer she had ever known in all her years as both a customer and a police officer had all made a fortune. How in the hell Chigger managed to merely eke out a living selling drugs was astonishing. Sure, he'd given up selling the hard drugs, but if you couldn't make enough money to support a family selling weed—

She stopped herself in mid-thought. She'd just watched Chigger behave with more character than she'd ever realized he had. She watched him be the man and the husband and the father that Georgia and those kids needed right now. She saw in those few moments what Georgia saw, what she called his "good side," which she sang the praises of whenever Rileigh got on a rant about her drug-dealing husband.

Never again. Someday, Rileigh would tell Chigger how proud she was of him. Someday she'd let him know that everything he had ever done in his whole life should be wiped off the slate of sins, and he should be declared pure and white based solely on how he had handled the last five minutes.

Mitch came to stand beside her, leaned over, and whispered in her ear. "I've just called in the FBI."

Rileigh didn't feel good about that, but she didn't blame him. He had no choice. The second kidnapping had elevated the situation to a whole new level of horror and a small Tennessee sheriff's department was in way over its head. Now they needed all the resources of the FBI's national network, because clearly they were dealing with way more than a local kidnapping. Something far worse and more sinister was happening and it was time to provoke the antipathy of the community toward the federal government and FBI agents. Yarmouth County would just have to suck it up and cope.

She hoped they would. She hoped that in this direst need, the people of Yarmouth County would rise to the occasion, just as Chigger Stump had, and behave as their very best selves. That they would set aside their distrust of strangers and away-from-heres, and cooperate fully with the battalion of FBI agents who were about to descend upon the county. She hoped that's what they'd do.

Hoped.

Chigger had enfolded his semi-hysterical wife and his terrified children into his arms, allowing Rileigh to extricate herself and do her job — help Mitch.

"How long?" she asked.

"They're coming from both the Knoxville and Nashville Field Offices," he said.

Knoxville was only a little over an hour's drive away. Nashville was three hours.

"But they'll send a chopper with the first wave," Mitch added, "so I'm thinking fifteen minutes, maybe a little longer. Between now and then, we keep the place locked down tight and do the things that locals–" He managed a small smile then. "—can do that the FBI can't."

"Whatever happened to Mason is already over. And the people in the store were very likely unaware of it when it was going down." Rileigh paused, tried to keep the sick terror she felt at that thought out of her voice. "Are we dealing with a pro? Somebody who snatches children?"

"I don't know." She saw the look of desolation in his eyes. "Rileigh, I flat out don't know. But I do know that our time is best spent going over the surveillance footage. It's not like it was at the school. There are cameras every three feet here."

Rileigh shook her head. "Yeah, but I wouldn't count on them all being functional." Mitch's eyebrows shot up. "I just know how easy it is to let things slide. I don't know the manager of this store. I'd imagine being assigned to Black Bear Forge is the Walmart equivalent of being sent to Siberia."

"Meaning you don't think the manager is the sharpest knife in the drawer."

"Meaning I doubt very much if he was a first-round draft pick for team Walmart. Keeping something as mundane as surveillance equipment up and running properly day in and day out is probably not on the top ten of his to-do list."

"The FBI's going to be all over that footage too, but

we'll be looking for what it could take them a week to find."

Now it was Rileigh's turn to raise an eyebrow. "And that is?"

"The people who were at *both* the carnival and this store today. The FBI can track that down comparing lists of names, or maybe using facial recognition software, but I'm betting we — and by 'we' I mean 'you'— can look at the faces on the video and pick them out."

That's how Rileigh spent the whole rest of her day, staring at monitors with grainy images of people trudging up and down the aisles of Walmart, filling up their shopping carts. It was as Rileigh had feared, the surveillance in the store was less than ideal. Several cameras didn't work at all. Several were dummy cameras positioned to make customers believe they were being watched. The lenses on a couple were so dirty it was hard to see anything clearly.

Most damning of all— one of the cameras at an entrance didn't work at all, meaning there was no reliable footage of people leaving, no smoking-gun image of a grownup walking out holding Mason's hand. Or, the more remote possibility that he'd been put in something — a box or a case — and carried out. The cameras mounted in the parking lot were trained on the front of the store, but they were hundreds of feet away. Very little was visible on the footage they'd recorded.

Mitch wanted Rileigh to review the footage from all the cameras, starting when the store opened that morning. The first thing she did was fast forward to the images of Georgia and her crew going into the store, to get an idea of what Mason looked like on the video. But they'd gone in the grocery side of the store rather than the housewares department, and it was the grocery store camera that was non-functional. She spotted them now and then in the footage, but got only one clear view of Mason trying on huge football helmets that looked like fishbowls sitting on his shoulders. Then hockey masks and baseball caps. He hadn't yet bailed on Eli, who could be seen in the background. She jotted down the time from the time stamp.

While she sat for hours glued to the replay monitors in the store's security room, the FBI showed up in force and took over the investigation. Deputy Mullins, who had "requisitioned" some snacks and soft drinks from the store to keep Rileigh's gears greased, summed up the meeting between Mitch and the agent in charge, Senior Special Agent Lamar Devereux.

"The sheriff stood his ground," he said. "The guy said something like, 'I value your input,' and Mitch asked, 'Is that code for we could use your help in crowd control? Because if it is, that's bullshit. It'll take your whole crew half a day's work to find out what I already know. That's a waste of resources. And if you think the locals in a little East Tennessee mountain town are going to open up to a bunch of suit-and-tie FBI agents, you best get used to disappointment.' Then Mitch spent an hour bringing the guy up to speed."

Mullins said he and the other deputies had spent their time setting up a command center for the agents in the sheriff's department.

"It was like they had a portable office that they picked up somewhere else and dropped here. You should have seen the tech equipment. They needed special phone lines and internet service. They've already churned out all kinds of information about the people who are still here, locked down. They brought their own K9 unit and have cleared all the cars in the parking lot."

Rileigh had heard the protests outside the confines of the little office in the back of the building. People didn't appreciate getting stuck at Walmart the whole day and they minced no words about it.

She had seen Mitch only once — when he came to check on her progress. He rolled his eyes when she asked him about relations with the FBI.

"The guy's a prick, but you don't get to be a senior special agent for twiddling your thumbs, so I hope he's good at what he does. I don't have any ego in this. I just want to find those kids and I don't care who gets the credit for it. If I see some task we can perform better than his agents … then, yeah, we'll butt heads over that."

Rileigh felt like she was mining for gold — every now and then she found a nugget. She spotted Evelyn and Clive Foster. Clive was using a walker, moving slow, breathing oxygen out of the canister in the satchel on his shoulder. His walker wasn't the fold-up kind. It fit in the back cargo area of the SUV.

About two hours into her surveillance marathon, she scored a two-for. Audrey Tatum was shopping in the store when she ran into Granny Maggie and Shiloh. Rileigh added their names to the meager list of people who'd been present at the scenes of both kidnappings.

Ben Pendergast came hurrying into the store about noon and was out through the U-Check-Out lane in ten minutes. He'd bought only one item, a bag of charcoal.

Hannah and Betty Marie Forrester appeared on the video, Betty Marie piloting her motorized wheelchair up and down the aisles and Hannah coming along behind with a cart.

Rileigh kept her eye peeled for the tall, dark stranger in the mask who'd been standing beside the booth with the pictures of teachers as small children. If he was in Walmart without a mask, Rileigh would have trouble recognizing him, but she peered so intently into the faces of all the men that she got a headache from eye strain. She only skimmed the footage from the outside cameras because it was too distorted to make out faces.

She saw children going into and coming out of the store for the whole day. She watched for Mason, sure she'd recognize him — a blond boy in a white tee shirt and jeans. Several children fit that general description. A little boy in a baseball cap whose hair might or might not have been blond came out of the building with a little girl in a floppy hat and flowers. An older man held the hand of a little boy about the right size, but for the life of her she couldn't tell whether or not it was Mason. Four other little boys came out the grocery store door during the time Mason would have been in the building, but the parking lot footage was too grainy to make out anything about their features.

By the time she was finished, she had a short list of people who'd been at both the carnival and Walmart. She phoned Mitch to tell him, but he couldn't talk, just texted back that he wanted her to go out and question every one of the people on the list.

Rileigh looked at her list — riiiight. It was insane to believe that one of these people had abducted two little kids. But the truth in long johns with the butt flap down was that *somebody* had taken those kids. Somebody she knew.

Surprised to see it was dark outside, she emerged like a mole from its hole into the store, list in hand. She'd start down the list first thing in the morning. But right now, she needed to go see Georgia.

Chapter Twenty-Seven

THE GROWN-UPS ARE in the next room fighting, screaming at each other. The little girl is so afraid she can barely breathe. She has figured out from what they're saying to each other what they're mad about: the kidnapper mother went out somewhere and kidnapped another child, a little boy. The kidnapper father is furious, screaming at her that she's crazy, that they're going to be caught, that she can't keep doing stuff like this.

"I just wanted a little brother for Margaret," the kidnapped mother wails.

"Little brother, are you serious?"

"I didn't want her to grow up by herself."

"So you went out and stole her one! What's wrong with you?"

"There's nothing wrong with me. I just want to be a mommy and I don't want Margaret to be lonely."

The little girl is sitting in the middle of the bed in the room that they have told her is her room, the one where the windows are nailed shut. They're screaming so loud she doesn't have to go to the door and sit next to it with her ear pressed against the wood to hear what they're saying. She wonders if the neighbors can hear.

She wonders if there are neighbors.

When she was brought here, the kidnapper mommy put a blindfold around her eyes so she couldn't see.

So maybe there are neighbors right next door. But she can't see any houses from the one window in her room. There is a bush on the other side of it that blocks her view of everything.

"What are you going to do?" the kidnap mommy whines.

"I'm going to get rid of him. That's what I'm going to do."

"Oh, no, please don't do that. I want a little brother for Margaret."

"Do you have any idea what will happen to us if we get caught?"

"We're not going to get caught."

"Oh, yes we are, if you keep doing insane things like stealing more children."

"Please don't yell at me anymore." The kidnapper mother's voice sounds small, not frightened but timid.

"I'm getting rid of him," the kidnapper father says.

The little girl wonders where the little boy is that the kidnapper mother stole. What did she do with him? The little girl hasn't seen him, hasn't heard him. Where is he?

"Jesus, you act like, 'he followed me home, mom, can I keep him?'"

The kidnapper mother said nothing then, but the little girl could hear her sniffling, and maybe she was crying.

"Look, you said you wanted a little girl and I got you a little girl. That's as far as this goes. No more. I'm getting rid of the little boy and don't you ever, ever pull something like that again."

The little girl didn't even get to see the little boy. And she's sorry that the kidnapper daddy is going to get rid of him because she would have liked a little brother. So she's not so alone here with these people who took her.

But the words "getting rid of the little boy" bounced around inside her head, because she couldn't put it together with what he meant. How do you get rid of a little boy? It's not like you can go put him out of the car on the side of the road like a dog. What did "get rid of" mean?

The kidnapper woman had started to cry when he said that. And he yelled at her to hush, that it was her fault, that everything that had happened with the little boy was her fault. Then he stormed out. The little girl heard the door slam. Then she heard the woman crying softly.

That's when it began to occur to the little girl what the man had meant when he said, "I'll get rid of him." He meant he was going to kill the little boy, didn't he?

Waves of terror washed over her. She was afraid she was going to throw up. The kidnapper daddy was going to take the little boy somewhere and kill him. That had to be what it meant.

Would they do the same thing with her if the kidnapper daddy decided they never should have gotten her in the first place?

The little girl was shaking all over. Even her teeth were chattering, like she was cold, but she wasn't cold. She was numb. She shoved her hand down into her pocket and grabbed the locket, squeezed it tight in her fist and pulled it out. The locket was such a beautiful thing. She'd thought so when she got it for Christmas, never dreaming how much it would come to matter to her, never dreaming that it would be the only thing she had left of her mommy and her daddy.

Her fingers were shaking so badly, she had trouble getting the clasp undone so that she could open the locket and look at the picture of her parents inside. The ache in her heart when she saw them, the ache for them to come and get her and take her home and put her in her own bed and love her and make her their little girl again was so strong, she felt like her heart was going to burst out of her chest.

She stroked the locket with her thumb, back and forth, back and forth, trying to feel her parents through the metal, trying not to think of the little boy that the kidnapper man was going out to kill.

Chapter Twenty-Eight

RILEIGH KNEW she would never be able to find a place to park at Georgia's house. And she was right. The whole road, for a quarter of a mile in both directions, was jammed with cars. Both Chigger's family and Georgia's come to offer support.

Rileigh hated that she sensed the same kind of quiet desperation in the living room of Georgia's house that she'd felt in the Malones house just two days ago. Almost Georgia's whole family was there, except for her father. He was a long-haul trucker, somewhere in Arizona when her mother called him and told him about Mason.

Georgia had called Rileigh maybe ten times, asking if Rileigh had any news. Georgia hadn't actually expected her to give out brand new information that Rileigh just hadn't bothered to call her about. Georgia was just touching base, drawing strength wherever she could.

Halfway across the yard, Rileigh could smell the aroma of roast and chicken, baked casseroles and pies, strong coffee and chili. She shook her head, not surprised herself, but surprised on behalf of Mitch, who couldn't understand two nights ago why anyone would come to the house with food at a time like this.

Chigger was sitting on the porch with his brothers. He looked up at her with anguished eyes. She would tell him someday how proud she was of how he had spared his eight-year-old son pain and guilt he'd have otherwise carried for the rest of his life, but now wasn't the time. He nodded and she nodded, then she opened the squeaking screen door and went into the house. Georgia was in her bedroom with two of her sisters. Rileigh could hear her sobs all the way from the living room. The family peppered her with questions about the FBI, what the FBI was doing, and what they had found out, and, and, and. She answered as fully as she could, mostly dodging the difficult questions, giving a hopeful-sounding "I don't know" to the others.

She rapped her knuckles gently on Georgia's bedroom door and pushed it open, and the look of joy and hope on Georgia's face broke her heart. She suspected that Georgia was coping by clinging to the belief Rileigh would find Mason ... because Rileigh had rescued her when she was a teenager facing spending the best years of her life in prison. Even if Georgia wouldn't admit it, she thought Rileigh would do the same thing now. Rileigh watched that hope die in her eyes.

Georgia got up off the bed, grabbed Rileigh's hand, led her through the tangle of relatives, all talking in subdued voices like it was a funeral.

"Where are the kids?" Rileigh asked.

"I farmed them out. I didn't want to come completely apart in front of them, so I sent them home with their grandparents and aunts." Georgia described which child had gone to what relative, as they stepped out onto the porch, smelling the chilled spring air. Georgia reached out her hand, just a touch, to Chigger, then she and Rileigh headed down the rickety steps to the yard, turned and went around the end of the trailer, and started up into the woods.

Rileigh didn't ask where Georgia was going because she already knew. She was making her way to the "waterfall." Creek water running down the mountainside spread out into the creek bed about fifty yards behind Georgia's trailer. And before it spread out, the water dropped off a ledge and fell about three feet. Rileigh had named it the first time she saw it and the name stuck. It was the Notmuchuva Waterfall.

Georgia went there sometimes for a bit of solitude in the blender of her raising-five-children life, and she marched to the spot like Sherman through Atlanta. It was where the two of them went the day Rileigh exploded on Georgia for taking Chigger back after he'd cheated on her.

Georgia clung to Rileigh's hand with the fierceness of a little child and it broke Rileigh's heart. It all broke Rileigh's heart. The unfathomable anguish of her best friend right now staggered the imagination. Georgia turned around when they got to the rock near the edge where they always sat.

"Do you believe in signs?"

"What kind of signs?"

"Like, I don't know. Not anything as formal as astrology, like the planets aligning or anything like that. I just mean, do you believe that sometimes, something in the world tells you what you need to know and you hear it, not with your ears, but with your heart?"

Rileigh patted the rock where she sat, pulled Georgia down beside her and wrapped her arm around her shoulders.

"It was the most awful thing I ever felt," Georgia said, her voice barely above a whisper.

"What was?"

"About half an hour ago, I was sitting at the kitchen table, just drinking a cup of hot chocolate, and suddenly I felt this horrible, horrible premonition that something terrible was happening to Mason right at that moment, and I couldn't do anything about it."

"If you want to know if I think that kind of message from beyond is something you can rely on, the answer is a big fat no. I don't believe in it."

Georgia reached up and put her fingers over Rileigh's lips, shushing her. "Listen to me." Her voice broke and cracked. "Something happened a little while ago. I don't know what it was, but *something* did. Something having to do with Mason, and it was not good. Something..." She shuddered and could barely get the next words out. "Something terrible happened to him, Rileigh, I'm sure of it. I could feel it. I could feel it in my heart."

She began to cry softly then, a weak mewling cry like a kitten left out in the rain. Rileigh hugged her tight, rocked her back and forth, and kissed her on the top of the head. She had no idea what to say. The statistics that she didn't want to know, that she would certainly never tell Georgia, were banging around in her head. Sixty percent of kidnapped children who didn't survive were killed less than three hours after they were taken. Mason had been gone now for more than twelve.

Georgia finally cried herself out, didn't have the strength to keep sobbing. She took Rileigh's hand, squeezing it so tight her fingers hurt.

"Do you believe in that kind of thing?"

"Absolutely, one hundred percent *not*," Rileigh said firmly. "You're scared shitless. Of course, you're scared shitless. Somebody kidnapped your little boy. And scared people think weird things. It's your mind attacking you, taking pot shots at you from behind a bush. It doesn't mean anything, Georgia." She grabbed Georgia's other hand in hers and leaned into her face. "Listen to me. It doesn't mean anything. Nothing bad has happened to Mason."

Georgia drew in a deep, ragged breath and let it out in a painfully slow sigh.

"Whatever happens to Mason, it's my fault."

Rileigh began. "Don't—"

Georgia held up her hand to stop her words.

"You can tell me anything you want. You can reassure me that I did nothing wrong, that I did nothing negligent, that I did nothing that put my little boy at risk. You can spew those words out like Mayella's projectile vomit when she's had too many bananas. It doesn't mean anything. In here—" Georgia tapped her chest. "—deep in here, I know the truth. I know that I should have been taking better care of my little boy. And because I didn't, he's gone."

She drew in another breath. "Something really bad has happened to him and whatever it is, it's my fault."

Chapter Twenty-Nine

RILEIGH WOULD HAVE SPENT the whole night at Georgia's, but eventually the strain and fear caught up with Georgia and she collapsed into her bed in exhaustion. So Rileigh went home, trying to think of anything that she could do that she hadn't already done as she drove the dark, lonely mountain roads. Or anything she could do to make Georgia's load lighter. But she knew there was nothing.

That family would never be the same again, even if Mason were returned to them with a red bow on his head first thing in the morning. The trauma they all had suffered, the terror, the mindless agony of worry, they would never fully recover from that, no matter what happened to Mason.

Rileigh flat out refused to countenance the thought that anything bad would. Georgia was wrong. Whatever stupid gut instinct she'd had about some awful thing happening to her little boy was wrong. Mason was fine and Mason was going to stay fine. He was going to come home.

Rileigh was going to find him!

She sucked in a breath, which was a strangled sob. It all fell in on her then. All the emotions came crashing down like an avalanche off the mountains, and she began to sob, cried so hard she could barely see to drive. Great gut-wrenching sobs that tore out of her soul into the world.

How could a thing like this could happen in Black Bear Forge? How is it possible that a child vanished out of the damned elementary school yard while every adult there was safe?

Rileigh stopped crying so abruptly then she almost choked. That was not true. And she needed to get rid of that misconception right now. *Somebody* took Chloe Malone and Mason Stump, kidnapped them. And that person was not safe. Someone in this community was harboring a horrible dark side that no one had ever dared imagine existed. Because it was not some random stranger who'd passed by the school and yanked Chloe into the trunk of his car. Chloe had left that carnival with someone she trusted. And the same was true of Mason Stump.

A small smile curled the corners of her lips when she thought about Mason. Whoever took him had convinced him to go without a struggle. *Nobody* got Mason Stump to do something he didn't want to do without a fight. Mason had left Walmart because he chose to leave with someone. And that someone was local.

Local.

The word pinballed around in her head. It used to conjure up an image of goodness and safety. Local meant *us,* the home team. Neighbors who would come to your aid at need as they would expect you to come to theirs. But somewhere out there in this local county was a monster who had been awakened by God knows what. Rileigh was sure that nobody in this community would ever again feel as safe as they had before this happened.

Rileigh hadn't wanted Mama to wait up for her. Never dreamed that she would. But there was a light on in the living room, and she found Mama curled up on the couch with a quilt spread over her. The squeaking of the screen door roused her. She looked at Rileigh for just a moment with hope that they'd found both of the children unharmed. Rileigh watched that hope die in her mother's eyes, just like she'd watched it die in Georgia's.

"You want some hot tea, sweetie?" Her mother asked. Without waiting for a reply, she got up, went into the kitchen, and put the tea kettle on the stove. Rileigh sat at the kitchen table a few minutes later, inhaling the pungent aroma of sweet tea —a cup into which she put two full teaspoons of sugar.

"What I can't make work in my head, Mama, is how it could happen here. A thing like this happening here is just inconceivable."

"Ain't the first time. Happened once before, when I was a little girl."

Rileigh sat the cup down carefully in the saucer on the table and looked with bloodshot eyes at her mother. She didn't know how to respond to that. The dying synapses in the old woman's brain had obviously conjured up a fictional horror. Rilieigh would've heard the story if it had happened before. "Let's not do this right now, Mama. I'm too tired."

"It ain't no story. I'm telling what's true. When I was a little girl, they was a kidnapping. A couple of tourists went into a grocery store outside Pigeon Forge to stock up on picnic supplies, and when they were ready to check out, their little girl was gone. I want you to know they never did find out what happened to that little girl."

Rileigh's mind couldn't process it, just flat out couldn't.

It could be true, it could be a crock of bullshit. And she knew that her mother had no idea which it was.

"It happened when I was about five or six years old, as I recall, and my mama and every other mama in this county used that as a club to beat us kids over the head with: 'Don't Talk to Strangers.'"

Her mother scratched her thinning white hair. "If I recall aright, it seems to me there was a baby boy who also got kidnapped 'bout the same time."

And probably a set of identical triplets, too. Some conjoined twins with two heads and no bodies. Or maybe—

"I ain't sure about that last part, but I am sure about the little girl. I remember my mama hauling that story out every time I left the house."

Rileigh finished her cup of tea, kissed her mother on the cheek, and went upstairs to try to get a few hours' sleep before she dragged herself back out of bed in the morning to start down the list of people whose names she had gleaned from staring at surveillance video for hours all afternoon. But more than that, she would do her dead level best to let go of the fantasy of this perfect little community with its perfectly safe place to raise perfectly healthy children who were never in any danger of any kind. She had to shake hands with the fact that *somebody* took those children, somebody she would never have dreamed capable of such a thing.

As she lay down, she couldn't help wondering if her mother had made up the kidnapping story. It kept itching in her mind until she finally reached over to the nightstand and picked up her phone. She dialed the office of the Black Bear Gazette, punched in the voicemail for Mrs. Sandusky, and left a message. "This is Rileigh Bishop. I'm working on the kidnapping cases with the sheriff. And my mother mentioned tonight that a little girl was kidnapped here years ago, when she was a child. You know how Mama is, she remembers things that never happened. Would you mind looking in the back issues to see if it's true, and if it is, would you please give me a call?"

Chapter Thirty

THE FBI HAD ARRIVED en masse less than 20 minutes after Mitch had called them. A helicopter full of agents dropped down in the parking lot of the post office and disgorged the vanguard, and a truckload of sophisticated electronic equipment arrived from Knoxville shortly afterward. Those in the helicopter had started setting up a command post in the sheriff's office taking the entire basement of the courthouse and expanding up into the first floor, effectively evicting most of the personnel of the Property Valuation Administrator's office.

Their organized chaos was impressive and intimidating and annoying as hell.

The agent in charge was brusque, no-nonsense Senior Special Agent (SSA) Lamar Devereux, recently transferred from the Baton Rouge field office. It wasn't that Devereux had moved in and moved Mitch out from a sense of superiority or even pecking order—and he was higher on it. The only thing that mattered to SSA Lamar Devereux was finding those missing children. He would have run through a brick wall and parked cars to do it. So in that regard, he and Mitch were totally on the same page. The issues that divided them were their very different views about how to accomplish that task.

Mitch handled things by learning how to be the guy from away-from-here in a small Tennessee town and still get something done. The FBI agent handled things by marching through the county like Sherman through Atlanta.

SSA Devereux had made his position clear from the git-go — "I'm not interested in getting in a pissing match with you over jurisdiction."

Mitch had made his position clear from the git-go, too. "You're running the show and my deputies and I will do whatever you think's necessary. But if you try to sideline us in parking lot duty when we're the most valuable resource you've got right now, then yeah, I'll start unzipping my pants."

The special agent had actually smiled a little at that, told him, "Fair enough," then grilled Mitch for two hours to get up to speed on the investigation Mitch had been conducting when he called in the FBI. At the end of the two hours, SSA Devereux had laid out what he and his phalanx of officers would need in order to do their jobs properly and Mitch set about filling every need — which included getting the librarian to open the county library in the middle of the night, where he "requisitioned" two big standing white-boards. By the time he'd finished unloading the second one into his office, the first had already been outfitted with a big picture of Chloe Malone and was jammed with information about her case.

Mitch had to admit he was overwhelmed by the mass of resources that had arrived on his doorstep in such short order. If he had really believed that all of this firepower was what was needed to find those children, he would have been cheered and encouraged by the sight of it. He didn't. He believed that good detective work and localized, on the ground information-gathering would accomplish the task, but he had to admit he'd tried that for two days and got nowhere.

After snagging a couple of hours of sleep on a couch in the circuit judge's chambers on the third floor, he shaved and put on a clean, unwrinkled uniform in the department's locker room. He had to keep reminding himself to stop rubbing his eyes — the red in them made him look like a pothead.

Special Agent Lamar Devereux was not in Mitch's office, but half a dozen other agents were scurrying around like ants building an anthill. The second-in-command on the FBI side was a tall, skinny, red-haired man named Philip Parsons, who informed Mitch that Devereux had taken two other agents with him and was out speaking to the Stump family and the Malone family. Mitch told Special Agent Parsons to tell Agent Devereux that Mitch and Rileigh were going this morning to speak to the people that Rileigh had picked out from the Walmart surveillance video, who had also been at the school picnic.

The agent said he'd deliver the message that Mitch was out interviewing suspects, and that grated like sand in Mitch's teeth. But he let it go. He didn't see these people as suspects, and that was probably part of his problem. Everybody, *anybody* was a suspect, even two sweet ladies, one of whom was confined to a motorized wheelchair because she had ALS, which was a fatal disease. It's hard to think why in the world either one of those women would have any motive to kidnap a child. But he and Rileigh had agreed they would chase down every lead, no matter how improbable.

Betty Marie and Hannah Forester lived in a beautiful

cabin deep in the woods outside Black Bear Forge. It was one of the older cabins, on a good chunk of a hillside. Apparently, it had belonged to Hannah's parents. It had the advantage of fully-grown landscaping all around and no neighbors in sight. Along the side of the house that was visible from the driveway was a colorful rose garden, red roses and yellow roses and white roses. There were pots lining the short walk from the driveway to the porch that filled the air with the fragrant smell of roses, so thick, you could almost taste it. Mitch inhaled it deeply and savored it.

The road passed in front of the house. The driveway swung by the right side of the house and around to the back. There was a wraparound porch with a railing around the building, which appeared to be a log cabin, but he suspected that the logs were only on the outside and it probably not interior walls. But who knew? The front door faced the driveway, but there was a second floor, a basement that was a walkout into the back part of the property. There was a small ramp up the two steps to the porch to accommodate Betty Marie's wheelchair.

When Mitch pulled his cruiser into the driveway, there were no other vehicles parked there. He knew, thanks to Buddy Russell's savant memory that the Forresters had a white van with side-opening doors to load and unload the motorized wheelchair. The van was nowhere in sight. Maybe nobody was home.

He stepped up onto the porch, and there were two tables beside the front door. They were rustic, had been constructed to match the front railing, and each had big vases with roses in them. The roses were wilted but still smelled glorious. Mitch knocked on the door, since there was no doorbell. He peered through the window into a large kitchen area that probably opened onto a great room at the back of the house, where he suspected there were floor-to-ceiling windows to capture the view. He knocked again, tried the doorknob, thinking he'd at least opened the door a crack and yell, but the door was locked.

Alright then, swing and a miss. He'd come back later. As he turned, he leaned over to smell one of the wilted yellow roses, and when he touched it, a few of the petals fell off. He picked one up and held it to his nose, inhaling deeply.

Back in his cruiser, he entered the address of the next person on his list into the GPS on his phone. He was going to talk to a man named Ben Pendergast, who Rileigh said had only been in Walmart a few minutes, and had left with a bag of charcoal. But he'd also been at the carnival.

Mitch wasn't sure exactly who he was. Lily and Rileigh had told him about so many people. Ben Pendergast was either the man who lost a son in Afghanistan or the man who had been engaged to Rileigh's sister before — no, the ex-fiancé's name was Hicks and he'd been with the woman with the Chinese Crested in a stroller. Hicks' name was not on the "both" list, but Pendergast was. Mitch took a big deep breath of rose-scented air before he rolled up his window and pulled back onto the road.

Chapter Thirty-One

WHEN RILEIGH OPENED HER EYES, she was surprised to discover that she really had gone to sleep. She hadn't thought she'd be able to, thought she'd be tossing and turning, tangling up the sheets in the bed. But the exhaustion had hit her a little like it had Georgia, and she'd slept long and deep for a few hours. She didn't feel exactly rested, but her eyes no longer felt like her eyelids were lined with sandpaper.

Rileigh went downstairs to make a pot of coffee, moving as quietly as she could so that she wouldn't wake Mama, who'd stayed up waiting for Rileigh last night, so she had to be exhausted, too.

"You want some eggs and bacon?" Mama said from behind her. Rileigh had been so lost in thought that she jumped.

"No, thanks, Mama. Just a little coffee and maybe a piece of toast. I'm not hungry."

Mama shuffled to the refrigerator and took out a carton of eggs, then went to the stove, and started heating a burner. She took a spatula off a hook above the burners and stabbed it into the butter in the butter dish, plopping a dollop of it down into the bottom of the pan.

"Scrambled or fried?"

"Neither. I said I don't want any eggs."

Mama nodded and went on. "Where are you going this morning?"

"The FBI totally took over the whole investigation yesterday afternoon. They're running the show and we're filling in the gaps."

Mama picked up an egg out of the carton, cracked it on the side of the pan, and dumped it into the splattering butter.

"I texted Mitch a list of the people I found in the Walmart surveillance videos who had also been at the carnival. We divided it up and we'll both spend today questioning them."

"Was there a whole lot of names on the list?"

"Yeah, several. I'm going to Granny Maggie's and he's going to Hannah and Betty Marie Forrester's, then—"

"Betty Marie has ALS, for cryin' out loud. Surely you don't think—"

Rileigh stopped her. "Of course not. But *somebody* took those children and I guarantee it was somebody we'd never dream would do a thing like that. Maybe somebody was forced to be a part of this against their will. Anything's possible. We are checking out EVERY lead, no exceptions."

Pouring herself a cup of coffee, Rileigh dumped what she called "a bucket" of creamer into it. She had never had a Starbucks coffee. Five dollars for a cup of coffee — *seriously?* But she was grateful to them for popularizing lattes, frappes, café au laits, and the general idea of dumping a bunch of extraneous ingredients into a perfectly good cup of coffee. Gave her permission to drink coffee that was just about half creamer.

"Did you know Granny Maggie when you were a girl?"

"Yeah, we's 'bout the same age, but she didn't start school regular 'til we was older, third or fourth grade. Her folks moved around a lot, in and out of the county and she was sickly, seems like."

"What happened to her husband? Was he local?"

"Almost local. Merrick County."

Merrick County bordered Yarmouth County on the north, and since the boundary was a creek with a tendency to flood, it shifted around some, so people who lived there were granted almost-local status.

Mama continued: "Maggie never socialized much and he was like a third or fourth cousin. There's a lot of McCullochs over in Merrick, so she didn't have to get no new monogramed towels."

It wasn't uncommon for couples with the same last name to marry. Big Catholic families with limited mobility for generations could fill up a whole page of the phone book with the same surname. Priests in the local parishes were tasked with making sure the kinship wasn't too close.

"They come back here and lived on her parents' farm. He died about twenty-five years ago when Becca was just a little bitty thing. I think it was some odd illness like congestive heart failure or some such that a young man hadn't ought to have got in the first place. That's when she moved back into her parents' old house."

Rileigh rose to leave, but Mama looked at her still-full plate and made a tut-tut gesture.

"Sit back down there and eat yore breakfast."

"I told you, Mama. I'm not hungry."

"Then why'd you ask me to fix you them eggs? Make up your mind."

Rileigh went back upstairs to grab a light jacket — mornings were still chilly — then went out to her car. Before she could drive away, Mama came running down the porch steps with a Tupperware container for her.

"A couple of pieces of toast," she said as Rileigh rolled down her window and took the container.

The shadow of the mountain stretched out all the way across the valley, receding up the hillsides as the sun climbed higher into the sky. Maggie didn't live in the middle of nowhere, some isolated place. Haskell Lane, which led to her house, stretched a mile or two from the state road back through the mountains. It must have had considerable traffic because it was smooth and well-kept, no potholes. Rileigh rolled down her window and enjoyed the feel of brisk morning air scented with pine and cedar trees.

When she pulled up in front of the house, she saw no vehicle and had second thoughts about not calling in advance to make sure Maggie would be home. But that's not what you do. You don't set up an appointment to go talk to suspects. (Is that what they were, suspects?) No, you show up unannounced, hoping surprise might kick loose some stray fact or another that a prepared person would have their guards up for. And just because there was no vehicle didn't mean Granny Maggie wasn't home. There were several different outbuildings on the property. Her truck could be in a garage out back, or maybe she'd put it in the barn.

Rileigh turned off the ignition, stuffed the keys into her pocket, and glanced at the Tupperware container on the seat beside her. She *had* wanted some toast, after all. The container was sealed tight, hard to open. Rileigh shrugged with it, but it wouldn't budge. She tugged hard and the lid came off suddenly, dumping two pieces of toast into her lap — toast slathered with grape jelly!

Dammit!

She picked up a piece of toast by the edge, but the crust came off in her hand and she dropped it again — on a different spot on her otherwise clean pants.

Mumbling a stream of obscenities, she tried to pick up the toast without getting jelly all over her hands, but it smeared everywhere. Dumping the gooey mess back into the Tupperware container, she tossed it into the floorboard, reached for her cell phone in its plastic holder on the dashboard, then stopped before she touched it. A *sticky* iPhone? No. She left it where it was. Just getting out of the car left the door handle sticky. *Thanks a bunch, Mama.*

Rileigh started up the walk and heard the child-guard locks click. She unconsciously patted her pocket to be sure she'd gotten her keys out of the ignition ... and smeared jelly on the pocket of her pants. How had she managed to stumble into an episode of Brer Rabbit and the Tar Baby?

Chapter Thirty-Two

MITCH WAS ALMOST HALF a mile away from the Forresters when it hit him, and the thought snagged all the rest of the thoughts in his head and wouldn't let anything else through. The flowers in the vase on the porch at the Forresters' house were roses, but they were *wilted*. They weren't fresh cut this morning. They'd been put there yesterday, maybe the day before. Mitch thought about the conversation he'd had with Rileigh and her mother at the elementary school carnival. Mama had said Betty Marie Forrester raised the most beautiful roses Mama had ever seen. Then she said that she had talked to the mailman who delivered mail on the Forresters' route, and he'd said: "First thing every morning for four years there's been fresh roses in a vase on the porch. Never missed once, not even in the snow. So, they must be raising some indoors somehow."

Every morning for four years, the women had put fresh roses on their porch, didn't miss a single time, even in the dead of winter. So why were there no fresh roses on the porch this morning?

Mitch pulled his cruiser into the next driveway he came to and turned around. He pulled off the road onto a barely discernible logging road about a quarter of a mile before the Forresters' house, got out and walked from there, went through the woods toward the back of the house where the basement was a walkout.

He had assumed, rightly so, that the whole backyard was full of rose bushes: red and yellow and white and pink. The smell was intoxicating. He'd also been right in the assumption that this cabin had floor-to-ceiling windows on the backside that looked out over the hillside and the rose garden. But most interesting of all, he'd been right about a garage in the back of the house —there were three vehicles parked in front of it. The van belonging to the Forrester's. A black Subaru, a rental with a Nashville inspection sticker on the plate. And a gray Mercedes with tinted windows and New York tags.

He carefully went from one tree to the next until he was close to the house, out of the sight line from the windows. He used the vehicles as cover then hurried to the side of the house and flattened himself up against it before moving slowly toward the big floor-to-ceiling windows. When he passed the Mercedes, he could hear the engine ticking as it cooled. That car hadn't been here long.

He could hear voices from inside. Hannah and Betty Marie Forester were indeed home after all, and not alone. The other voices voices were male.

Crouching low, he edged around the corner of the house, keeping behind the firewood stacked up against the wall. Then he rose up slowly and peeked out over the wood pile into the basement of the house.

What he saw there chilled him. He quickly ducked back down and drew his weapon.

RILEIGH WENT UP to the porch and knocked firmly on the door. No one came. She knocked again. Still no answer. She knocked louder the third time out of frustration — she needed to wash her hands!

And surprisingly, the door opened — just enough to reveal the little girl, Shiloh. Rileigh was struck anew by how ethereal she was — tall and willowy, but at the same time delicate in a way that seemed too perfect for the world. Her hair was like corn silk, hanging all the way to her waist. Her skin was porcelain white. And her eyes, when she would look at Rileigh, appeared to be a beautiful robin's egg blue.

"Hi Shiloh, I came to talk to Granny Maggie."

"Granny Maggie's not here." Shiloh started to close the door.

"Wait! She left you here all by yourself?" That stopped her.

"Oh no, she wouldn't … I mean …"

"You remember me? Rileigh Bishop?" The little girl looked down at the floor. "I met you at the carnival the other day. Your grandmother brought you around to introduce you."

"I met lots of people that day," Shiloh said, still not meeting Rileigh's eyes.

"And we remembered you a whole lot better than you remember all of us, I'm sure. I need to talk to Granny Maggie. Is she here or not?"

Shiloh's eyes grew wide. The question had clearly unnerved her, and she looked … frightened. Then she straightened, pushed open the screen door and stepped out onto the porch.

"She's not *here*, in the house, I mean. She's out back."

The little girl made a come-on gesture. "I'll show you. A fox got in our chicken house last night, tore a hole through the screen, killed a whole bunch of hens. Made an awful racket, so loud it woke both of us up."

Rileigh was astonished at the number of words that suddenly bubbled out of the child's mouth. Beckoning Rileigh, she crossed the porch to the steps and started down, continuing the almost frantic come-on gestures. "Granny Maggie is out there trying to fix the screen. She's been working on it all morning. She should be done by now, though and—"

"Just give me a minute, I need to wash my hands. Got jelly all over them."

The little girl whirled toward her and Rileigh held up sticky fingers. "There's a water hose outside. This way, I'll show you."

"That's ok. This won't take but a second." Opening the screen door with only one finger to keep from getting it sticky, Rileigh stepped into the house. Old houses always had a bathroom beside the front door. This one was no exception. Leaving the door open, she went to the sink and washed her hands thoroughly. She used a washcloth to clean the jelly off the sink, then dabbed at the jelly stains on her pants. Useless. She'd need spot remover. The little girl had come back into the house and was standing right outside the bathroom, waiting anxiously.

Rileigh smiled. "Thanks. I'll need to borrow some paper towels to clean the sticky off the door handles on my car."

"I'll go get some. You wait right here."

The little girl turned and bolted for the kitchen.

Ok. Something wasn't right here. Something was bothering this little girl beyond simple shyness.

She started toward the kitchen and collided in the

dining room with the little girl as she returned, clutching a handful of paper towels.

"Here!" she said, breathless.

She might as well have started shoving Rileigh toward the front door. Instead, Rileigh moved past her into the kitchen.

"If you want some more towels, I can get them for you!"

What Rileigh wanted was a look around.

As soon as they got into the kitchen the little girl began to babble, "We have cookies. Do you want some cookies. They're real good. Granny Maggie made them this morning fresh—"

Rileigh scanned the room as the girl talked. Besides the doorway into the dining room, there was a door leading out to the back porch and a small door on the far side of the room, probably to the basement. When she moved in that direction, the little girl stepped in front of her and talked louder.

"… chocolate chips and pecans and …"

Rileigh was on high alert now.

Putting her finger to her lips, she whispered sternly "Shiloh, hush!"

The child stopped chattering in mid word.

Putting her hand on her holstered weapon, Rileigh walked quietly to the door, tried the knob. It wasn't locked. She pushed it slowly inward. It was dim and shadowy in the basement, no lights on, but there were windows high up near the basement ceiling that opened onto the ground outside and sunlight was shining in through them.

Rileigh took two steps out onto the landing in front of the door to see what might be down there. Her breath caught in her throat at what she saw and her heart banged into the walls of her chest. She quickly drew her 9mm Glock. Shiloh gasped when she saw the gun.

Rileigh told her quietly, but sternly, "Stay behind me."

Chapter Thirty-Three

MITCH SAT where he was for a few seconds, his heart hammering like a lunatic woodpecker in his chest. Then he slowly crept back from his hiding place behind the woodpile to the side of the house, where he could see the vehicles. Once there, out of earshot, he keyed his microphone and spoke to the dispatcher.

"This is Unit One. Patch me through to Agent Devereux."

He was sure that Connie heard the urgency in his voice. It was only seconds before Devereux was on the line.

"What's up?"

"I went out this morning to interview the people that Rileigh picked out of the Walmart video who had also been at the carnival. I'm at the home of Betty Marie and Hannah Forrester, 2709 Brook Lane, Caucasian females, mid-50s. Betty Marie has ALS and uses a motorized wheelchair."

"When I arrived, they didn't answer the door. I went around to the back and found their vehicle, along with two

224

others, a rental car from Nashville, plate number—" He leaned so he could see it. "—K29-WW5, and a Mercedes with New York plates, number 7821LB. The engine on the Mercedes was still warm. I looked through the basement patio glass doors, I saw two men and two women. One was the man I believe to be the masked man in the dark T-shirt that I told you about, who was a stranger to everyone at the carnival. There was also an older man with a gun drawn, appeared to be a Glock 18." Glock 18 pistols were illegal in the US. With the flip of a selector switch, the gun could become an automatic pistol capable of firing 1200 rounds per minute. "Betty Marie had a black eye and a split lip, and Hannah appeared to have a broken nose. Both were sitting on the couch with the men standing in front of them, backs to the glass doors. I saw no evidence of the children anywhere. I stepped out of sight, calling for backup."

That was as succinct a report as Mitch could make it. There was only a slight pause on Devereux's part before he asked, "What's the best approach to that location?"

Mitch didn't allow himself enough time to be pleased that the man had sense enough to ask for his advice.

"Get Deputies Mullins and Rawlings to take you and your agents to the house at 2709 Brook Lane. It sits by itself on a couple of acres, woods surrounding on three sides. Bring Rawlings in from the north, Crawford from the south. Don't approach the house where you can be seen. Send Rawlings and Crawford through the woods to the back of the property. Two more officers approach from the front, one from each direction, out of sight behind the hedge. I'm concealed behind a woodpile on the south side of the patio. I need one officer at my position as backup. Once we're all in position, a coordinated assault from the front and back."

There was dead silence on Devereux's end. For two, three seconds. Then he responded.

"Seven agents, including myself. Two others will wait at the road to stop traffic."

This guy was the real deal. When you're willing to let FBI agents take the traffic duty, you've put the big rocks in first.

"Harding will go with Mullins, Gregory with Rawlings, I'll take Haddux with me from the south out front, send Conseco and Papadopoulos to approach in the front from the north. Parsons will provide your backup from the trees west of you." Mitch hadn't yet gotten all the FBI agents' names straight yet, but he knew Parsons was the tall, red-headed second in command.

"Sounds good."

"How long will it take us to get there?"

"Code 52—"

Before he could go on, Devereux said, "What's code 52?"

"Sorry. Lights, no sirens — it should take 10-12 minutes. I will monitor the situation and I won't inter-vene." He paused. "Unless I have to."

"10-4," Devereux said and clicked off.

Mitch crouched again and went back to the spot where he had been hiding behind the woodpile. Dared a peek over the top of it and saw that Betty Marie was crying.

Where were Chloe Malone and Mason Stump? And why had either the two women, or the men, or a combina-tion of both, taken the children?

He didn't want to do this on his own, but he would if he had to. He couldn't stand by and allow the men to harm Betty Marie and Hannah. He couldn't allow the men to leave the room and go somewhere to threaten the welfare of the children, wherever they'd been stashed away.

There was no way to know how many other people might be in the house — surely they'd left someone with the kids upstairs. But maybe not. Maybe they'd locked them in somewhere.

Unless there were no kids. Unless they were already gone, shipped off somewhere to … god only knew what.

The only outside entrance to the basement were the sliding glass doors in the middle of the wall facing the woods, and there was certainly no way to get through those without being noticed. He was stuck hiding behind the woodpile. So he held his breath and concentrated on listening to what they were talking about.

RILEIGH CROUCHED INSTANTLY, her head on a swivel, her eyes sweeping the basement and kitchen behind her, ready for an attack.

She'd seen the vague outline of what appeared to be two big dog kennels in the basement and there was *something* in both of them— a dark shape in each one. If the something was a dog, the dogs would have been barking their heads off right now. The silence was deafening. So, what *was* in the kennels?

Rileigh edged a little farther out onto the landing to get a better look into the basement, her mind whirring, assessing the situation and her options.

She needed to call immediately for backup. But her cell phone was in the car. Right now, she was flying solo. She was on the hook for this one.

First priority was to find the children, make sure they were all right, protect them. She turned to Shiloh and barked "Who else is in the house?"

Shiloh just looked at her, a true deer in the headlights.

"Is there somebody else here besides you and Granny Maggie?" She might as well have been talking to a Barbie doll. "Shiloh, stay right behind me. Do you hear me?"

This time, at least, the little girl nodded mutely.

Keeping her gun in a two-hand grip, sweeping the room, she started to ease sideways down the steps. *Anybody* could be hiding down there, armed and just waiting to get a good view of her before they fired. Granny Maggie could be in the basement or somewhere else in the house. The most important thing right now was to find out what was in those dog kennels, the dark shapes she couldn't make out in the gloom.

If there were children in them — as great a leap of the imagination as that might be, she had to get them out of the kennels, out of the basement, and all *three* children out of the house to safety. Then, and only then, would she worry about the kidnapper.

When Rileigh put out her foot, she saw that the steps leading into the basement were old and worn and didn't look particularly sturdy. She eased her weight onto the first step, and it held. And then...

Rileigh wasn't sure afterward exactly what happened then. She lost her footing somehow. Either a step had broken out from under her or she had simply lost her balance. But before she could do anything to stop her fall, she banged into the wall, tried to find something to grab there, clawing with her fingernails, then tumbled all the rest of the way down to the floor, where she lay still in front of two big dog kennels and the shapes inside them.

Chapter Thirty-Four

MITCH COULD HEAR Betty Marie crying, and he could hear snatches of her words, then the old man's words. He heard enough to note that the older man had an accent, sounded possibly Russian, at least Eastern European.

"...don't know what you want."

"I prefer not to beat it out of you, but I will hurt you."

The old man spoke harshly, and Betty Marie stifled her tears. It was only then that Mitch noticed she wasn't sitting in the wheelchair. It was next to the couch where she was sitting. He wondered why she had gotten out of it. And how?

When the older man continued, his voice was louder, and Mitch could catch much of what he said. "... did good work on that face. Subtle changes, but very different."

"Please, I don't know what—"

"I'm tired of listening to the lies." The old man held the pistol loosely, pointed at nothing. If he lifted the pistol to fire, Mitch would take him out. "I tracked you down." He indicated Hannah as he spoke to Betty Marie. "You tell me the truth, we'll let her live."

Mitch hoped they weren't stupid enough to buy the offer. Clearly, the man was threatening to kill Betty Marie unless she told him what he wanted to know. She couldn't possibly be dumb enough to believe that he'd allow Hannah to live after Hannah watched him commit murder.

Hannah began to sob then, and the man who'd worn a black tee-shirt and a mask at the carnival, took one step forward and slapped her, knocking her back onto the couch. Mitch could hear Betty Marie's voice then.

"All right, I'll tell you. Yes, it's me." She said a name. It was too garbled, and Mitch missed it. The tension went out of the older man, and he turned to confer privately with tee-shirt man. When they turned, they were facing outward, and Mitch had no trouble hearing what they said.

"I've looked around, this forest goes on for miles. We take them out into the woods, shoot them, and leave them there. There's a lot of acreage out here. It ought to be a long time before anybody finds them."

The older man nodded.

Once they'd killed the two women, what were they going to do with the children? Where were the children? It didn't appear anybody was thinking of them at all.

"Yes, the woods. Silenced."

Mitch tensed. This was going to get ugly before backup arrived. He had no idea where the kids were, but right now, his concern was the safety of the two women in the room. Obviously, the men planned to kill them both.

With the two men near the windows, the women were not in Mitch's line of fire. But they would be if he allowed the men to approach them.

Time to act.

Mitch stepped out from hiding behind the woodpile and stood up tall in front of the floor-to-ceiling windows.

He saw Betty Marie and Hannah respond to seeing him outside the windows, knew the men would read the expression on their faces quick. His feet spread apart, his gun in a two-hand grip. He called out, "I'm Sheriff Mitchell Webster. Drop your weapons."

He knew they wouldn't and was prepared for what happened next —they whirled toward him. He took aim at the older man in front, carrying the Glock 18. He wouldn't have to aim at Mitch, just spray bullets in his direction, so before he had a chance to lift his weapon, Mitch fired two shots mid-chest. The glass of the windows shattered, exploded inward with his first shot, scattering shards of it in every direction. Mitch swung his gun toward the other man, but tee-shirt man got off a shot first. Mitch felt the impact of the bullet striking his Kevlar vest. It knocked him backward a step and off balance. But before he fell, he squeezed off a shot of his own and caught the man in black somewhere on his upper body. He was knocked sideways and the gun flew out of his hands as Mitch hit the ground, rolled, and came back up with his gun pointed at the man.

It was over almost before it began. Both men were down. Mitch was standing, swaying, and to his utter surprise, Betty Marie leapt to her feet and hurried to where the old man had dropped his gun and kicked it away from him. The other man had lost his gun too, but he wasn't hurt as bad, and he was crawling toward it. Mitch leveled his pistol again.

"Don't try it, buddy. I won't put another one in your chest. This will be a headshot."

The man froze for a moment, then relaxed back onto the floor. Mitch called out to Betty Marie and Hannah, who was sprawled on her back on the couch where she lay after the man had slapped her.

"You two, come out here with me — *right now*, move!"

Mitch kept his gun trained on the man who was way too close to his own gun, moved to keep the women out of the line of fire as Betty Marie went to Hannah and helped her to her feet. The two women hurried outside to where Mitch stood.

Mitch clicked his mic and spoke into it. "This is Unit One. I need a bus. Code 23, two suspects down."

"Roger, bus at 2709, two subjects down."

"Tell Devereux, Crawford, and Mullins, Code 39," which meant lights and sirens "Two subjects are down but location has not been cleared. Repeat, *not* cleared."

Mitch had no idea how many other suspects might be in the house.

He drew a breath then, surveying. The old man was lying on his back, apparently hurt bad, maybe dead. The younger man lay on his belly with his hands stretched out toward where his gun lay. It was still three feet away. Mitch kept his pistol trained on him. But he spoke to Hannah and Betty Marie over his shoulder. "Are there others, did they bring anyone else with them?"

"No, they…" Betty Marie began and stopped. "I don't know. Maybe. I didn't see. There could be others."

Then the children were still in danger.

"Where are they? Where are the kids?"

Mitch was focused on the man inside, wasn't looking at the women's faces, but he could hear Betty Marie's response clearly.

"Kids? What kids?"

Chapter Thirty-Five

Whum!

Whum!

Whum!

Rileigh knew that sound.

Whum, whum, whum. It was a sound you heard inside your head, not with your ears, a pulsing rhythm that kept time with your heart.

The sound pulsed louder and then softer. Louder and then softer. And as it grew softer, she could hear other sounds behind it, sounds it had been masking. One of them was the sound of someone crying. A child.

That meant something. She knew it did, but all of it was so jumbled up in her head. And the world was spinning around and around. She opened her eyes and immediately closed them, the world a dizzying spiral out there beyond her eyelids.

And there was a terrible pain at the base of her skull. She'd felt that before, too. Some part of her knew what was going on, what was happening. But she couldn't manage to get the rest of her to understand.

"Wi-leigh." Rileigh heard a child's voice call her name. "Wi-leigh, help me, I want to go home."

It all came crashing down on her then. Realization, understanding. She was lying on her stomach with her face pressed against dirty, cold, concrete. She smelled sawdust, motor oil, too. All of the smells overlaid on a background of damp mildew, the signature smell of basements everywhere.

She risked opening her eyes just a little, peered out through the forest of eyelashes. The world kept spinning and she had to close her eyes and take deep breaths to make it stop. She opened them carefully again and peered out into a dark, dank, shadowy basement where she could see one large dog kennel and the edge of another one. But she would have to move her head to see the second one. The one she could see was jammed with blankets and pillows and all manner of junk food. Cookies and chips, crumbs everywhere, ho-hos and ding-dongs. The wrappers lay on the floor beside the kennel.

"Wi-leigh," Mason Stump said softly. She blinked her eyes, opened them, looked full at him. It was Mason. He was right there only a few feet away. He was *fine*, alive, unharmed. Her heart leapt out of her chest and did a jig around the moon.

Then the little boy started to cry again. "Wi-leigh, take me home to Mommy and Daddy. I'll be a good boy. I won't never run off again, never ever, I promise."

"I want to go home, too," cried the voice of a child she couldn't see, somewhere beyond Mason.

Chloe Malone. Both of them.

Rileigh had to get them out of here!

She raised up onto her elbows and looked around. She could see both the dog kennels now. The little girl in the farthest kennel was seated in the back corner, pushed up against the bars as if she were trying to be as small as she possibly could. Mason, on the other hand, was being loud, his demands that she take him home alternated with pleas that she tell his mommy and daddy to come and get him. There were toys of every conceivable kind — spaceships, and action figure dolls, baby dolls, Legos, puzzles, and kitchen playsets — all over the basement.

The doors on the dog kennels were held shut with more than metal latches. Ziplock ties fastened the doors to the bars on both sides. Rileigh raised up a little farther onto her elbows. She wasn't ready to stand up yet, but she could at least crawl over to Mason. She made the first crawling effort, but her foot was hung on something. She didn't know what. And the world spun around and around and around.

Glancing over her shoulder, her heart froze in her chest. Her foot wasn't hung on anything. What was keeping her from moving was her own handcuffs. One side clamped to her right ankle, the other side to a three-inch water pipe coming out of the wall. Rileigh still couldn't put together in her head what was going on, but she had to think. She had to get these kids out of here.

She groped her holster. It was empty, her gun was gone. She patted her pockets for her phone. Where was her phone?

She wasn't processing information properly. She knew where she was, but not how she'd gotten there. She remembered taking a step down the stairs … and then …

She must have tripped, or the stair tread gave out underneath her — something! — but clearly, she had fallen down the stairs onto a concrete floor. Though she felt the ache of bruises all over, she supposed she ought to be grateful that she wasn't seriously injured. But she couldn't just lie here. A kidnapper had taken these children.

Someone had forced Granny Maggie and poor little Shiloh to be a part of the plot. Who? Who had snatched the children … and what for?

Rileigh heard a sound from above, up on the landing of the stairs leading down to the basement. She looked up and was almost sure she caught a glimpse of Shiloh.

"Shiloh," she called out. No response. "Shiloh, can you hear me? You have to help me. I need a phone."

The little girl edged very carefully out to a point where she could look down into the basement. Her eyes were saucers of abject terror.

"Sweetheart, listen to me. We have to get out of here. All of us. My cell phone is in my…" In her car. *Locked* in her car. She reached down to feel for her keys in her pants pocket — the outside of the pocket was still a little sticky with jelly, but the keys were gone.

Somewhere in the recesses of her mind, she tried to figure out what had happened. Obviously, one of the steps had collapsed out from under her, but who had come down those stairs and handcuffed her ankle to a water pipe while she was unconscious? Who had taken her gun, her car keys, and the key to the cuffs out of her pockets?

The image of the man in the mask from the carnival flashed through her mind like a comet and then was gone.

"Shiloh," she called out. The little girl said nothing. Mason had dissolved into sniffles and hiccups, and Chloe Malone was as silent as a little mouse. "Shiloh, honey, Listen to me. You have to come down here and bring me a phone or bring me the key to these handcuffs. I have to get all of us out of here. Shiloh, do you understand?"

The little girl peered down at Rileigh and the other two children. Her face was as white as a sheet and her eyes were huge. It was like she didn't hear … no, didn't understand what Rileigh was saying.

Rileigh tried a different approach. "Shiloh, honey, does your grandmother have land line — a normal telephone? Do you know how to call 911?" The little girl looked at her as if she were speaking Swahili. She took another breath and tried to calm her voice. "Shiloh, I know this is all bewildering, but you are in danger here and you have to let me out so I can help you. I know you're frightened of ... whoever ... did this, but you need to hurry before they come back."

Rileigh drew another breath.

"Do you know how to dial 911?" Surely she did. Every kid knew how. But she explained anyway. "If it's a dial phone, you just dial the number 9 and then the number one, twice. If it's a cell phone, punch the 9 icon and then the number 1, twice."

The little girl just stared at her with wide, terrified eyes. And Rileigh realized then that the kid had obviously been traumatized by the monster who'd kidnapped the children and forced her grandmother to put them in her basement. Who knew what other horrors Shiloh had been subjected to? Who knew what had happened to Granny Maggie? Rileigh doubted she was in the back yard repairing a chicken coop with two kidnapped children in her basement.

Had the kidnapper threatened to hurt Granny Maggie if Shiloh didn't do what he wanted? Shiloh was just a *little girl* and Rileigh had no right to expect her to climb on a white horse and come riding to the rescue.

But there was no one else.

"Shiloh, listen to me. Are you listening to me? Nod your head if you can hear me."

She nodded slowly.

"You have to find a phone and dial 911. You have to *call the police!*"

The little girl responded like she'd been jabbed with a cattle prod— jumped backward, her face bleached of all color. She looked like Rileigh had slapped her, and horror now battled terror for dominion on her face. She shook her head vehemently, backing slowly away. Her lips formed the word "no," but there was no sound as she backed across the landing, out the basement door and slammed it shut behind her.

Chapter Thirty-Six

MITCH STOOD with Special Agent Devereux as the EMTs loaded the two men he had shot into an ambulance under the watchful eyes of half a dozen FBI agents.

"I've alerted the Federal Marshal Service," Agent Devereux said, "let them know they dropped the ball on Sylvia Steinman, AKA Betty Marie Forrester. They've obviously got a leak somewhere and they need to plug it."

"Color me naive," Mitch said. "I thought the Witness Protection Program was something like sacred, that nobody ever broke that code."

Devereux let out a sigh. "Nothing in federal law enforcement is without its leaks. You plug one and another one pops up somewhere else."

Mitch had given command of the kidnapping case over to Agent Devereux, but as soon as it became clear this wasn't a kidnapping case and had nothing to do with the missing children, Mitch was back at the helm of the ship. Devereux stood on the sidelines as Mitch got the story from the Forresters. As soon as the danger was passed and

Betty Marie/Sylvia realized that she and Hannah were safe, she imploded.

Mitch figured she was entitled, given what she'd gone through. He let her cry herself out, Hannah sitting stoically by her side with her arm around her. And when she was finally able to answer questions, he started with as basic a question as it gets. "What's going on here, Ms. Steinman?"

"No, please … Betty Marie." She glanced at Hannah. "Betty Marie *Forrester* — that's who I am now."

She said that the cover story — that she had ALS — was made up. She had been partially paralyzed by a bullet fired by one of the bag men in a bank robbery. She'd gotten a look at his face, and as soon as she gave a description to authorities, they knew they had more than a simple bank robbery case. The man whose face matched in the facial recognition software with the artist's sketch Betty Marie had provided was a member of the Russian mafia — the son, in fact, of one of the mafia bosses. They'd been trying to pin something on him for years, and this was their shot. But they knew that, like the other two times they'd tried to take him down, the witness against him wouldn't last through the trial unless they put her into protective custody. And so...

"And so, with a bullet lodged in my spine and paralyzed from the waist down, I found myself shunted off to Lincoln, Nebraska, a rehab center there, and that's where I met Hannah." She reached up and patted Hannah's hand on her shoulder. "She was my therapist. She gave me hope that one day I would walk again. I had plastic surgery on my face there and she took care of me. When I was dismissed from the hospital, we were married and came back here to live in Hannah's parents' house until I was called to testify."

Hannah barked out a sarcastic laugh. "Right, called to testify."

Betty Marie gave her a smile and said, "It's over now."

The case couldn't go to trial without the defendant. As soon as the mafia boss got wind of the possible prosecution, he'd sent his son back home to Russia.

"Then he vanished off the face of the earth," Hannah said.

"And left me hanging in limbo," Betty Marie said. "So for the past two and a half years, Hannah has continued my physical therapy sessions. She built a therapy room onto the back of the house when she renovated it. And slowly, I got better and better. I can walk now with a cane. And when I got here, I couldn't even stand on my own."

"So you had no idea that your cover was blown, is that right?" Mitch asked.

"We didn't know a thing. I remember the tall guy from the carnival. I remember seeing him watching us and thinking, I don't know who he is," Betty Marie said. "So I asked people, and nobody else knew who he was either. And then he showed up last night at the house." Betty Marie began to tremble and Hannah took up the story.

"He forced his way in, demanded that Betty Marie tell him her real name. We've been told to lie. We've gotten pretty good at it over the years. I never call her Sylvia anymore, not even in private. And we stuck with that."

"I think he had orders not to hurt us."

"He made a phone call then, and this morning, that other man, the one with the Russian accent, showed up. He'd been in the bank that day, acting like a customer when they robbed it. He saw his son shoot Betty Marie. He got a good look at her face. And he came to identify her, to see if... and of course, as soon as she saw him, and he saw her..."

"The plastic surgery changed the shape of my nose and my jawline, and I've colored my hair, cut it short and left it curly. But he knew as soon as he saw me."

Hannah turned to Mitch. "If you hadn't shown up, if you hadn't come, he was gonna kill us both, take us out into the woods and shoot us and leave our bodies there."

If you hadn't come.

The words reverberated in Mitch's head as he stood with Agent Devereux, watching them load the two injured men into an ambulance. Devereux pushed off from the wall. "Good job, Sheriff."

"Didn't put us an inch closer to finding those children, though."

Devereux shook his head. "No, it didn't."

"Truth," Mitch said. "Stays between us. What do you think happened to those kids?"

"Two different children, both blondes with blue eyes, snatched out of one little town in a place where everybody knows everybody, their motives and their past …"

Mitch barked out in a laugh. "Well, not everybody."

"True that. But most everybody. I think it's a professional job."

"Professionals as in?"

"Professionals as in sex trafficking."

Mitch was sick to his stomach and asked no more questions.

"I'm going to give it another 24 hours," Devereux said. "Then I'll call in our Special Victims Unit, the ones who handle cases of children kidnapped for the sex industry."

He shook his head.

"This place is so isolated and insulated. It's hard to conceive that there's a motive here that you and yours didn't find in the first thirty-six hours — you were thorough." Devereux looked at his watch, did the math in his head. "Chloe Malone has been missing now for seventy-six hours." Devereux dipped his head. "And you didn't hear that from me, Sheriff Webster."

"Hear what?" Mitch said, dully.

Then the FBI agent went to join the other agents getting in their cars. Mitch walked slowly to his cruiser and pulled up the list on his phone. The only rails he had to run on were protocol. Protocol, even when it didn't make any sense. His job was to check out the list of people who had been at both kidnapping sites when the children were taken. He'd been to the first on the list. Next was Granny Maggie, and Rileigh was checking her out. Third was Ben Pendergast. He punched Ben's address into his GPS, pulled slowly out onto Brook Lane and turned as it directed.

If you hadn't come.

Hannah Forrester's words rang in his head again. His mother always told him things happened for a reason. He liked that sentiment, but he wasn't sure he believed it even when he'd been told it as a child, and he didn't know if he believed it now. But the truth — he smiled thinking of Rileigh's Aunt Daisy, who'd used the phrase — the truth in long johns with the butt flap down was that two women were alive right now because he'd come here this morning for the wrong reason.

But two small children were still missing.

Chapter Thirty-Seven

THE *BAM!* of the door banging shut went off like a rifle shot, seemed like it was so loud you could have heard it on the other side of the mountain. The sound shocked the two children and they fell silent. But that didn't last long. The little girl tuned up and started crying again, softly whining, the sound a baby rabbit might make when caught in a hay baler.

Both dog kennels were stuffed with soft, fluffy blankets and pillows, and the little girl reached out to one of the blankets, put the corner of it in her mouth and started sucking on it.

Mason was as much angry as he was frightened.

"Mommieeeee! Daddieeee, get me out of here," he demanded. "This is a cage for dogs. Get me out of this cage." He grabbed the sides of the cage, sticking his little fingers through the metal bars, and shook it as hard as he could, yelling at the same time, "I want out, out! Mommieee, I want *out!*"

He turned toward Rileigh and the anger vanished in a puff of smoke, like it'd never been there at all. "Wylie, unhook this door, pleeeease, so I can get out," he *pleaded*, not demanded. "I don't like it here. I wanna go home."

And even with all that was going on it clicked with Rileigh, what she'd never said to Georgia.

She'd noticed when she was home on leave and Liam was two that all he had to do to get his way was throw a tantrum. She almost said "behavior that's rewarded is repeated" ... but didn't, made a decision that day that she'd stuck to ever since. Georgia was her best friend and Rileigh would lay down her life for her, but how Georgia raised her children was *none of Rileigh's business.*

"Everything's going to be all right, Mason."

"I want Mommieeee," he wailed, his genuine distress breaking Rileigh's heart. Of course, he wanted his mommy. He was four years old, and somebody had *kidnapped* him and locked him in a cage!

"I'll take you home to Mommy and Daddy. I promise."

To keep that promise, Rileigh had to act fast! Because, as God made little green apples, whoever had kidnapped these children had heard that door slam and would come to investigate the sound.

She surveyed her surroundings, frantically looking for anything she could grab to use as a weapon. She wiggled and squirmed, but her ankle was held firm with the handcuffs. Nothing short of gnawing off her own foot would get her out of them. So she crawled as far as she could stretch out with the cuffs, and then moved to the sides, seeing what she could reach. But it wasn't as if there were all manner of weapons that just happened to be out of her reach. There was not much of anything at all in the basement except children's toys all over the floor.

The two kennels rested in the center of the room, each wire crate four feet long and three high. On his knees, leaned back on his heels, Mason's head cleared the top. Bending over, he could stand in it.

Some taped-shut cardboard boxes had been pushed against the walls under the windows that ran along the ground above. Beside the boxes were four plastic storage boxes stacked two on two, three red and one green. In one corner was a broom and a mop, but they were too far away to reach. In the other corner, too gloomy to get a good look at, was a pile of something. Maybe rags. Maybe old clothes, sheets, or blankets.

There was a water heater next to an almost-new washer and dryer. Sitting beside the dryer was a white plastic clothes basket. Detergent, dryer softener sheets, and spray to get out spots was on a shelf above them. Rileigh continued searching the gloom, but there was nothing that would serve her needs. No stick, no wrench, no pipe, nothing.

She moved as carefully as she could to a sitting position, the best she could manage with her ankle handcuffed to the pipe. Her head swam and when she closed her eyes, she grew dizzy. Waves of vertigo washed over her and she had to concentrate to keep her balance, to keep from toppling over on her side. She could see nothing sitting up that she'd missed surveying the room from the floor.

The crying of both children echoed in her head like an empty oil drum.

"Hey now, shhhhh," she told them. "Stop crying. Everything's going to be all right."

"I want to go home," Mason wailed. "Please Wylie. Take me home."

"Hush now, both of you. I'm going to get you out of here, but you need to be quiet now. Can you do that for me? Can you stop crying?" She wanted to plead with them to hush as Mason had pleaded with her to take him home.

The noise was hammering into her temples and she had to think.

What would she do when the kidnapper returned?

How could she possibly escape and get the children away safely?

The children continued to cry.

If she just knew what she was dealing with — *who* she was dealing with. Who had taken these children and penned them up in dog kennels? And why? Granny Maggie would never do such a thing, at least not voluntarily. She had no motive. So, who had forced her to do it and what did they want? What was the end game here?

Rileigh heard that awful mental clock tick, tick, ticking, the one that had started when Chloe Malone had disappeared. Statistically, these children had survived longer than seventy percent of kidnapped children. But their continued survival was dependent on a woman handcuffed to a pipe with no weapon and no phone.

She froze. Above the din of both children crying, she thought she heard a voice.

"Hush, Mason!" she demanded. And to her utter surprise, he did just that. She put her finger to her lips, and Chloe stopped crying, too. Now she could hear voices, but she couldn't make out what they were saying. Then the basement door opened. And Rileigh steeled herself for who might be standing there — a small, irrational part of her mind certain it would be the tall man with the angular face who'd been wearing a mask at the carnival.

It wasn't.

It was Granny Maggie! Obviously, she was *not* locked away somewhere, tied up, incapacitated.

She came out onto the landing, speaking over her shoulder, something about slamming doors, making too much noise. When she turned to look down into the basement, her face registered shocked surprise.

"What … why … what in God's name are *you* doing here?" she demanded.

Granny Maggie could help!

"My ankle is handcuffed to this water pipe," Rileigh told Granny Maggie "You have to get the key — hurry!"

The woman had taken two steps down the stairs, then stopped, wouldn't go any farther. Her eyes were huge as they surveyed what lay below her and Rileigh didn't think she'd heard a word Rileigh had just said to her.

"Granny Maggie, listen to me!"

But the old woman's face was blank. Nothing was registering.

Rileigh remembered Mama saying that the last time she'd seen the old woman, Granny Maggie's dress was on wrong side out. Was she so far gone she didn't know what had happened here?

Then Rileigh watched something like realization dawn on Granny Maggie's face. The old woman looked from Shiloh to Rileigh, and back to Shiloh.

Then she asked the little girl, her voice soft, like she didn't have enough air to say it any louder, like she'd taken a boot to the belly that'd knocked the wind out of her — "Shiloh, what did you *do?*"

"I pushed her," the little girl said. "Just like Mommy did. Mommy pushed the handyman down the basement stairs."

Chapter Thirty-Eight

SHILOH LOOKS through the crack between the curtains, and he's there. Her cat has come home!

She named him Cinnamon because she doesn't know how to tell the difference between a boy cat and a girl cat, and Cinnamon works for either. And that's what color he is. He is the color of cinnamon. Not just an ugly brown, his fluffy fur looks like maybe he started out as a white cat, but then somebody sprinkled cinnamon all over him. Shiloh liked to think that's what happened What a wonderful job — to be a cinnamon sprinkler, the person who gets to turn white cats into cinnamon-colored cats. Maybe black cats too. Maybe the cinnamon would work on a black cat. She doesn't know. Cinnamon is the only real cat — not just a picture, but alive — she has ever seen.

It has taken her weeks of patience to get Cinnamon to come down off the fence into the backyard, then out of the backyard onto the back porch. And it has taken longer than that to get the cat to allow her to pet him. That had been the hardest part. It had taken a really, really long time. There had been snow on the ground when she started trying. All the trees had green leaves on them by the time she could reach out her hand toward him and he didn't jump back or raise his hackles and hiss.

In the beginning, she used to wonder whose cat it was that walked like a trapeze artist along the top of the fence in the backyard. A tall fence. So tall nobody could see over it. Nobody could see into the backyard. And that's why Shiloh couldn't understand why Mommy wouldn't let her play out here. With that tall fence, nobody would see her. But Mommy said no.

Mommy doesn't know about Cinnamon, though.

Shiloh had decided that Cinnamon wasn't anybody else's cat. Cinnamon was his own cat. He did what he wanted whenever he wanted, and nobody owned him. But after a while, she thought of him as her cat. And now he is her cat. He comes to her house almost every day, up onto the back porch so she can feed him. Little pieces of cheese. He really likes cheese. Little pieces of lunch meat. Whatever she can steal out of the leftovers in the kitchen. When she'd first seen him on the fence, she'd wanted so badly to pet him, to feel his soft fur. That's when she decided to break the rule. The SACRED rule. Shiloh's mommy has told her over and over and over again: Don't EVER let anybody see you! If anybody found out that Shiloh lived with her mommy, they would come and take Shiloh away.

"They'll put you in an orphanage. Do you know what an orphanage is?" Her mommy had said. She hadn't known what an orphanage was. Then mommy told her it was a terrible place where they put bad children. They got spankings every day. They didn't get enough to eat. And they were cold in the wintertime because they doesn't have shoes or coats. Most of them died.

The day Shiloh decided to break the rule to go downstairs into the kitchen to get some food for the cat who was on the fence every day, she'd been so scared she was afraid she would throw up. But nothing bad happened. Nobody could see into the backyard, not with that fence. It was too tall.

The sight of Cinnamon puts a broad smile on Shiloh's face so wide she can feel it stretching her lips. Mommy is busy. She's always busy this time of day in her office. Shiloh doesn't know what she does, but she stays in there for a long time and she never comes out until lunchtime. It's a long time until lunchtime. Shiloh sneaks silently down the stairs to the kitchen. She opens the refrigerator door to see what's inside and sees a carton of half-and-half, what mommy puts in her coffee. She lifts it and can tell it's almost full. Mommy won't miss a small bowl of it, and Cinnamon would love some half and half. She quietly gets a bowl out of the cabinet, pours some half-and-half into it, and walks carefully to the back door.

She sets the bowl down on the table beside the door and unlocks all three locks quietly, so they don't make the snapping noise. Then she pushes the back door open and steps out onto the porch. It's early morning, still cool, and she loves the smells of outside.

She'd never been able to get Cinnamon to come all the way up onto the porch, so she'd moved the food she used as bait to the top porch step. That was fine. That is close enough. She takes the bowl of half-and-half and sets it down on the top porch step, then sits down on the porch beside it and watches Cinnamon jump off the fence to the ground. So far, but he never hurts himself jumping down. He pads up to the bowl of half-and-half with his tail sticking straight up in the air and begins to lap it up. Shiloh reaches out slowly, gently, and begins to stroke his fur. It is so soft. She's never felt anything as soft. Oh, how she wishes he would let her pick him up, cuddle him to her face as she petted him, feel the sound of his purring. But whenever she tries, he jumps away. Petting him will have to do, and that is enough.

Suddenly, she hears a sound and she freezes. Cinnamon freezes, too. It's the door to the basement. Before she can think what to do, the door opens and a man comes out of the basement and walks up the steps into the backyard. Cinnamon bolts, leaps back up onto the fence and down off the other side, gone. But Shiloh isn't a cat. She can't leap on the fence and jump over it to hide from the man. She sits frozen in absolute horror as he stops at the top of the steps and begins to scrape something off the thing in his hand onto the grass. He's cleaning something. He is a small man, with a gray mustache and short gray hair. She thinks maybe he won't see her just as he turns his head a little, glances her way, and smiles.

"Well, hello there," the man says.

Shiloh says nothing. She sits frozen with terror. Wants to bolt back into the house. but she's so scared she can't even move.

"What's your name?" the man asks. Still, she says nothing.

"Cat got your tongue?" the man chuckles, then notices the bowl sitting beside Shiloh on the step. "The brown cat that ran, is that your cat?"

Still scraping something off, chunks of it into the grass beside the basement steps, he keeps talking to her as he works. He doesn't look at her. His attention is focused on whatever gunk he's trying to clean out of the thing in his hands. He's dressed in blue coveralls with words above the pockets and a leather belt at his waist with tools dangling off it. The knees on the pants of the coveralls are dirty, as if he's been kneeling somewhere.

"I used to have a cat," he says. "Name was Buttons. But she got hit by a car. You better be careful with that cat of yours or it's a—"

Shiloh has been so struck dumb and terrified by the man emerging out of the basement that she didn't even notice the back door behind her opening. She jumps when she hears her mother's voice.

"You about finished?" Mommy calls out to the man in the backyard.

"Just about. This your little girl? She sure is a pretty one."

Mommy doesn't answer. Just tells Shiloh, "Go in the house now."

It isn't her mean and angry voice. It is almost cheerful. But Shiloh doesn't think it is real. She thinks Mommy is being cheerful because the man is there. Shiloh stands up and starts across the porch.

"Get that bowl," her mother says. She turns and picks up the now-empty bowl and walks past her mother into the kitchen, sets the bowl on the counter and stands waiting to see what Mommy will do.

"Come on in the house and I'll write you a check," she says to the man.

Shiloh can hear the man from inside the kitchen.

"This was your problem," he says. "Got all rusted up, but I

cleaned it out. You'll be fine now. Won't take me but a minute to put it all back together good as new."

Mommy comes back into the house and closes the kitchen door behind her. She won't even look at Shiloh. Just marches to the door at the top of the basement stairs, opens it, and stands there waiting for the man to come up the steps.

"I'm sorry, Mommy," Shiloh's voice is quavering. "I…"

Her mother shoots her a look, and she falls silent. In a couple of minutes, she hears the clomp of a man's feet on the stairs as he comes up, talking to her mother as he comes.

"I could have got a new part, but that would have cost you a lot of money. It wasn't all that hard to clean the old one." He's at the top of the stairs now and Mommy is blocking his way into the room.

"I'm so sorry," Mommy says, sounding embarrassed. "I should have said something when you were still down there. You were standing right beside it. Would you mind checking the furnace filter? The latch that holds it shut is stuck and I can't open it."

"Glad to."

Shiloh can hear the man start back down the steps, and she watches in horror as Mommy leans back on her left foot and kicks viciously out with the right—the way she learned in that kick boxing class. Shiloh hears a grunt. Mommy's foot must have hit the man in the middle of the back because Shiloh hears a small cry, then a crash as the man tumbles down the basement stairs. Mommy follows along behind him, and Shiloh hears sounds from the man grunting or moaning or something.

"Hey, what are you —" His words are cut off, and there's a whop sound. There are other sounds, too, but Shiloh doesn't know what would make a squishy sound like that. In a few minutes, Mommy comes back up the stairs. She has blood splattered on her jeans and her white t-shirt. There are even some spots in her hair, and she's carrying a bloody hammer. She tosses the bloody hammer into the sink and then turns to Shiloh, her face a mask of rage.

"*What have I told you?*" *she snarls. Shiloh's so scared she says nothing.*

"*Answer me, child. What have I told you?*"

"*Not to let anybody see me,*" *she says in a very small voice.*

"*And why can't you let anybody see you?*"

"*Because if somebody sees me, then they'll know. Somebody will come get me and take me away and they'll be mean to me and not give me enough to eat and I'll be cold and … and I'll never see you again.*"

The last words ride a sob out of her throat.

Mommy holds up the bloody hammer.

"*This,*" *she says,* "*is all your fault. What I had to do is all your fault for disobeying me, for coming downstairs when I told you not to.*"

Shiloh starts to say she's sorry, but before she can speak Mommy slaps her so hard it knocks her down on the floor, but she doesn't burst out crying. Mommy doesn't like it when she cries, so she bites her lip and says nothing and waits for Mommy to finish saying what she has to say.

"*Do you know how much trouble we're in right now? How much trouble you caused?*"

Shiloh shakes her head. Shiloh is afraid Mommy is going to hit her again and she cringes away from the blow.

"*Now you get your ass up those stairs and you stay there, young lady, until I call you back down. Is that understood?*"

"*Yes ma'am.*" *She turns on her heel, runs up the stairs to her room, and closes the door behind her. She is shaking all over, shaking so hard her teeth are chattering, so afraid in the pit of her stomach, she's afraid she'll throw up. She reaches up to her stinging cheek and feels wet, looks at her fingers and there's blood on them. That man's blood.*

Will they get in trouble? Will they come and get Shiloh and take her away? She vows to herself she'll never do anything like that again. She'll never disobey Mommy again.

And when Mommy calls up the stairs, "get your things together, we're leaving," she knows how to grab everything she owns fast and shove it into the suitcase. She's done that lots of times before. The suitcase has wheels on the bottom and it bumps along behind her on the stairs when she comes down.

She'll never see Cinnamon again, never feel Cinnamon's soft fur, never have a chance to pick the cat up and cuddle it to her face. She'll miss Cinnamon. As she goes through the living room to the door into the garage, she smells something funny, a strong smell she recognizes but can't place.

Glancing out the window, she can see Cinnamon sitting on top of the fence, somehow balancing there, licking one paw. She hopes he liked the half-and-half, wishes she could give him more of it.

"Goodbye, Cinnamon," she says, but not out loud. "I love you."

Chapter Thirty-Nine

GRANNY MAGGIE LOOKED in horror at the little girl whose hair was the color and consistency of corn silk.

"What are you saying, child?" It was clear that Granny Maggie was so staggered by the little girl's revelation that she couldn't even speak. She sat down abruptly on the step above where she stood, probably because her knees collapsed out from under her.

"You're saying your mommy…?" She tried again. "You're saying my Becca *pushed*…"

"She *had to*," the little girl cried, her voice high pitched and terrified. Looking down at her grandmother, her face was twisted in anguish, and tears ran down her cheeks and dripped off her chin. "She had to, he *saw* me, she had to push him down the stairs."

"Who?" Granny asked.

"He was a handyman. Mommy said she called him because something was broke in the basement, and he came to fix it, but I didn't know he was there. If I'd known he was there, I would never have gone out, but, but I had to feed my cat." She said the last part as if that somehow explained everything. "When mommy came out on the porch and saw him, she made him go back in the house and come up the stairs inside the house, then she pushed him down the stairs, and she went down and she hit him with a hammer. When she brought the hammer back up with her, it had blood all over it, and she told me it was all my fault because I let him see me, because I disobeyed. She said we were in trouble, that the police would come and take me away from Mommy and put me in an orphanage where there wasn't enough to eat and it was too cold, and most of the children die. If she hadn't pushed him down the stairs, the police would have come and taken me away. She *had to*."

The little girl shot a look at Rileigh. "Just like I had to push her. She's going to *tell*, Grandma Maggie, she's going to *tell*."

Rileigh felt like she'd fallen down more than a staircase. She'd fallen down Alice's rabbit hole into Wonderland, right smack out of the world of reality into what couldn't possibly be.

That little girl had *pushed* Rileigh down the stairs. What was she — nine? Ten years old, maybe? And she'd pushed Rileigh down the stairs because she'd watched her mother do the same thing — had watched her mother kill a handyman just because he saw Shiloh? None of that made any sense — surely the little girl had made it up. Dear god, that child was more than just socially awkward and painfully shy. She was a deeply disturbed little girl, living with a grandmother who was so crazy she'd kidnapped two children. Why? None of it make sense.

The old woman let out a trembling breath. Then she reached into the collar of her dress and drew a necklace out and held it in front of her. On the end of a gold chain was a gold locket. It looked like an antique, tarnished and worn.

"Becca seen this every day her whole life and kept asking about it," Granny Maggie said, barely a whisper, as if that somehow explained something. The old woman fiddled with the locket for a moment with her arthritic fingers. Then it opened up and she sat staring at what was inside. "Becca wanted to know why I wore it every day. And I did — every day. Still do. I probably ain't taken this locket off more'n half a dozen times in sixty, maybe sixty-five years. Becca kept pestering me, so finally I told her."

Chloe and Mason had stopped crying when Rileigh told them to hush and now the two of them sat silent and wide-eyed, looking at the old woman sitting on the basement stairs. Shiloh stood in the shadows above her.

"Granny Maggie, I need for you to listen to what I'm saying," Rileigh said, her tone kind, but firm and commanding.

The woman gave no indication that she'd heard a word Rileigh had said. Her eyes were fixed in a thousand-yard stare. She brought the locket to her lips and kissed it tenderly, shaking her head. "But that was a bad, bad thing. I had never ought to have told her, no matter how much she pestered me. I had never ought to have told nobody. I should have took that secret with me to the grave. But one day we were sitting on the back porch, and she kept asking me, 'What's that locket? Why does it matter to you?' And finally, I broke down and told her."

Granny Maggie shook her head again. "That there's the single worst mistake I ever made in my whole life. I had never ought to have told Becca what this is and why I treasure it so."

"Granny Maggie!" Rileigh spoke loud and abruptly, a

verbal slap on the face to bring the old woman back from wherever she'd gone. "Listen to me, Granny Maggie!"

"'Your name's Margaret,' that's what they said." The old woman went on, oblivious to Rileigh's words. "Told me to say it out loud, to say, 'My name's Margaret McCulloch.' So I said it. I was afraid not to. But that wasn't true. That was a lie. My name wasn't Margaret. My name was Marilee Nicole Bratcher ..." Her voice grew faint and childlike. "And sometimes Mommy called me Nicky."

The magnitude of the old woman's words hit Rileigh in the chest like a wrecking ball, knocking the wind out of her so she couldn't have formed words around the thousands of questions exploding in her mind even if she'd known which one to ask first.

"They didn't know about the locket, though. I kept it hidden from 'em, or they would have took it away from me. They'd never have let me keep a locket with a picture of my real mommy and daddy in it. At night, when they was asleep, I'd take it out and look at the faces and it'd make me feel better. I'd look at those faces and remember Daddy putting me on his shoulders at the parade so I could see, or Mommy singing to me when she put me to bed ..."

The old woman sang in a quiet but remarkably clear, voice. "Hush little baby, don't say a word. Mama's gonna buy you a mockingbird. And if that mockingbird don't sing, Mama's gonna buy you a diamond ring ..."

She rocked back and forth on the step, looking at the locket in her hand, oblivious to her surroundings. Maggie McCulloch ... no, *Marilee Nicole Bratcher* ... was in her own world, transported by the locket away from the pain and terror and loss in this world, as she had probably escaped dozens, maybe hundreds of times before.

Chapter Forty

GRANNY MAGGIE SAT on the step, rocking slowly back and forth, looking at the locket in her hand and singing a song she hadn't heard in more than six decades.

"If that diamond ring don't shine, Mama's gonna buy you a valentine ..."

Rileigh kept silent, left Granny Maggie there where she was in her world as she tried to sort out her own thoughts in light of the incredible revelation that Maggie McCulloch wasn't Maggie McCulloch at all. Her parents had kidnapped her when she was a little girl.

Rileigh remembered then what she'd said that day at the carnival: "I was the only kid in my class didn't know Tennessee, my homeland, and all the other kids made fun of me." Maggie hadn't known the words to the song because she hadn't learned them, and maybe she'd learned the words to some other state song. Who knew?

So many things fell together in Rileigh's head and made sense as they hadn't before. No wonder Granny Maggie had raised such a fearful little girl. She was terrified somebody was going to come and steal Becca just like someone had stolen her. That's why she wouldn't let Becca go anywhere or do anything. That's why she had the big dogs. She'd turned Becca into a terrified little mouse who grew up to be a paranoid grownup. No, more than paranoid — unbalanced … insane. Start with a neurotic woman, add in years of alcohol and drug abuse, mix with a generous portion of late-stage syphilis and stir. Unless Shiloh had made the whole thing up — and maybe she had — Becca had been so conditioned to fear she'd be kidnapped that she took her fear to the next level with her own little girl. She kept Shiloh from being kidnapped by not letting the world know she existed. Becca had been so afraid somebody would take Shiloh from her that she hid her, didn't let anyone know she even had a child!

Rileigh could square up now what she knew in her head. What she couldn't square up was how that had led Granny Maggie to kidnap Chloe and Mason. That made absolutely no sense. But right now, it really didn't matter why or even how she'd managed to pull it off. The only thing that mattered was getting those children out of here as fast as possible,

"Granny Maggie," Rileigh said as kindly and tenderly as she could. "It's me, Rileigh. Do you know who I am?"

Granny Maggie took her eyes off the locket in her hand and turned them toward Rileigh, but they were like a camera pointed in the right direction with the lens unfocused. "I'm Lily Bishop's girl, remember me?"

Rileigh continued to speak softly to the old woman, dragging her slowly back to reality, watching awareness return to Granny Maggie's eyes. Finally, she looked at Rileigh for the first time since she'd sat down on that step and really saw her. She had the locket in her hand and turned it around so Rileigh could see the picture in it. "These are my real parents. I haven't seen them in 70

years. I don't even know their names. All I know about
them is what I was told, and I know wasn't none of that
the truth. At the time, I believed it, but I know now it was
never true, none of it."

"What wasn't true?"

"They told me my parents was tourists that had come
to the Smoky Mountains from somewhere way off out
there on the flat, and that they didn't want me. They said
my parents went into a grocery store, and while I was
looking at the comic books, they went out and got in the
car and drove away and left me like you'd leave a dog on
the side of the road when you don't want it no more.

"'Course they told me that so as I wouldn't run off, so I
wouldn't tell nobody what they'd done, you know, when I
got older and maybe people would have believed me. They
said since my parents didn't want me, if I told the police
what happened to me, they'd take me away and put me in
an orphanage somewhere — that's what they did with kids
who didn't have no parents." Granny Maggie let out a
sigh. "Somewhere along the line, I decided having the
parents I had was better than no parents at all."

She shifted a little on the step and Rileigh tried to grab
the conversation and change direction. "Granny Maggie, I
need for you to–"

But Granny Maggie wasn't finished.

"They weren't bad people, Mama and Daddy. I found
out later Mama had four or five miscarriages, had two
babies stillborn. She wanted a child so bad and was so
miserable, my father couldn't hardly stand it. I heard him
talking about it once, about seeing me in that grocery store,
how pretty I was, how I looked so much like Mama it'd be
real easy to pass me off as her little girl."

"So how did they get you out of the grocery store?"

"He had a puppy. It had a big white spot over one eye

and was black all over with a little white tip on his tail. Cutest thing you ever saw, and he asked did I want to pet it, and I said sure, so he gave me the puppy, and I petted it. Then I gave it back to him, and he said, 'I got three or four more in the truck if you'd like to see them. They're even cuter than this one.' And I wanted to see the puppies, so I went with him. It was that simple. I'm sure my parents went to the sheriff and reported me missing. But they was from away from here, accusing the people of Yarmouth County of stealing their little girl — you know how that musta gone over with the locals."

Granny Maggie's eyes filled with tears.

"I always wondered how long they waited, how long my mother and father stayed here in Yarmouth County hoping somebody would find me and bring me back. And I still wonder what happened to the mama whose arms was aching to hold me — but I was gone."

She looked at Rileigh and shook her head.

"That part ain't a thing you can understand. I felt Becca growing inside me all them long months, and when she was born and I looked down at her, I realized I didn't even know what love was till that moment. I'd have given my life for her in a heartbeat, and the thought that somebody might steal her away, kept me awake night after night. I knew how easy it was to take a child. I warned Becca, I told her time and again, 'Don't talk to strangers, don't go look at nobody's dog. You stay right here with me.' And she was a good girl, she did." Granny Maggie let out a sigh. "But all them warnings … being scared all the time, that done something to her, broke something inside her. My Becca, she wasn't right in the head."

Anybody who'd pretend she didn't have a child to keep her from being kidnapped definitely had a busted main-spring. But there were way more important things to talk about right now. She sensed how fragile Granny Maggie was, though, and she needed the old woman. She needed the old woman to get her out of these handcuffs *now*, because if Shiloh had pushed Rileigh and handcuffed her to the pipe, then it was Shiloh who had taken her gun. What had Shiloh done with Rileigh's gun? The thought of that unstable little girl with a loaded gun was horrifying. She had to keep the situation calm, had to keep a lid on until Granny Maggie got her out of these handcuffs. She had to be free to deal with that little girl, or no telling what she might do. So she sat and listened as Granny Maggie rambled on.

"I was so excited when Becca told me she had a little girl. I can't even tell you how much my heart just swelled up in my chest to think my Becca was finding out what real love was, feeling what I'd felt for her when she was in my arms. I wanted that for her."

Granny Maggie took a deep breath, shot a glance up at Shiloh, then looked into Rileigh's eyes. "But my Becca didn't never have that feeling," she said carefully. "My Becca didn't never know what that was like."

Rileigh's head was reeling. What did she mean? She was clearly being intentionally vague in an effort to hide what she was saying from the little girl standing on the landing, but Rileigh was lost.

"Sometimes I think the happiest I ever was in my life was when I was driving back here with Shiloh from California. Them days on the road, them was happy days," she let out a sigh. "But other times, I know that I was happiest before I found out what my Becca had done."

Chapter Forty-One

RILEIGH HAD LISTENED as Granny Maggie poured out the horror story of what had happened to her when she was a little girl and what she'd found when she got to California. She said nothing, just listened. It was as if Granny Maggie had held it in for so long that once she started spilling it out, she couldn't stop until she had vomited all the horror out of her soul.

Rileigh had a thousand unanswered questions, and maybe they never would be answered. Rileigh understood the old woman's wish to give the beautiful little girl a good life. But there was nowhere inside Rileigh that understood the rest of it. And she couldn't stop the question before it left her lips.

"You just got your granddaughter back. Why did you take Chloe?"

Granny Maggie looked surprised and confused.

"Oh, you got this all wrong. You don't understand—"

"I understand all I need to understand. You kidnapped Chloe Malone—*why?*"

"I didn't."

Rileigh's mind stumbled. "What …?"

"I didn't kidnap her." Granny Maggie let out a long sigh and she looked up to the little girl on the landing. "Shiloh did."

Just when you thought it was safe to go back in the water.

"Are you telling me–" Rileigh was actually sputtering. "—that you didn't take Chloe from the carnival?"

Granny Maggie nodded. "I didn't know she was in the back of the truck until we got back to the house. My hearing aids was going in and out and I couldn't hear nothing. I don't know if she was making any noise back there, but she could have been leading a brass band in the back of that truck and I wouldn't have heard a thing."

Whoa, whoa, whoa, whoa. Rileigh's mind stumbled, tripping over her own lack of understanding.

"*Shiloh* took her?"

"I opened up the back door of that camper and there she was. I thought, did she climb in the truck and we didn't notice? And then Shiloh said, 'You told me I could have anything I wanted when I came to live in the mountains and what I wanted is a little sister. Mommy always promised me one.'"

"Ok fine. All right, I get it. *Shiloh* took her. Why didn't *you* take her home?" Rileigh tried to keep the rage and accusation out of her voice. "Why didn't you call her parents and tell them that Chloe was with you? Shiloh's what, ten, eleven years old? She wanted a little sister and did something stupid. And Shiloh definitely needs some counseling — but it could have, it *should* have ended right there."

"It wouldn't have ended there. They'd have took Shiloh from me."

Rileigh blew by her words.

"What were you planning on doing with Chloe? She's a five-year-old child and you kept her locked her up in a dog kennel." Rileigh had been holding tight to her growing anger, but she felt her control over it slipping through her fingers. She was so outraged that she sputtered to a stop, couldn't even finish. She dragged in a breath and looked at the old woman whose eyes were wide with confusion and shock. "Why did you take Mason?"

"Well, see, Chloe wet her pants. She, you know, she didn't make it to the... She wet her pants and I didn't have no clothes that would fit her. So I had to go into Walmart and buy some clothes for her."

"So you went into town to Walmart to buy her some clothes. And then ... what?"

"Then we got home, and the same thing happened as happened before."

Rileigh was certain that Mason had not been sitting quietly in the back of the camper as Chloe had been.

"Only this time, I heard hollering in the back of the camper, and I looked over at Shiloh and I said, 'No, you *didn't.'* She just smiled at me, said she wanted a little brother too. I got out of the truck and I ran around to the back and opened the door, and there was that little boy. He was pitching a fit. Said he wanted to go home, wanted his mommy."

"Can you blame him? You'd just kidnapped him. *Kidnapped* him! Are you crazy?"

Granny Maggie looked like someone had slapped her. "I was trying to figure out some way that I could undo what Shiloh done. Some way I could take the children home and it would be like it never happened."

Rileigh was incredulous. "Like it never happened? You have traumatized these children. They'll never get over what you did to them. How could you do a thing like that?

Especially after the same thing had happened to you. How could you?"

"I was just trying to save my Shiloh. The police woulda took her away and I wouldn't never, ever see her again. She'd be *gone.*"

"That's a ridiculous overreaction. Of course you'd see her again. You're her grandmother."

"No, I ain't."

Rileigh couldn't breathe. She tried to speak. Her lips formed the word, "What...?" but she had no air to propel it out of her mouth.

"Becca *took* her. That picture I was showing everybody of Shiloh in a stroller? Becca took the picture. Then she took Shiloh. Snatched her right out of that stroller in a park."

Granny Maggie looked up at Shiloh, whose face was as white as a new gym sock. The old woman mouthed, "I'm sorry," but didn't say the words out loud. Maybe she couldn't.

"That's why Becca had to hide her away. Not 'cause she was afraid somebody would kidnap Shiloh. Becca was afraid somebody'd find out she already had. That's why we had to come back to the mountains, why I left my Becca there—" The rest of the words rode a sob out of her throat. "—to *die alone,* 'cause soon as she died, they'd have found Shiloh. Becca wasn't her mother. And I didn't have no right to her, cause I ain't her grandmother."

Rileigh looked up at Shiloh. She was as still as a statue, catatonic, no look of any kind on her face.

"I never meant to hurt nobody," Grandma Maggie said, wonder in her voice that anyone would suspect she would.

And Rileigh was reminded how she had described Granny Maggie to Mitch when she came up to their booth that day to introduce Shiloh. She'd said, "She's a crazy old lady." And that's what she was. That didn't excuse what she did, but it might have explained a little of it. Granny Maggie obviously had some form of dementia, like Mama did.

When she saw her wildest dream suddenly come true — a beautiful little girl to raise — she couldn't let it go.

All of that— the whys and the hows — was to sort out later. Right now, Rileigh had to get these children — all *three* of them — back to *their parents*.

"Granny Maggie, you need to call the police *right now*. These children need to go home."

As soon as Rileigh said that, it was like she had reanimated the two children sitting despondent in dog kennels. Both children began to cry at the same time. Surprisingly, Mason didn't throw some kind of tantrum. He was just a scared little boy who wanted his mommy, sobbing inconsolably.

Rileigh put steel in her voice. *"Now,* Granny Maggie, right now, you go up those stairs and you dial 911. Do you hear me? *Now!"*

It was like Rileigh had flipped a light back on inside some dark recess in the old woman's mind. Granny Maggie nodded her head and rose to shaky legs, then stepped back up the stairs to the landing. She turned then, the tears flowing again down her cheeks.

"I'm so sorry. I didn't ever mean for nobody to get hurt. I was just trying to rescue my little Shiloh. I didn't mean to hurt two other children. I'm so sorry," she read the cold, stern look on Rileigh's face and hung her head. "I'll call the police, tell them to get here fast as they can."

Shiloh moved as quick as a rabbit. She rushed the two steps to her grandmother, screaming, *"Noooo!"* She hit the old woman in the chest, knocked her backwards, and

Granny Maggie tumbled head over heels until the bottom two steps broke beneath her, then she fell with a clattering crash to the basement floor and lay still.

"No!" screamed the little girl. "No, no, no, no. You can't call the police. I don't want to go to some orphanage where it's cold and I'll be hungry! No!"

She turned and ran out of the basement, slamming the door shut behind her. The second slam silenced the crying children for a second time. Rileigh sat shocked, looking at the old woman lying in a crumpled heap a few feet from the dog kennel where Chloe Malone cringed in a corner.

Now what was Rileigh going to do?

Chapter Forty-Two

RILEIGH and both of the children sat in stunned silence, the sound of the slamming door echoing off the concrete basement walls. Rileigh looked at the crumpled body of the old woman lying at the foot of the stairs. There was a trickle of blood seeping out the corner of her mouth, and her head was twisted on her neck at an unnatural angle. Maggie McCullough ... no, Marilee Nicole Bratcher, was dead.

The enormity of that took a second to absorb, but Rileigh shook off the shock. She had to find a way to get out of here, without Granny Maggie's help. She turned and examined the handcuff fixing her ankle to the water pipe again. The cuffs would hold firm, and the pipe wasn't going anywhere, and neither was Rileigh, not until somebody found her — somebody packing a hack saw, or a key to the cuffs.

"Rileigh, I want to go home," Mason said, and for the first time, Chloe spoke up. Her voice was trembling, but she sounded remarkably calm. "Will you please call

Mommy and tell her to come and get me? I want to go home now."

Rileigh looked at both of the children, and her heart broke. These poor kids had been locked up in dog cages.

But, in actual fact, it's not like they were in small boxes. The cages were large. The bottoms of the cages were covered in soft blankets and pillows. And obviously, they had been fed. You could see the remains of sandwiches and chip wrappers and soft drinks everywhere, and the toys all over the basement floor seemed to indicate that they hadn't been kept in the kennels all the time. But just because they were comfortable didn't mitigate the fact that they were kidnapped children and Rileigh had to get them out of here.

"You'll be going home real soon, Chloe," Rileigh said. "Mason, honey, I'll call your Mommy and Daddy just... as soon as I can. It won't be long now."

She couldn't see any way to free herself from the handcuffs or the water pipe. But maybe she could get the kids out of the kennels. She could remove the zip lock ties if she could reach them. But she was too far away to reach the nearest kennel, which was Mason's.

Rileigh thought for a moment, then unfastened her belt, pulling it out of the belt loops on her pants.

"Mason, honey, I need you to listen. I'm going to toss the end of this belt over to you. You need to reach out through the bars to grab it and pull the belt back into the kennel with you. Do you understand?"

"Uh-huh," he said, sniffling and wiping his nose on the back of his hand as he nodded his head.

Rileigh reached out as far as she could, holding onto the belt buckle with one hand and tossing the other end of the belt toward Mason. It clumped down on the floor too far from the kennel for him to reach. She tried again and again. Finally, it landed only a few inches away from the kennel, and the little boy stuck his fingers out between the bars, managing to hook one around the belt and draw it back through the bars.

"Good job, Mason, good job," she said.

It flashed across her mind like a comet through the night sky, the image of Georgia's face last night when she sat on the rock beside the Notmuchuva Waterfall, sobbing, believing her little boy was dead.

Rileigh would get this kid home somehow. She would get all of these children out of this … somehow.

"Mason, what I'm going to do is use this belt to drag the kennel close enough to me so that I can get those zip ties off and let you out. That means you're going to have to hold onto the belt really tight when I start pulling. Can you do that?"

"Uh-huh, I can hold real tight. I'm strong."

"Yes, you are, you're very strong. Now grab it with both hands." As soon as Mason had a firm grip on the belt with both hands, Rileigh began to put pressure on the belt, trying to pull the crate across the floor toward her without pulling the belt out of Mason's hands. It didn't work. Mason couldn't hold on tight enough, and the belt came out of his hands and snapped back out through the bars to the floor. She tossed it back at him, and he tried again. It still didn't work. Mason wasn't strong enough to hold onto the belt while she pulled the kennel.

"We're going to do something different this time," Rileigh said and tossed the end of the belt toward the kennel again. When Mason had pulled it inside the kennel, she told him. "I want you to pull the whole belt into the kennel."

Mason pulled the belt through the bars until the buckle stuck.

"You'll have to turn the buckle sideways, sweetheart, to get it to fit through the bars." Mason turned the belt sideways and eased the buckle through. Now he had the whole belt inside the kennel with him.

"Mason, do you know how to fasten a belt?"

"Of course I know how to fasten a belt. I'm a big boy." With more alacrity than Rileigh would have expected, he shoved the end of the belt through the buckle and poked the stem through a hole beyond it.

"Okay, Mason, listen carefully. I want you to unfasten the belt from the buckle." He did. "Now, push the end of the belt out of the kennel and then pull it back in *around one of the bars*. Do you know what I mean?"

"Uh-uh." He shook his head in confusion.

Rileigh kept the frustration out of her voice. "It's simple, sweetie. Can you stick your tongue out at me?"

Mason didn't move.

"Go on, do it." She stuck her tongue out at him and the little boy stuck his tongue out at her.

"Ok, now stick the end of the belt out between the bars like you just stuck your tongue out between your teeth, just a little way."

He poked his tongue out of his mouth … and the end of the belt out between the bars.

"Now, with your other hand, grab the end of the belt on the outside and pull it back into the kennel *around the bar* …"

He'd already figured out what she wanted. His little fingers reached out and grabbed the end of the belt, then pulled it back into the kennel.

"Yay, Sweetie, you're doing great. Now, fasten the belt buckle — but don't stick the thing through any of the holes. Just pull the whole belt through the buckle and keep pulling until the belt is tight around the bar." His hands were clumsy, but Mason got the drift of what she wanted and he finally managed to pull the belt tight around the bar. Now she had to get him to toss her the end of the belt so she could —

Rileigh heard a sound from the landing above and looked up.

Shiloh stood just inside the basement door, looking down at Rileigh and the other two children. She held Rileigh's pistol in her right hand, her finger inside the trigger guard.

Chapter Forty-Three

RILEIGH FROZE WITH TERROR. But she grabbed hold of it and kept the fear out of her voice.

With her heart pounding so hard she could hear each beat thud in her ears, Rileigh said calmly, "Have you ever held a real gun before, Shiloh?"

"No, but I've seen guns on TV."

"Do you understand that you have to be very careful with a gun or it might go off accidentally?"

"It won't go off if you don't pull the trigger."

"That's right, it won't. But sometimes people accidentally pull the trigger when they don't mean to. Do you know how to keep that from happening?"

"No."

"Move your finger out of that circle where the trigger is and wrap your finger around the *outside* of the circle. Then you won't accidentally pull the trigger."

The little girl did as Rileigh instructed and tried to put her finger around the outside of the trigger guard, but her finger wasn't long enough and she couldn't do it.

"It won't reach."

"Okay, your finger's not long enough to hook it around the outside of the circle. So here's what you have to do. You need to lay your finger down along the top of the circle, so you're pointing your finger the same direction that you're pointing the gun."

The little girl stretched her index finger out along the bottom of the barrel.

Rileigh gasped in relief.

Then Shiloh turned the barrel of the gun back toward herself and Rileigh managed not to scream.

"Sweetheart, don't point the gun at your face!" she said, her voice shaking.

The child was looking down the barrel, examining it. Rileigh couldn't tell where her finger was.

"The hole on the end where the bullet comes out isn't very big. The bullets must be real little."

"*Please,*" Rileigh pleaded, "point the gun at the ceiling or the wall, not at your face. Okay?"

The little girl shrugged her shoulders and sighed, and then to Rileigh's utter horror, she tossed the gun on the floor. Rileigh cringed, but the gun didn't fire.

"I don't have time to play with the gun." And then for the first time, she seemed to notice Granny Maggie. "Is Granny Maggie still asleep?"

Rileigh responded calmly. "Yeah, she's still asleep."

"Good, I want her to be asleep. I want you all to be asleep. Because it'll be ugly if you're not."

"What will be ugly, sweetheart?"

"I've decided to run away. I'm going to go live in the woods so the police can't come and get me and take me to an orphanage—"

"Sweetheart, that's not true." The little girl stopped. "Honey, it isn't true. The police won't take you away—"

"Yes, they will. My mommy said they will. She said

they would take me away and put me…" The little girl was getting upset. And an upset little girl with a loaded gun on the floor in front of her was not an ideal situation.

"Okay, I'm sorry. I didn't mean to contradict your mother. I just meant that, well…"

She looked over at Mason. "Mason knows the sheriff. Don't you, Mason?"

"Uh-huh, his name is Mitch. He's Wylie's boyfriend." Rileigh couldn't help a small smile. Little pitchers have big ears.

"That's right, Mason. The sheriff of the county is my … boyfriend. He's a really, really nice man. You'd like him."

"No, I wouldn't. He's the police. The police are bad. Mommy said they're always bad. She said they'd would take me away and—"

"Okay, okay. I'd love for you to meet my boyfriend, the sheriff. But if you don't want to—"

"I got a pillowcase off the bed and put stuff in it. Some bread and two Dr. Peppers and the candy out of the bowl and the cookies that Granny Maggie made this morning."

"Are you going on a picnic?"

"Weren't you listening? I'm going to run away. And I'll need some food if I'm going to live in the woods. You know, like Tarzan."

"Sure, just like Tarzan."

"And I'm going to have a cat. I'm going to have two cats. Two cats that are the color of cinnamon. Have you ever seen a cinnamon cat?"

"No, I never have."

"Well, I have and they're beautiful. I had a cat that was cinnamon. I named him Cinnamon. But then the handyman came and …"

The little girl looked like she was about to cry.

"What happened to your cat named Cinnamon?"

"He ran away. Just like I'm going to do now. And not just cats. I'm going to have puppies, lots of puppies. Puppies that have little white spots on their tails."

Rileigh wasn't sure exactly how old Shiloh was. She was a big kid, so it was hard to tell. But however old she was, she was enormously immature. She reasoned like a five- or six-year-old.

"What's going to happen to *us* when you run away and live in the woods?"

"You won't care," she said, shaking her head. "By then you won't care about anything."

Rileigh felt a chunk of lead descend into the bottom of her belly. "Why won't we care, Shiloh?"

"I just came to tell Mason and Chloe goodbye." Shiloh looked down at Mason. "I wanted a little brother. And you're so cute, I thought —"

"I don't want you to be my big sister." Mason sneered. "I don't like you. You made me come here and I didn't want to."

"Mason ...." Rileigh tried to sound calm and commanding at the same time.

"Oh, you would have liked it after a while," Shiloh said.

"No, I wouldn't. I'd never like it. I'd never like you! I want my mommy and my daddy. I want to go home."

All Rileigh needed right now was for Mason to have a meltdown.

"You are going to go home, sweetheart. It's okay," Rileigh said, as soothing as she could.

Shiloh went on as if she hadn't heard a word the little boy said.

"We'd have had a good time, me being your big sister."
She looked at Chloe. "Mommy always told me I could
have a little sister." Chloe said nothing. Just looked up at
Shiloh with big, frightened eyes. "We could have played
dolls. I've never had anybody to play dolls with."

Mason began to yell louder. "I want to go home. I want
my mommy and daddy."

"We'd have had fun, all three of us. We'd have played
and played all day, every day. I've never had anybody to
play with."

"I want to go home."

"Mason, honey," Rileigh said, with as much sternness
as she dared put in her voice. "You need to hush now,
sweetheart, okay?"

"I don't want to hush. I want to go home."

Shiloh let out a big sigh. "But it's too late now. We'll
never get to play now. I need to go find a place in the
woods that will make a good house to live in. Somewhere
way far into the woods so that the police will never find me
there."

"I hope the bears eat you up," Mason yelled.

Shiloh's eyes flew open wide. "Bears?"

"Yeah, big black bears. Their teeth are sharp and they
have claws."

"Mason, honey, you need to hush."

"I hope they eat you up. I hope they bite your nose off
and —"

"They won't eat me up," the little girl said, and she
reached down and picked the gun back up. Rileigh gasped.
"If the bears come at me, I'll shoot them with the gun."

"Shiloh, honey, remember what I said about accidentally pulling the trigger."

"I'll shoot the bears if they try to eat me up. I'll
shoot—"

Bang!

The gunshot echoed around the walls of the basement, ten times louder than the door slam. Everything was quiet then. Until Chloe started to cry.

Chapter Forty-Four

MITCH DIDN'T KNOW anybody named Mildred Sandusky. But the dispatcher said the woman had asked for him specifically, said she wanted to talk to him about Rileigh. So he told the dispatcher to give the woman his cell number. He'd talk to her while he drove to the home of the person next on his list — the man who'd bought charcoal at Walmart, Ben Pendergast.

"This is Sheriff Webster. What can I do for you?"

"My name is Mildred Sandusky and I'm calling because Rileigh needed some information from me, told me to give her a call if I found anything, but I've tried and tried, and I can't reach her."

Mitch had tried a couple of times to reach Rileigh as well, but her phone went to voicemail.

"What was it she asked you, Mrs. Sandusky?"

"She said her mother remembered a kidnapping case from when she was a girl, which would have been more than sixty years ago. Rileigh asked if I would mind looking in the back issues to see if Lily was remembering correctly."

Translate that: Rileigh was checking to see if her mother was making it up.

"What did you find?"

"On June 17, 1956, a little girl disappeared out of a grocery store here in Black Bear Forge."

Mitch sat up straighter in the seat.

"Tell me about it."

"Her name was Marilee Nicole Bratcher. She was the daughter of a tourist. They had stopped at the Get 'n Go Convenience Store to stock up on picnicking supplies. The little girl went into the store with them, but when it was time to leave, they couldn't find her. The sheriff was called, and from what I can determine, they pretty much turned Black Bear Forge wrong-side out looking for that little girl, but they never found her."

Mitch didn't like the sound of that.

"There's more. A couple of days after the kidnapping, eight-month-old Samuel Hansford disappeared out of his car seat while his mother was paying for her gasoline. She pumped it, went in to pay for it, and when she came back out, the baby was gone. As you could imagine, she went postal. But the strange thing was that the baby boy was found unharmed on the steps of St. Michael's Church only a couple of hours after he was taken."

"And nobody saw anything?"

" It certainly didn't say anything in the newspaper stories about witnesses or arrests or anything. They never found the kidnappers for either one of those children. They never made an arrest in either case. And they never found Marilee Nicole Bratcher."

Never found her. The words were chilling.

"Thank you so much for giving me a call, Mrs. Sandusky. I appreciate the information. If you think of anything else, anything at all involving the kidnappings, please let me know."

There was a moment of silence.

"Well … oh, I'm sure it's nothing."

"It's something or you wouldn't have thought of it. Tell me."

"It's not about the kidnapping. It's about the *story* of the kidnapping. It happened about twenty years ago, right after I went to work at the Gazette. I started right out of high school, at the bottom, selling classified ads, and one afternoon, Granny Maggie… you'd know her as Margaret McCulloch, came in, said she was going to have a garage sale. As we were filling out the form, the teenagers who'd been going through the bound volumes came down out of the attic. That's where all the old newspapers are kept. They had been working on some class assignment, doing genealogical research on their families. But that's not what they were talking about. They'd come upon that newspaper, the June 17 issue of 1956, and the kidnapping was all over the front page. One of them said something about the little girl who was kidnapped, something like, 'You think maybe she's still alive, that Marilee Bratcher?' And another one answered. 'No, but I bet she's buried here, like somebody kidnapped her and then killed her and her body's somewhere in these mountains.' Something like that. Then the first kid said, 'You reckon her family's still looking for her?' I'm not getting what they said exactly right — it was twenty years ago."

"You're doing just fine Mrs. Sandusky, please go on."

"I don't know exactly how to describe it, but Granny Maggie went off on those kids. Went nuts. She screamed at them that the little girl wasn't dead, that her body wasn't buried up in the mountains. Said the girl's parents never gave up on her, waited their whole lives for their little girl to be found and brought home to them, that they died waiting. Then she just ran out of the office. Didn't finish filling out the classified ad form, and she'd already paid for the ad. Just left the form laying on the counter and ran out."

Mitch ended the call with Mrs. Sandusky, trying to make sense of this new information. Ok, not new information — old information, more than sixty years old. The daughter of a tourist couple from Indiana vanished in Black Bear Forge and nobody ever saw her again. Then a local baby snatched out of a car seat and returned to church steps within hours. What possible connection could there have been between the two kidnappings? Did law enforcement ever find a connection? What possible connection could there be to the cases he was investigating now? None of the incidents were even remotely similar. And six decades ago …

Still … he called the dispatcher and told her to get Deputy Rawlings to dig around in the records in the basement of the courthouse and see if he could locate the original police reports about the kidnappings. Maybe Rileigh had talked to Granny Maggie and could shed some light on her strange reaction to the newspaper story. He punched favorites and then Rileigh's name, listened to the call go directly to voice mail.

He'd try to call her again after he talked to Ben Pendergast.

Chapter Forty-Five

THE BULLET from the gun in Shiloh's hands knocked a big chunk of concrete off the wall a few feet above where Chloe sat, exploding tiny bits of stinging shrapnel. Pieces of it peppered Chloe's head and arms — Rileigh knew from experience that it felt like bee stings — and she burst into tears. Shiloh dropped the gun again with a clatter. It slid across the landing, and for a wild moment Rileigh thought maybe it would slide off the edge and down to the basement floor where maybe Rileigh could grab it, keep it away from Shiloh ... but it didn't. It went to the edge and stopped there.

"I didn't know guns made such a big noise," Shiloh said, breathless, then she started tentatively toward the gun on the floor.

"Shiloh, honey, Mason was teasing. There aren't any bears in those woods. He was just kidding."

"No, I wasn't." Mason was indignant. "There are, too—"

Rileigh glowered at him. "Mason. *Shut! Up!*"

To her astonishment, he did.

She turned back to Shiloh. "There aren't any bears, really, I promise. No bears in the woods. You don't need the gun to protect yourself." Shiloh stopped, indecisive. "And every time you pull the trigger on a gun, the sound is twice as loud as the time before. You knew that, didn't you?"

Rileigh's heart was hammering in her ears, and she held her breath.

The little girl looked fearfully at the gun, then turned away.

Chloe had stopped crying and Mason was silent. Shiloh spoke into that silence, looking at the two children in dog kennels.

"I came to tell you goodbye. I wanted to be your big sister, and I'm sorry that I couldn't be. I will miss you."

Then she turned her eyes on Rileigh. "I'm sorry," she said.

Rileigh did not like the sound of that.

"Sorry for what, sweetheart?"

"Sorry that I have to do what Mommy did when she pushed the handyman down the stairs."

For a moment, Rileigh wondered if the little girl meant that she was going to go get a hammer and hit Rileigh in the head with it. But that's not what she meant.

"Mommy had to do it. Had to fix it so nobody would know what she did, that she pushed him down the stairs and hit him with the hammer."

Even though she really didn't want to hear the answer to the question, Rileigh asked it anyway. "What did your Mommy do so nobody would know that she had killed the handyman?"

"She set the house on fire."

The little girl turned on her heel and did *not* go to the stairs to pick up the gun. She just walked out of the basement and closed the door behind her. Rileigh heard the sound of the deadbolt clicking shut.

Rileigh figured Mason and Chloe didn't understand what Shiloh had threatened.

"She said she was going to set the house on fire," Mason said, awe in his voice. "Are we all going to burn up?"

So much for not understanding.

"It's okay, Mason."

"It's not okay if she burns the house down with us in it. We'll die!"

"She's not going to set the house on fire. It's okay. Starting a big fire is really hard. She'll just burn her fingers on something and give up." Rileigh hoped that was true, then she changed the subject. "Now we need to get back to you handing me the end of that belt so that I can pull the kennel close enough to get that plastic zip tie off and open the door."

Mason poked the end of the belt out between the bars and started scooting it toward Rileigh. Rileigh lay on her belly and stretched out as far as the handcuffed ankle would allow, reached as far as she could stretch out her arm … and was finally able to hook the belt with her fingers. Then she sat up and dragged Mason's kennel across the floor to her. Up on one knee, she turned the kennel around so she could reach the plastic zip ties on the front that kept the door shut. Plastic zip ties were a bear, the method of choice for criminals to tie up their victims these days. But with considerable effort, it was possible to work the plastic back around and unhook the fastener.

When Rileigh got the last of the zip ties off and the door swung open, Mason leapt out and into her arms and started sobbing. She held the little boy tight, rocking him back and forth, kissing the top of his head and his face, crooning the kinds of things she knew Georgia would be crooning to him as soon as she got her hands on him. "It's okay, sweetie, it's okay, you're gonna be just fine. It's all right, baby. Don't cry, sweetie, you'll be home soon."

She held him that way for as long as he wanted to hold on, rocking him gently back and forth until he finally calmed down.

"I love you, Wylie," he said and planted a big kiss on her face.

"I love you too, sweetheart, and I'm gonna take you home to Mommy and Daddy just as soon as I can, but you have to help me just like you did before. Will you be a big boy and help me?"

"I'm a big boy," he said and doubled his hands into fists and curled his arms up like a weightlifter. It was so adorable it made her heart ache.

"Here's what I need you to do. Go over there and push Chloe's kennel to me so I can get the ties off and let her out. Are you strong enough to do that?"

"I'm a big boy. I'm strong."

The boy ran to the back side of the kennel. He shoved with all his might and moved it an inch, two inches.

"You're doing great, Mason. You're strong."

"I'm strong. I'm a big boy." He shoved, and the kennel moved another couple of inches.

"I'm so proud of you, Mason," Rileigh said. "I'm going to tell your mommy how big and strong you are."

Mason kept pushing. His face turned red with effort.

"And Eli?" he gasped. "Because he thinks he's stronger than me, and he's not."

"I'll tell Eli ... and *Liam*, too." That built a fire under Mason. The thought of besting his oldest brother at anything was a mighty incentive.

With lots of encouragement, lots of stopping to rest,

and lots more encouragement, eventually Mason got the kennel close enough that Rileigh could grab it and pull it the rest of the way. She had less trouble with the plastic zip ties on Chloe's because she'd figured out how to do it by then. In short order, she had unhooked the ties, opened the door, and held out her arms to the little girl. Chloe crawled out of the kennel and leapt into her arms and started to cry. Rileigh did as she had done with Mason, holding the child close.

"Hey there, sweetie pie. Everything's going to be fine now, just fine." She patted the little girl on the back and kissed her, hugged her tight, and rocked her back and forth as she cried. "You need to hush now, sweetie. Everything's going to be fine now. I'm going to take you home to mommy and daddy and tonight you can sleep in your own bed … with Mittens."

The little girl sniffled and snuffled, her breathing hitching in her throat.

"Mittens!"

Chloe stopped crying.

"I smell something funny," Mason said.

Suddenly, Rileigh did, too.

Smoke.

Chapter Forty-Six

RILEIGH STOPPED ROCKING Chloe and sniffed. She smelled smoke all right. Somehow Shiloh had managed it. She'd set something on fire. Maybe not the whole house, but she had definitely started a fire. She had to get these kids out of this basement. Thankfully, as she had been rocking Chloe, she had come up with a plan.

"I need you to come over here and stand by me, out of the way," Rileigh told the children. They both obeyed. Rileigh got a good grip on Chloe's kennel and shoved it as hard as she could toward the wall. It slid across the floor and stopped a few feet short of the wall. "Both of you — scoot that kennel all way to the wall. Can you do that?"

The two children grabbed hold of the empty kennel, it took no time at all to scoot it the last few feet against the wall.

"Mason, you see those boxes over there, the plastic ones stacked on top of each other?"

"Uh-huh."

"Go see what's in them."

He and Chloe both ran to the boxes. It took him a minute to figure out how to get the plastic lids off, but as soon as he did, Mason turned back to her and smiled.

"It's Christmas decorations."

Perfect.

"Okay, empty that box. Take everything out of it — just dump it on the floor." The children had a good time doing that, pulling out tinsel and boxes of Christmas lights and a tattered tree skirt. They had the first box almost unloaded when a smoke alarm somewhere in the house began to wail.

The children stopped, looked at Rileigh with big, frightened eyes.

"Go on now, get the rest of the decorations out of the box."

Before long, the other alarms in the house joined in the cry. The smoke smell was getting stronger.

Once the children had the box empty, she instructed them to turn it upside down and put it on top of the dog kennel, next to the wall. It was a big, sturdy plastic storage tub, but with the two of them to accomplish the task, they managed it.

As soon as they had it in place, Rileigh could tell it wouldn't be tall enough, so she told them to empty out another box.

The children tore into the second box of Christmas decorations, throwing wreaths and plastic holly and garlands every which way. As they worked, Rileigh looked up at the landing. All the smoke alarms in the house were shrieking, and now she could see smoke sliding like gray fog under the closed basement door.

"Put that box next to the other one, on top of the kennel."

The children were getting tired now, and they struggled to lift the box up onto the kennel, even with both them working on it.

When she announced, "One more!" both children started whining.

Mason plopped down on the floor beside the kennel. "Those boxes are heavy."

"I can't pick up another one," Chloe said.

And of course, the ever popular "I want to go home now!" from both of them.

"If you want to go home, you have to empty the boxes and stack them up. That's how you're going to get out of here."

Mason looked at the kennel with boxes on top of it and he got it.

"We're going to climb on the boxes and then out the window!" he cried.

"That's right. But you'll need one more box to make the stack tall enough."

Mason tore into the third box, with Chloe helping, but without his enthusiasm. The pile of Christmas junk on the floor grew taller ... as a gray haze began to spread across the ceiling of the basement. The smell of smoke was pungent now. The shrieking of the alarms was not as loud now, as the fire reached one after another of them and silenced it. Rileigh could hear the sound of the fire itself now, a hungry, growling sound.

When the third box was empty, Rileigh told the children how to position it on top of the other two, making a pyramid.

"Can you climb up on top of the boxes now, Mason?"

The little boy started up on top of the two boxes.

"Be care—"

Then he was on top of the third, reaching up to the window. The window opened out, with a latch at the top. Mason could easily reach the window ledge, but not the latch on the top of the window.

"Let me try. I'm taller," Chloe said.

"She told *me* to do it," Mason said.

"Mason, move and let Chloe try," Rileigh told him. The little boy stuck out his lower lip and climbed down to the first row of boxes to make room for Chloe on the top box. Then he began to cough. The smoke was sinking down from the ceiling, and it was low enough to reach the children. They had to hurry!

Chloe was not a little monkey like Mason. She took her time, careful to get her balance as she climbed. The box stack was wobbly and unstable, and she was tentative, ready to step back down.

"You can do it, Chloe. I know you can!"

Then she was on her hands and knees on the top box. She stood up slowly into the lowering smoke and started coughing. She stretched her hand up as high as she could. But she couldn't reach the latch either. She began to cough too.

If they had time, they could empty another couple of boxes, make the pyramid wider at the bottom so they could add a third level. But they were running out of time. The smoke was getting thicker and the rumble of the fire was unmistakable now.

"Okay kids, this is what we're going to do. Mason, you're going to help Chloe reach that window latch."

"I want to go home," Mason said, "I want Mommy."

The time for reassurance was gone.

"The only way for you to go home is to climb out that window. If you won't do that, you're stuck here with me … and the fire."

Both children looked terrified.

"Can you be a big boy? You need to get down on your knees and let Chloe climb on your back to reach the latch."

"Why can't Chloe get down on her knees and let *me* climb on top of *her*?"

Rileigh was done.

"Listen up, Mason, you're going to do this my way because I said so. Do you understand me? And unless you want to have your little butt busted worse than you've ever had it busted in your entire life, you get down on your hands and knees and you let Chloe climb up on your back."

Mason dropped to his hands and knees.

"I'm scared!" Chloe cried.

"So am I sweetie pie. But you have to be brave."

The children were squinting in the thickening smoke, both coughing.

If Chloe didn't climb right now, Mason would start coughing, wiggling and …

Chloe put one knee on Mason's back, then climbed up on top of him. Using the wall to keep her balance, she slowly stood up. She could reach the latch easily now. She shoved. It didn't move. It was stuck.

"It won't open."

"Try again. Try harder. *Push!*"

Chloe pushed again, shoved as hard as—

The catch let go and the window flopped out onto the ground. When it did, the opening instantly became a chimney, sucking smoke out of the house. Within seconds, the thin layer on the basement ceiling became a boiling gray mass.

"Climb out!" Rileigh cried. "Do it *now*."

Chloe scrambled up over the ledge and out the

window. Mason leapt to his feet, tall enough to grab hold of the window ledge. He tried to lift himself up on it, but there was nothing to hold onto, nothing to … then Chloe was there, pulling on his arm, dragging him.

Suddenly, they were out! They were free!

Rileigh didn't even realize she'd been holding her breath until she let it out. She sagged back onto the floor and wanted to cry. They were out. But they weren't *safe*, not yet. Right now, they were two little kids standing beside a house that was on fire.

"Mason, Mason, listen to me." Mason stuck his head back in the window and started coughing.

"You and Chloe have to get away from the house. Run! Run into the woods and wait there. Someone will come when they see the smoke."

And that was true as far as it went. But the mountains had been named "the Smokies" for a reason. The mists that hung above the trees, in hollows and valleys looked just like smoke. Even trained rangers in fire towers had trouble telling the difference.

"You have to get out, Wylie," Mason said.

Rileigh was coughing hard now.

"Don't worry about me. I'm fine. Go on now, Mason. Chloe— run!"

"But—"

"*Run!*"

And then they were gone. The children were gone. Rileigh sat where she was, staring up at the window where the children had been, and realized *she'd done it*. She'd rescued both children and they were *unharmed*, and soon they'd be back home with their families.

Settling back onto the floor, she started to cough and let herself face the ugly reality she'd been avoiding. She'd gotten *them* out, but there was no way to get herself out. She was handcuffed to that water pipe, and she wasn't going anywhere. And the way smoke was bubbling under that basement door, it wouldn't be long before the flames caught the kitchen floor on fire.

Chapter Forty-Seven

As Mitch headed toward Ben Pendergast's house, he rolled around in his head what Mildred Sandusky had told him, trying to make the pieces fit. It was strange that no one else had bothered to mention that kidnapping all those years ago to him, and there were certainly plenty of people still around who were old enough to remember it. He hated to think... but it was possible... maybe because the child who was taken was a tourist child, not a local, an away-from-here like himself, maybe her kidnapping just hadn't been a big deal in their lives.

He couldn't figure out Granny Maggie's response to the teenagers who'd read the newspaper account of the kidnapping. She had unloaded on them, then ran off, didn't finish her classified ad. Why had the story so upset her? Rileigh had told him that Granny Maggie was a "crazy old lady." But the incident had happened twenty years ago. Surely she hadn't had dementia then. So why was she so freaked out?

It was just a small mystery. But it *itched* in his mind until he couldn't stand it anymore. He had to scratch it. Whipping his cruiser around in the road, he headed back the way he'd come. His mind wouldn't settle until he went to Granny Maggie's house and asked her to explain it.

When he came around the curve on the state road and slowed, preparing to turn off on Haskell Lane, he saw a pickup truck parked square in the middle of the road. Just stopped there. A man in overalls was standing beside it, talking to two small children.

A little blonde girl.

A little boy in a white tee-shirt and jeans.

Mitch's heart began to gallop. He drew closer and the little girl lifted her head and saw the police car. And he saw her. Got a good look. It was *Chloe Malone!*

Mitch instantly flipped on his lights and turned his cruiser crossways in the road to stop traffic — and to keep that pickup truck from going anywhere. As soon as he leapt out of the cruiser, the farmer came running to him, babbling.

"These kids, these is the ones that was took!" he cried. "The little boy says his name's Mason Stump and it was one of the Stumps that was took, wasn't it?"

Mason caught sight of the sheriff then and raced to him, threw his arms around his legs, and burst into tears. Chloe was only a couple of steps behind. Mitch's heart swelled in his chest and he felt a lump in his throat. *Both* the children, here. Neither one of them had a mark on them that he could see. They seemed to be fine, just fine. He dropped to his knees and enveloped them in a huge hug. Holding them too tight, he supposed, but they didn't seem to mind.

With his eyes wet, Mitch pulled away enough from the two crying children to key his mic.

"Patch me through to Devereux —now!" he said. Connie could hear the urgency in his voice, but she knew him well enough now to know the situation wasn't dire. Even so, Devereux was on the line in a heartbeat.

"What's up?"

"What's up is I found them, I found both children *unharmed*."

"Say that again, slow," Devereux said.

"Repeat, both children alive and well and no longer in harm's way."

"Where are you?"

Mitch gave him the address and was about to call him on his cell phone to explain further when Mason's insistent little voice finally penetrated, and he listened to what the child was saying.

"Sheriff, Sheriff, you got to go, you got to go right now. The house is on fire!" He pointed back down the lane and Mitch could see smoke rising above the hillside.

"Wylie's in there and she can't get out!"

Mitch froze.

"What did you say?"

"Wylie came with her gun and then the girl pushed her down the stairs and she fell and bumped her head. Then the girl set the house on fire."

The little boy was talking so fast, babbling and crying at the same time, that Mitch couldn't make sense of what he was saying.

"Mason, listen to me. What did you say about Rileigh?"

"I said, she's in that house that's on fire," and he pointed back down the road.

Chloe spoke up then. "We climbed out the basement window, but she can't. That girl handcuffed her foot to a pipe."

Mason was nodding his head frantically up and down. "With her own handcuffs, to a pipe."

Mitch didn't know whether to believe a word they said, but it was clear that Mason Stump believed Rileigh was in a burning house, and that was really all Mitch needed to know.

He looked at the farmer, whose eyes were as big as saucers.

"I got 'em," the farmer said. "I'll see to these young-uns, won't let no harm come to 'em, swear on the souls of my grandkids. You go, you go see who's in that burnin' house and can't get out."

Mitch could hear the wail of sirens, the beautiful symphony of help on the way. He nodded at the farmer, ran to his cruiser, and tore out for the house. As soon as he rounded the last corner, he could see the blazing building. It was a big old house on fire, red and yellow flames consuming it, black smoke lifting up into the blue sky. He screeched to a halt, leapt out of his car, and raced toward the flames.

Basement.

Chloe said she and Mason climbed out a basement window. They both said Rileigh was still there, in the basement of the house.

He ran around the burning building, looking at the windows at ground level. They were all closed .... no, one was open.

The wind was whipping the flames and smoke the other direction, but smoke was pouring out of the window like a chimney. He ran into the heat of the flames, ducking under the curling smoke, dropped to his knees, and called out into the window.

"Rileigh, Rileigh, are you in there?"

Nothing.

"Rileigh! Answer me. Ri—"

He heard a sound. Wasn't sure what it was, but it

sounded like a voice. He didn't know who it was. But it was human, and it was in distress. The window opening was small, but he dropped to his belly, shoved his feet into the opening and began scooting himself backward through the opening. When he was in far enough to bend at the waist, his feet hit something. It felt solid and he stood on it as he pulled the rest of his body inside.

Coughing, gagging on the smoke, he could hear someone else coughing, too. Blinded by smoke, he dropped to the floor where the air was still barely breathable. Through the haze, he could see Rileigh lying on her side. He crawled to her, shook her. She opened her eyes and tried to speak, her words distorted by coughing. But he understood one word. "Cuffs."

She pointed to her ankle, handcuffed to a pipe. Shoving his hand into his pocket, he pulled out the key to his cuffs — the same key opened all the handcuffs — and jabbed it at the hole, coughing now, his eyes watering so he could barely see. It took three jabs before he finally hit it right. He turned the key, and the cuffs unlocked.

Rileigh was only semi-conscious, coughing and coughing. He dragged her across the floor to what he could now see was a dog kennel with plastic storage tubs stacked on it. Lifting her up onto the kennel, he shouted into her face.

"Rileigh, you have to help me." He rolled her over. "Climb!" She struggled, clawing her way up onto the boxes, with him steadying her. She made it to her knees on the top box, the smoke boiling out around them, "Stand up! Up! Out the window!"

Somehow she managed to remain on wobbling legs long enough to push the top portion of her body out through the opening. Coming up behind her, he grabbed her hips and shoved hard, pushing her out the rest of the way so he could lurch out the window behind her.

Couldn't stay here.

"Crawl!" he commanded. Her breathing was nothing but coughing and his was little better. Together, they crawled away from the burning house. He heard the crash when the kitchen floor fell into the basement, belching flames out the opening behind them.

"Crawl!" he said again, but she was all the way out now. Lurching to his feet, he dragged her, staggering. Heard sounds around him. Voices, cries. Felt hands on him and allowed himself to collapse into them.

Chapter Forty-Eight

MASON STUMP'S birthday wasn't really until July 25th, but there was no reason to let a little thing like the wrong date get in the way of a birthday party. Georgia and Chigger had decided to throw out all the stops and host a big celebration with the whole family — a party staged at Butler Park Pavilion, because there was no way they could fit both their families into that little double-wide trailer on Carter's Mill Road.

When Rileigh pulled around the bend and looked down on Butler Park to the right, she saw that the parking lot was jammed. Everybody who was related to Georgia — Georgia's parents, aunts, uncles, cousins, her sisters, their husbands and kids, their husbands' families and their kids — or to Chigger, who had brothers and sisters and aunts and uncles all over the mountains. It appeared that every single member of the Stump and McGinnis clans had shown up for the affair.

The first person Rileigh ran into as she crossed the parking lot was Georgia's brother, Ian, who was unloading sacks of ice from the trunk of his car.

With a sweeping gesture to include all the cars in the parking lot and along the road, Rileigh said, "I might as well have left my car at home and walked."

To her utter surprise, Ian dropped the bag of ice and grabbed her in a bear hug, lifting her feet off the ground and swinging her around and around.

"I love you, Rileigh Bishop," he said. "And the whole family is so grateful, we—"

Rileigh pulled back away from him so she could put her hand over his mouth.

"No," she said, "we're *not* doing that, we're not doing the how-grateful-we-are thing. I was doing my job, and that was my job. It was not some uniquely heroic act. As a matter of fact, I was pretty stupid to turn my back on that little girl and let her push me down the stairs."

She said all that as Ian eased her back down to the ground, grinning his gums dry and shaking his head.

"You think you're going to get out of it that easy?" he said. "Seriously? This whole family owes you more—"

Rileigh held her hand up. "*Stop!* stop with the 'owes' and the 'gratefuls.' You don't *owe* me anything."

She tilted her head to the side, "… except maybe… oh, I don't know … Mama's got this chair with a broken leg and maybe you could cut us a special deal to repair it."

Ian shook his head. "I *always* charge you half price. This repair will be free."

"I'm not asking for free, just a discount—"

Georgia's children spotted Rileigh then and came squealing at her, a herd of happy, grinning children who'd been scrubbed up and put in their Sunday best clothes… to go play in the park. Georgia probably hadn't thought that all the way through to the end, but Rileigh couldn't blame her. It'd been almost two weeks since Special FBI Agent Lamar Delacroix had taken Mason home. Rileigh had spent three days in the hospital, with Georgia heli-coptering — no other way to describe it, *hovering* over her right beside Rileigh's mother. Rileigh finally had to demand Georgia go home and expend all that energy on Mason.

After that, Georgia had called her at least a dozen times. Make that two dozen times. Make that she barely hung up from one call before she called back, just babbling. Too full of happiness to contain it all, so it spilled out all over everybody she knew.

Rileigh hadn't been there to see Mason returned to his parents. But she didn't need to be. She could imagine exactly what it looked like.

Georgia, her face aged and tired, lank hair hanging in her eyes, cheeks tear-streaked — and beaming a light of joy so bright it could lead a whole fleet of oil tankers out of the fog to shore.

Mason falling into her arms. Chigger and the other kids piling on.

Tears, tears, so many tears. Healing tears, Rileigh hoped, because the family had been shattered. It would take years for all the wounds to heal, but she was sure that joyous reunion at least put sturdy scabs on them all.

Rileigh had stopped at Georgia's on her way home from the hospital and Georgia had grabbed her hand, dragged her out of the trailer and up to Not Muchuva Waterfall, where she'd hugged Rileigh so tight, she almost cracked a rib. Then the two of them stood there in each other's arms, both crying with joy. Georgia mumbled things about how much she owed to Rileigh, her life, her son's life, and Rileigh protesting the whole way for her to shut up. It did no good, of course, but Rileigh tried.

She'd gone to visit Chloe the next day. The little girl surprised her by running across the room and throwing her arms around Rileigh's waist. Then, wonder of wonders, she began to chatter, just babble, five-year-old babble. Mason had done all the talking for both of them, and Chloe had been submissive and let him. But now... her Mommy got her a kitten, even though Daddy had said she couldn't have one, but then he said she could. And maybe she was even going to get a puppy.

Rileigh had been less able to fend off the effusive gratitude of the Malone family. She couldn't tell Chloe's mother to shut up the way she could Georgia, but she smiled through it, and said all those things you say about it not being anything more than doing your job.

Rileigh had had a considerable amount of time to think about all that, in the hospital and the rest of a week off wandering around the house with nothing to do, and she realized how good it felt, how right in that way that goes click in your soul and fits perfect. How snugly her life fit together now with her return to being a police officer. It had never been just a job with her, it had been a calling. She was profoundly grateful, yeah there was that word again, grateful, to be able to do it again.

The kids collided with Rileigh and almost knocked her down, laughing. Mayella squealed, "Wylie, Wylie!" and Mason held onto her leg as if his life depended on it. She had to peel him off and pick him up into her arms.

"Hey, dude, how's my favorite big boy?"

"I'm a big boy," he said, then put his arms around Rileigh's neck as he had done when she saw him that first night at Georgia's, and hugged her tight and told her, "I love you, Wylie."

Rileigh owed him, too. Owed her life to his cantankerous personality.

If Mason had done what Rileigh told him to do — go into the woods and wait for somebody to come — Rileigh would be dead.

But that kind of obedience just wasn't how Mason Stump rolled. He didn't care what Rileigh said. He knew he had to get somebody to help her get out of the basement, so he had marched defiantly down the lane to the highway, dragging Chloe along beside him, then stood in the middle of the state road until the farmer in a pickup truck stopped to avoid running over him.

Mason Stump was destined for great things.

Mitch peeled out of the crowd and came to stand beside her, watching the Stumps and McGinnises weave in and out among themselves, chattering and talking and laughing and celebrating.

"I heard from the Department of Human Resources today," he said, and Rileigh perked up. "They're going to put Shiloh into a children's psychiatric hospital in Nashville while the FBI tries to find her family."

In the photograph Granny Maggie had shown everybody in town, Shiloh looked to be maybe 14 or 15 months old. That helped to establish a timeframe for her kidnapping.

Mitch continued: "Special Agent Delacroix told me he would personally look under every rock in California until the found her parents."

Rileigh wished she'd asked Granny Maggie more questions when she'd had the chance. She didn't know exactly where in California Becca had lived, and wherever it was, it was the last in a series of moves. She wasn't even completely certain that Becca had been in California when she kidnapped Shiloh. But the FBI would spread its net far and wide.

"I don't think I'd count on that if I were you," Mitch said.

"Count on what?"

"Sometimes you're as easy to read as the front page of

the newspaper. You were hoping someday there'd be this kind of celebration for Shiloh. But a lot of water has gone under the bridge, and that child has been damaged for a really long time. It's not like she can go home, settle back into her world, and live a normal life."

Rileigh shook her head. "None of it was her fault."

"You can say the same thing about a lot of people in this story — it wasn't their fault."

Georgia spotted her then and came running, threw her arms around her, and gave her the customary too-tight hug that lasted too long.

"We've got a birthday cake," she said, "we're about to cut it. Come on."

Mama suddenly burst out of the crowd and moved faster than Rileigh had any idea she could move. Almost knocked Emma Cummings off her feet as she barreled toward Rileigh squealing.

"Mama?"

Rileigh had left the house early for Mason's party so that she could go by Shuster's Shoe Store to pick up the shoes that she had ordered. Clunky work shoes that went with the uniform that had been ordered for her and would be in sometime next week. Mama grabbed Rileigh in a bear hug and squealed. And Rileigh considered that she'd gotten more big hugs in the last ten days than the whole rest of her life put together.

"Mama, calm down, what are you so excited about?"

"This, this, *this!*" She squealed and waved something in Rileigh's face that she couldn't see.

"What is that?"

"Look at it!" Mama cried, and she stopped waving it back and forth.

The whole world went very still then. The voices of chattering people and squealing children receded into the background, and all Rileigh could hear was a humming sound in her ears. She reached for what Mama held in her hand, but her movement seemed to be in slow motion. She took it. She had to pry it out of Mama's fingers, and Mama was jumping up and down and squealing and saying something. Rileigh didn't know what it was. Her eyes were fixed on the postcard in her hand. It was a picture of the sign outside the "authentic" log cabin on the edge of town. Rileigh had seen the postcard in the racks in various souvenir shops. The last time she'd seen one was in the rack at Souvenirs, Souvenirs, Souvenirs, where she'd been on stakeout. That seemed like a lifetime ago.

The sign in the picture was hand-lettered in that style you knew wasn't really hand-lettered at all, was just meant to look like it was. Written on a log where the bark had been stripped away was the East Tennessee version of "Welcome!"

"You're here now, by golly!"

And below that, printed on the bottom of the card, were the words "Black Bear Forge, Tennessee."

The words blurred a little, either because her eyes had suddenly filled with tears or because her hand was shaking. It seemed to take a hundred years to turn the card over and see what was on the back. The smiley face she'd expected to see grinned up at her from the back of the postcard. But for the first time in more than a quarter of a century, that wasn't the only thing written there.

In bold, all capital letters, was the word "HOME."

The End

What To Read Next

When a bullet strikes Rileigh Bishop's car and sends her careening into a river, she barely escapes with her life.

Convinced that her sister's disappearance, the postcards, and the assassination attempt are tied together, Rileigh and Mitch tear into cold cases, exposing bones that were better left buried.

Pick up your copy of Too Far Gone today.

About The Author

Lauren Street has always loved a mystery. As a kid growing up in bible belt country she devoured every whodunit book she could get her sticky little hands on and secretly investigated all of her (seemingly) normal boring neighbors. Sometimes their pets and farm animals too. All grown up now and living in the UK with her thoroughly unsuspicious (and often unsuspecting) husband, she writes domestic psychological thrillers about families torn apart by secrets and lies. And she sometimes still peers over garden walls to check up on the neighbors.

Also By Lauren Street

The Bishop Smoky Mountain Thrillers

Hide Me Away

Fuel To The Flame

Closer By The Hour

A Gamble Either Way

Calling My Children Home

Too Far Gone

Replaced with Nolon King

Replaced

In Her Place